# Qbits

## THE PERSEIDS
## ADVENTURE

*Graham —
Here it is !
See you soon "QFitz"*

## Peter Fitzgerald

# Science AND Fiction

*The Qbits think they are the world's greatest ever scientists, and they are back to save the planet!*

# About the author

A very boring man having an unusual midlife crisis.

OR maybe less true is:

Peter Fitzgerald is a businessman with a passion for science. He has degrees in economics, accounting and physics.

An avid traveller and adventure seeker, limited by dodgy knees, Peter is mad about kayaking, Australian Rules Football and cricket. He has kayaked in the Arctic and Antartica and many countries in between.

Married with two teenage children he believes science holds the key to solving world issues, not finance!

The goal of Qbits is to hopefully inspire one teenager or adult to pursue a career in science.

Scientists are rightfully remembered forever—it's a great way to be famous.

We have forgotten that.

Published in Australia by Sid Harta Publishers Pty Ltd,
ABN: 46 119 415 842
23 Stirling Crescent, Glen Waverley, Victoria 3150 Australia
Telephone: +61 3 9560 9920, Facsimile: +61 3 9545 1742
E-mail: author@sidharta.com.au

First published in Australia February 2012
This edition published February 2012
Copyright © Peter Fitzgerald 2012
Cover design, typesetting: Chameleon Print Design

The right of Peter Fitzgerald to be identified as the
Author of the Work has been asserted in accordance with
the Copyright, Designs and Patents Act 1988.

Fitzgerald, Peter
Qbits: The Perseids Adventure
ISBN: 1-921829-82-6
EAN13: 978-1-921829-82-6
pp352

# Acknowledgements

*I'd like to thank the Qbits team Tara, Matt and Simone for helping create this reality.*

# Chapter 1

## Harry's Cafe de Wheels

### 28 February 2015
### 7.15 am + 12 seconds

Tom Jackson was hitting his full jogging stride. Just as he passed his favourite coffee hangout, which was a ramshackle cart situated on a wharf in central Sydney, he huffed and puffed as he pulled out all the stops, his oversized feet pounding the pavement, arms rhythmically slicing through the air beside him. A brisk 5-kilometre wake-up run along the harbour before the party tonight was just what he needed, with his jogging music belting in his head as he waved a theatrical greeting to the staff at Harry's Cafe de Wheels.

A shout immediately bellowed out. 'Good morning, you're up early!' sang Chin from behind the counter. Chin was credited

1

with regularly resuscitating Tom from his coma each morning with his extra strong cappuccinos.

'Yup! Catch you later,' gasped Tom as he headed off along the harbour's edge towards the naval military base, where a massive American aircraft carrier had docked.

Suddenly, just 50 metres from Harry's, Tom stopped dead in his tracks, as if he had momentarily forgotten how to run.

'Not again!' he whined, as quantum teleportation whisked him instantly into another world. At this very moment, Tom was transported to the Great Hall, even though he was still simultaneously out running along the harbourfront on a lovely sunny morning. Teleported, his 'real' world entangled with another chaotic random universe.

# Chapter 2

## Great Hall

### 28 February 2015
### 7.15 am + 15 seconds

Almost instantly, Tom found himself in the Great Hall, sitting in his usual seat at the head of the table.

'Guys, I'm out for a run. Surely this can wait!' he implored.

Four unsympathetic faces stared at him blankly. The Qbits didn't like to wait for anything.

The Great Hall looked like the kind of medieval English banquet hall that kings would have dined in, with a long table that would easily seat thirty guests. Tom was wearing his daggy running shorts and sweat-ringed shirt, and therefore totally under dressed for any medieval festivity. The table was laid with an array of regal finery, with freshly spat upon and polished silver cutlery and immaculately starched and pressed white tablecloths. The thing was it was not even close to dinnertime; the table was always like that. In fact, no one ever ate at that table, other than when perhaps having biscuits with a coffee.

On the wall hung a massive tapestry that on close inspection did not depict grand kings and queens of times gone by, nor pious religious icons casting judgment on mankind; it displayed bizarre and ever-changing information on everything from flourless chocolate cake baking to the mysteries of the electronic universe. This was the Qbit portal to the real universe, they could be 'Anywhere, Anytime, Instantly'.

Seated at one end of the long table were four wannabe people— Qbits. One looked like a monk in a terry towelling dressing gown hanging in folds from his stubby feet, which were perched upon the table before him, as he dangled a half empty wine glass in one bunch of sausage-like fingers. He raised his glass to Tom, but his expression remained firm.

This man, known as GG, was under the mistaken impression he was Galileo Galilei. However, that gifted scientist had long been well and truly deceased, and although this slovenly creature did sound and look *remarkably* like that great man of times gone by, he was far too undignified lounging about all over the fine cutlery to measure up to such a great man. GG's behaviour was just as rebellious as that of his namesake, and indeed he was quite as wild as could be expected considering he had been awoken from a coma 373 years posthumously and told by mankind,

'Oops—sorry! All that stuff you said which we put you in prison for turned out to be correct.' As a result, GG was now determined to enjoy both his galaxy and his wine to the full. He was adamant that in this incarnation, nothing would stand in his way.

The Great Hall didn't exist in the real world as you or I know it. The Qbit world was a virtual world merely 'based on' something known in the real world, like a poorly adapted telemovie. The Great Tapestry, and indeed the entire room, could transform with merely a thought. And while the four Qbits' strong personalities couldn't easily agree on anything, they all felt comfortable settling down in a Cambridge-style university library with a large table for research and a big screen to project ideas and visualise concepts. And when they got bored, with no more than a thought they could flit about the cyber world or into outer space. They had plenty of time to surf the Internet as in Qbits time slowed, a real world second was nearly an hour—in fact to be precise 1 second in the real world was the same as 53 minutes and 5 seconds in Qbit time.

The Great Tapestry was now showing a magnificent picture of a huge mountain peak bathed in blue sky.

'Ok, yes, that's very impressive. Can I go back now? I'm trying to jog.' Tom feigned a yawn but was really trying to get his breath back after his speedy turn past Harry's.

The Qbits had become as excited as young children at a school show-and-tell session.

'But it's the Himalayas! Magnificent Mount Everest, to be precise,' replied GG. 'Mac thought you'd want to see it.'

Mac, the quantum incarnation of Marie Curie, seemed every bit as excited about the vision as GG. 'Isn't it just incredible?' she chirped. 'Look, you can see some adventurers climbing the peak. Must be so difficult with such low oxygen.'

Watto, the odd-looking feline assistant who only ever appeared as a smiling face on the large screen dispensing information, beamed at the Qbits helpfully. Schrödinger's cat, as Watto was known, was always poised to assist with the provision of knowledge.

Instantly, the lower part of the Great Tapestry filled with data on Mount Everest.

 **Great Tapestry**

'Hi guys, here it is. Mount Everest.'

**Drone Vision of Mount Everest**

Mount Everest is about 60 million years old.

The mountain range, the Himalayas, divides the countries of Nepal and Tibet.

Height: about 8,800 metres and getting taller every year due to geological forces.

Nepalese name: Sagarmatha 'goddess of the sky'.

Tibetan name: Chomolungma 'goddess of the universe'.

Western name is after Sir George Everest in 1865.

First climbed on 29 May 1953 by Sir Edmund Hillary and Tenzing Norgay.

The 'death zone' is above 8,000 metres—there are over 100 corpses on Everest.

'Excellent, guys, but I can watch National Geographic anytime. See you later,' said Tom dismissively.

The German voice coming from Tom's right was very matter-of-fact. He seemed to be one of the more sensible of the Qbits. 'Yes, of course, but this is live—we are streaming from the drone,' said Alby. Alby had the QED, or Quantum Electronic DNA, of Albert Einstein.

This statement alerted Tom's senses; the run would have to wait a few more seconds. What were they up to this time? Lately the Qbits had proven to be more random and uncontrollable than ever, as they cruised the seemingly limitless electronic world. Real world laws and rules seemed not to have much effect on the Qbits, who were basically quantum iterations of past famous scientists.

Tom turned towards GG, the apparent instigator of this latest jaunt.

'Live from the drone?' Tom asked anxiously.

'Yes, it's the drone's video feed,' chipped in Newts. 'It was GG's idea.' He sounded like a regular tattletale. Newts, who had Sir Isaac Newton's QED, considered GG's behaviour erratic, unpredictable and uncontrollable.

Tom nodded for a second, before giving in. 'Um, what exactly is "the drone"?'

They all looked at GG.

GG pulled uncomfortably at his collar. 'What? We just borrowed it for a few hours. We will return it after we do a lap around the mountains. We will have it back before dark, if they miss it ...'

'Borrowed it?' repeated Tom sternly. 'From whom?'

There was a faint titter as the Qbits mocked his overly correct grammar.

'Watto,' Tom knew the obedient Watto had no choice but to deliver actual facts, 'information on the drone, on screen now.'

The Great Tapestry quickly switched to footage of an unusual looking grey aircraft loaded up with missiles and guns.

**Predator Drone**

US military weapon.

Length: 8 metres.

Wingspan: 15 metres.

Engine: 4-cylinder turbocharged engine.

Extended flying range: up to 20 hours.

Weaponry: laser-guided hellfire missiles and 20 millimetre rapid-fire cannon.

Controlled by: Secure Communications Tactical Data link in California.

Developed by: Vextron Systems.

Estimated cost: over $10 million.

Tom slumped in his chair. 'What the hell is that? Who is flying it?'

GG had no choice but to answer. 'Me, I'm your pilot on this National Geographic adventure,' he chuckled.

Tom was aghast. 'You? GG, we can't just take someone's military weapon and go on a holiday!'

They all looked at Tom with scepticism. After all, it seemed as if they could in fact do precisely that.

Alby quickly attempted to justify the frolic. 'It took Newts less than a nanosecond to get through their security system and the flight manual is just like any Xbox game.'

GG made a peace offering to Tom. 'Here, you want to take the controls?'

Horrified by the offer and stunned by the whole concept, Tom recoiled. 'What? No! Of course I don't want to take the controls! I don't want to be here and I don't want to be flying a $10 million armed US military weapon on a joy flight to Mount Everest! Where did you get it?'

'Technically, it came from some base in Pakistan, but we had to hack US Airforce operations in California to seize control. Come and look—we are nearly at Mount Everest's peak now. Watto, just switch back to drone cam,' said GG.

The others turned excitedly toward the screen as a group of startled climbers attempting their once in a lifetime voyage caught sight of the large funny-looking oversized model of an aircraft and, unsure of how to respond, calmly waved and gave the internationally renowned thumbs up 'we are ok' signal. As clear as day, the drone zoomed in on the smiles on the climbers' faces. Mac found herself wanting to wave back.

'They probably think this is their tour company checking to see they are ok,' remarked Newts without emotion, before scoffing coldly.

Tom was reluctant to admit how cool it all was. It felt like they were right there on the peak of Mount Everest with the climbers, at the ceiling of the world. The sky was a crisp blue and the white clouds were like wisps of fairy floss draped along the mountain peaks. On the 3D Great Tapestry screen it felt as real as if they were actually there.

Tom snapped out of it and regained his focus. 'Now,' he said, clearing his throat, 'turn this thing around and take it back to wherever you stole it from. Tour is over.'

Like a scorned puppy, GG again mumbled 'Borrowed' just loud enough to be heard and then instructed Watto to engage autopilot and send the drone back to the secret US military base on the Pakistan border.

Admittedly, Mount Everest was impressive but the Qbits never thought about the consequences of their actions. Stealing an armed military weapon to visit Mount Everest? Where on earth had they got the idea? And what next? Air Force 1?

*Run harder* was all Tom could think to do as he teleported back to Sydney harbour.

# Chapter 3

## Great Hall

28 February 2015
7.15 am + 35 seconds

The violent explosion shook the Great Hall. Tom had taken barely two steps and he was back at the table, glaring at GG.

'What the bloody hell was that?' yelled Tom, as the paintings on the walls rattled on their hooks.

'It seems we are under attack,' Newts replied matter-of-factly, as a missile sped past and exploded behind the drone. 'But GG shot it down with the 20 millimetre cannon before it had a chance to impact our drone.' Newts pulled at a piece of thread that had come loose on his coat, tsking quietly to himself.

Wasting no time, GG began shouting instructions like a general in battle. 'All weapons systems live, Watto!'

Meanwhile, back in California some 12,000 kilometres away, after the disappearance of the drone some hours earlier, a red alert had been issued. The General in charge was now in the control room watching his pilots at the US Remote Air Force control base preparing to shoot and destroy the renegade drone.

Everyone in the operator's room was scared, not because of the drone or the firing of the missiles, but because of the inevitable witch-hunt that would follow. How had a $10 million fully armed weapon found its way to the Himalayas in a civilian area, with no discernible means controlling it? Someone would be made a scapegoat. But for now, downing the renegade drone was all that mattered.

The craft was heading towards Chinese airspace. Instructions were clear: 'It must not enter. Destroy at all costs.' The systems, the stealth construction, the missile systems could be reverse engineered but the self-destruct button had failed; it had been overridden.

'Watto, enter stealth mode,' GG commanded. 'I will show them General GG is ready for battle. Engage hellfire missiles laser guidance system. Arm 20 millimetre cannons. Let's settle this now.'

Watto responded, 'Check, done, check, engaged,' all in perfect military speak. It was war.

'Show satellite vision of the other drone's location and weaponry.'

'They are also in stealth mode,' chipped in Newts.

12

'So now it's visual warfare for both of us—just like on Xbox, Tom. Here we go!' said GG.

Tom's now purple face looked like it was about to spontaneously combust. Instead, it yelled very loudly. 'What! You are an idiot! GG, you are not a general, you are a complete idiot! This is *not* like Xbox! This is a multimillion-dollar weapon owned by the US Government! They will find us—sorry, find *me*—and stick me in Guantanamo Bay, and *torture* me, and then when they've finished *torturing* me, they will *electrocute* me for treason! What have you *done?*' If there was a darker shade of purple than dark purple, then Tom's face was now it.

'We are all going to die.' Tom's last exasperation just hung— the Qbits couldn't die and well, really the battle now in full swing was just a video game with real world robots. No one was going to die.

GG, who had some moments earlier stuck his finger in his ear being closest to Tom's tirade, now removed it and spoke in his alluring Italian purr. 'Relax, they will never find us. The channel we are using is untraceable.'

The other Qbits all nodded dumbly as if that had been obvious all along.

What ensued on the screen was two model aircraft weaving through the sky trying to gain a clear shot on the other with real and deadly weapons. Flashes occurred as bullets raced past the hull.

Suddenly GG's drone entered a vertical ascent. They all tilted back in their chairs as GG firstly climbed straight up and then looped back and dived.

'What the hell?'

'They aren't programmed to go above 40,000 feet. We are out of visibility. I'm looping back and going to take them out with a missile or the cannon.' GG was in charge. General GG—he liked the sound of that.

The sound of cannon fire filled the room as GG shouted, 'Fire, fire, fire!' and launched one of the two hellfire missiles with heat signature lock on the signal of the other drone. Meanwhile, the two US Air Force Lieutenants were seated in an air-conditioned room in a secure high-tech military facility in California, only about 30 minutes from the beach with a joystick in hand and a massive screen in front of them showing a view of the renegade drone darting around the Himalayan sky evading them, clearly in someone else's control. This definitely made for a more interesting shift than the usual surveillance flights.

The highly trained US Air Force pilots' adrenaline was pumping with lightning fast reflexes. The systems and weapons were the same as the full-sized stealth bomber. The main difference was that in an hour their shift would end and one would be at his son's basketball game, and the other was going to dinner near the beach. In fact, the impossibility of losing their lives made them want the battle to end quickly so they wouldn't be late. This was modern warfare, fighting the enemy from the comfort of an ergonomic chair, machine versus machine.

They both had their fingers poised on the joystick triggers as they tried to blast GG's drone out of the sky. The senior officer had his finger on the remaining hellfire missile, trying to lock onto the heat signature of GG's drone. The hellfire missiles were known as 'tank busters', capable of blasting through the hull of tanks. As GG's hellfire missile appeared on the screen, they immediately engaged the cannons and destroyed the missile just before impact.

The missile explosion was deafening. The screen flashed as if a huge firework had gone off in the room. There was an awkward silence of failure. GG snarled with the loss of his missile. The score was now one miss all.

Elsewhere the Pentagon was also alerted about the rogue drone and had assembled in the bunker at the Whitehouse. Next to the Chief of Staff was the President, Bob Neil, who anxiously watched the showdown. The drone must not enter Chinese airspace was the clear instruction. Many in the room believed it must be a Chinese hacker that stole the weapon; it would never be proved.

As the drones wove across the sky giving off occasional 20 millimetre cannon bursts, the adventurers on Mount Everest briefly watched, even though they weren't sure exactly what they were watching. More pressing matters such as surviving climbing the highest mountain in the world were more immediate than their curiosity about this confrontation taking place in the distance.

Alby tried to speak but GG kept interrupting, with Newts as his wingman, shouting instructions, 'Go left, bank right!'

'Gentlemen,' Alby stood up from the table.

'Not now, Alby, just going to take this mother out with a combination of the last missile and cannons together and blow the missile as it nears them to blind them, then use the 20 millimetre cannons to down them. Launching in 10 seconds 10, 9, 8 ...' counted GG, with Mac and Newts and even Tom leaning with every twist and turn.

'But—'

'Just a few more seconds until they are in sight again, Alby.'

'No, stop!' Alby stood in front of the screen, blocking their view; they all tried to see around him as this was the critical battle moment.

'Why not just take control of the other drone and fly them both back? I have the codes. Watto, enter the codes.' Alby's arms were crossed over his chest, exuding authority.

There was immediate silence. The deafening cannon fire

ceased. The clear sky returned, and Mount Everest was as it was before the battle. In some ways even the confused Tom was a little disappointed, as it was just getting exciting and they were all caught in the adrenalin of battle; they were about to score a kill on the other drone in the Battle of Everest.

Across the world, panic set in as the pilots looked at each other and spoke calmly and precisely into the direct link to the Pentagon. The message was simple and clear.

'We have lost contact with our drone; both drones are now rogue.'

The General on duty thumped the desk near the controls as his voice immediately filled the room. 'Scramble all available real aircraft in the area and obliterate both drones, now.'

Then, from out of nowhere, a message appeared on the control screen. 'Drone autopilot on and returning to base.' A second identical message appeared for the other aircraft. No one was game enough to say or touch anything. The pilots simply sat back in their chairs.

Furious, all Tom wanted to do was get back to his running. Scolding the Qbits could wait. What else could he realistically do? As he returned to the real world, he waved to Chin again as he gathered full speed and disappeared round the corner.

The next message from the Pentagon left a hush of silence in the Great Hall.

GG saw the communiqué but thought it best not to worry Tom with it. No harm done, both drones were on their way back to base. Let him run.

'Watto, file message under R Neil,' he instructed.

It was time for a relaxing glass of wine, and maybe a movie. Yes, he would watch *Top Gun* again, that would be good. After all, that was where he had got the idea for the flight. And he smiled as he pondered what a great day out they had enjoyed. No real harm done.

**From:** RNeil@presidentusa.com
**To:** Chiefs@presidentusa.com
**Sent:** 27 February 2015 5.30 pm
**Subject:** Everest drone incident

Trace all signals and find who stole our birds. Find them, put every tech head and special ops person in the area and get whoever did this and bring them in. This was an attack on our military.

I don't care which country, bring them in. All resources, all departments.

Security Chiefs, my office at 7.00 am tomorrow with answers.

Classified need-to-know basis.

R Neil
**President**

# Chapter 4

## Great Hall

### 1 March 2015
### 8.01 am + 32 seconds

'Good morning, all!' GG was chirpy as ever. Alby sighed at the tedium; GG knew as well as anyone that there wasn't really any morning or night in Qbits. GG shrugged as he parked his rear at the long table, looking around at the others for a more positive response.

With his customary glass of wine in one hand, he snapped his fingers together and as if by magic a magazine appeared in the other, whereupon his eyes lit up and he gulped contentedly from his glass and caught up on the latest issue of *Time* magazine.

'Hey guys, check this out! We all get a mention!' GG exclaimed excitedly in his thick Italian accent. 'Greatest scientists of all time named,' he started reading aloud. 'Hell, how good is that? We all get into the top 10—take a look at what it says. It's 100 years since Einstein published the theory that we reckon might be wrong. And Newts, they are calling you the father of mathematics—how cool is that? Very impressive.'

As GG took a slug of his wine, Newts gave a smirk in acknowledgement of the repulsive overweight rebel whose behaviour was mostly intolerable to him. He just wasn't proper at all.

'Hey, Mac, it rates you in the top 10 with your two Nobel Prizes—the only person ever to get a prize in both physics and chemistry ...' He paused to look over at Alby, 'ever.'

Mac blushed as GG shook his head and pursed his lips in a way that said her two trophies beat all of them put together.

'In my day we didn't *have* a Nobel Prize so it was a little more than difficult to procure one in any field,' Newts sniffled pompously.

'Are these grapes sour?' Mac interjected, sniffing GG's wine.

'*Che cretino!*' replied GG rudely.

'Why do you talk so rapscallionishly, GG? Can't we as thinkers and esteemed scientists use the Queen's English?' scolded Newts, his smirk gone.

'She might be your queen, *amico*, but she ain't no queen of mine,' replied GG, slurping his wine and returning to the magazine. 'It says I was the first to stand up against the Church and changed the whole basis of science.' He raised his eyebrows to signify the importance of that recognition. Then mimicking Newts' pompous voice, he added, 'We must take care not to communicate to *Herr* Alby that he is being celebrated in the real world, lest he become conceited.'

All nodded their heads in agreement. They didn't want Alby getting a big head; he already behaved like he was the leader of the Qbits, even though the little pipsqueak was some 300 years younger than GG.

'Where is the big kahuna, anyway?' GG asked, returning to his love of modern turns of phrase. 'Let's wake him up—I'm bored.'

In the real world, Tom's room in Kings Cross, Sydney, appeared far less remarkable. A young man lay sound asleep, snoring, with a few dog-eared posters on the wall and what seemed to be the contents of his entire wardrobe scattered all over the floor. Tom attempted to stir himself when he heard the excited gibbering Qbit voices but it was the night after a huge party and he had a pounding headache that was playing like a game of Xbox at full volume inside his head.

Your room obeys the Third Law of Thermodynamics —entropy. All systems go from a state of order to disorder.

At 28 years old, Tom Jackson was usually a first-year lecturer and research physicist at the University of Sydney, and a very good rugby player. But today he was just a young guy wanting this day to end before it had even begun.

Tom rolled over, putting a pillow over his head and trying to go back to sleep, but quantum teleportation is random and uncontrollable, and he felt the familiar pull of the Qbits as he was instantly transferred into their electron universe.

Suddenly Tom was back in the Great Hall, sitting in his usual seat at the head of the table. 'What is it now? Couldn't you guys deal with this alone? You are all living on borrowed time–c'mon you are all adults.' They all looked curiously at each other, as if to ask 'How do you borrow time?' Alby looked particularly disturbed, as he hadn't thought of a theory of BT. They all looked curiously at each other, wondering whether they had heard him correctly.

'Ah, Tom, we have something to discuss with you,' began GG.

Tom glanced around sourly at the motley bunch, who peered at him silently, waiting for someone else to pick up the train of thought.

'I need a coffee,' mumbled Tom, who suddenly realised he could see eight Qbits in total.

'He's useless today!' exclaimed GG, relieved beyond measure.

A barely perceptible collective sigh seeped from those present.

'And Watto, can you stop sending me all this random crap? It's driving me mad!' Tom's brow furrowed as he glanced disapprovingly up at the Great Tapestry.

'But I'm a totally random Qbit. I suffer from bit slip and decoherence. I send and find information. It is what I do. And I get bored. Need any information—anything?'

'Can't I just make you stop?' Tom retorted, exasperated.

'He can't, he doesn't have any logic functions,' replied Alby disdainfully. 'He is merely a bunch of happy excited electrons sending you random information to please you. When you created him, that was his mission—find information. Now it's random, all totally random. He is one happy cat.'

Watto was flitting about on the virtual screen, not quite as aesthetically pleasing as a real tapestry, but perhaps a lot more useful.

'Sorry, Watto, didn't mean to bite your head off,' said Tom.

'Some of it is kinda interesting,' conceded Newts.

'Yes, yes, anyway, it can't be helped. But we need you here to discuss other much more important things, Tom,' Mac stressed.

'That's right, Mac,' Alby said, stretching his grizzled arms. 'Tom, you are our portal to the world. We are you—you are we. Quantum entanglement.'

Tom managed to raise an eyebrow, but actually wanted to pull out each of their eyeballs to give them some impression of the pain he himself was in right now. He struggled to be civil.

'Mhmrrgmm.'

'Lights are on but nobody's home,' quipped GG.

Ants do not sleep.

Mac handed Tom a juice. He nodded in thanks, took a sip and almost instantly felt uplifted. His headache, tiredness and hangover were all gone.

'Wow, thanks for the recovery tonic, Mac! I feel energised, how did that work?'

'Curiosity; that's what all scientists have in common. They need answers to everything, searching for reasons, for the why, how and what. Immediate, reasoned, logical, supported answers.'

'You can solve that later,' dismissed Alby, who hated sitting still, and so sprang up.

GG too, now in his stylish waistcoat and frilled eighteenth century shirt, rose majestically to his feet, to reveal bright board shorts and crocs, and trashing any credibility he may have been mercifully granted despite his wine-swilling loutishness. Looking neither left nor right, GG sashayed daintily, as if on a high wire, to the tall stained glass window at the far end of the table.

Alby took the floor, with Watto obediently hovering on the Great Tapestry above him, awaiting the next instruction. GG, gazing out the window, raised his faded leather-tubed telescope to his wizened eye, whilst Alby prepared himself to explain the situation, as if this preposterous collective pose were the marking of some unvoiced cue.

'The calculations have been verified but we needed observational proof,' stated Newts.

All nodded and looked towards GG, who was now interrupting.

'Talk to the hand, Newts,' he said, holding up his telescope and stopping Newts mid sentence. GG had Watto link the Great Tapestry to his telescope, which he pointed back out of the portal. The tapestry operated like 3D TV, a window to the world and the Internet—this time it channelled the view from GG's telescope.

'What the hell?' Tom screwed up his face. 'What a ridiculously outdated telescope—surely it can't work?'

'Quantum magic, Tom,' GG muttered without straying from his target. 'The telescope is how I choose to see it, but the vision is from NASA's satellite located 500 kilometres above the Earth.'

Finally, after several protracted Qbit moments, Newts, who had left the room briefly, returned. He was carrying a silver tray bearing steaming hot coffees. He carefully lowered it onto the table. Beneath the prickly exterior he was very shy and found it very difficult to relate to anyone, other than cats and pigeons.

'I've made it strong.'

Tom smiled dimly in thanks. 'Fantastic—you must be psychic, Newts.'

Newts' modest head inclined ever so subtly at the praise.

'While you've been baristaing we've been looking at the bigger picture,' jibed GG.

Newts ignored him, as he was busy micromanaging their refreshments; each item on the colonial tray had been meticulously selected and distributed by him. He held the small silver galleon aloft. 'Sugar, anyone?'

The other three scientists all politely declined, patting their varying degrees of paunch, while Tom seized the galleon and poured a handful of sugar into his cup, the steam bathing Tom in the familiar smell of good coffee. Alby relinquished the floor to GG and resumed his seat, leaning back in all his subdued European elegance, his soft white shirt limp and spotless, a half Windsor knot in his necktie, and his coffee sitting idly in front of him, decreasing in temperature at an average rate of 0.03 °C per second.

As Tom stirred the sugar into his coffee, he glanced up at the Great Tapestry screen, which showed the current locations of two massive satellites, with a combined weight of over 1,000 kilograms and travelling at 28,675 kilometres per hour, but at different altitudes. As he squinted at the mind-boggling footage before him, he could see the two satellites' trajectories, which indicated they would be travelling within 100 metres of each other in the not too distant future.

Gravity is the master of the Universe

'Ok, cutting to the chase,' began Alby. 'We have been keeping an eye on these two satellites.'

Tom swallowed nervously.

The other Qbits were silent.

'More coffee?' suggested Mac.

'Shush!' Alby said abruptly. 'GG, we need to acquaint ourselves with the finer details of the situation.'

GG responded in his thick Italian accent. 'It's not the first time that such an observation has been made, yet modern science relies on causation and past event data. But this event is somewhat probabilistic and what you would call a random event. That is what we specialise in—quantum physics—and in here we can see the outcome that others think impossible or can't evaluate until after they know how it happened. Take quantum tunnelling, for instance, where electrons tunnel through walls and appear in impossible places. Look at us. We exist and we don't, quantum magic and—'

Alby put up his hand to stem the tide of tangency. 'Ok, Mr Mathemagician, get on with it. Move on to the facts.'

'Perhaps it would be easier if I just show you?' suggested GG, suddenly losing heart in his longwinded explanation. 'Want to go into "hyperspace"? C'mon, a quick trip into outer space?' asked GG enthusiastically. 'Perfect start to your day!'

They all knew even Tom loved their trips into space; it was every scientist's dream and the view on the Great Tapestry was like being there.

'Where to? Will it take long?' Tom wasn't even going to ask how.

'Watto, let's take the next available electromagnetic transmissions and hitch a ride,' instructed GG. 'How long have you got?'

Tom thought for a moment. 'Let's say 5 seconds, or 5 hours in here, give or take.' He quickly put his hand up to quell any pedantic clarifications on the exact time dilation. Time ran slow, very slow in Qbits' universe, they all understood that—operating at light speed seconds in the real world were hours in Qbits.

The Great Tapestry transformed into a 3D image of space as they hitched a ride on the electromagnetic transmission wave from NASA to the International Space Station.

# Chapter 5

## Great Tapestry

'All aboard the Q-xpress.
First stop International Space Station then on to the Hubble telescope.'

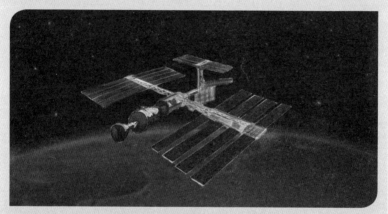

**International Space Station**

The International Space Station orbits at 400 kilometres above the Earth.

The Hubble Space Telescope weighs about 11,000 kilograms and is 13 metres long.

They both orbit the planet at about 28,000 kilometres per hour.

'We are linking in to NASA's secure in craft video link—we look out at them like you would on a video conference, but they can't look in.'

'So we can see them but they can't see us,' played back Tom.

'Correct,' confirmed Alby.

Each of them worked their way around the various internal cameras, looking into space in quiet wonderment.

GG was rabbiting on constantly, reeling off facts about the Universe. 'Big bang explosion began the Universe about 14 billion years ago. The Universe is expanding forever—what was that constant you invented, Alby?' he teased Alby, who had theorised it wasn't expanding at all.

He continued. 'All stars in the galaxy rotate around a galactic centre but not with the same period. Stars at the centre have a shorter rotation than those farther out. Our Sun is located in the outer part of the Milky Way galaxy. The speed of our solar system rotating around the black hole in the middle is about 792,000 kilometres per hour, based on a distance of 30,000 light years around the Sun's orbit around the centre of the Milky Way once every 225 million years. The period of time is called a cosmic year. The Sun has orbited the galaxy about 20 times during its 4.5 billion-year lifetime.'

GG just stared into the blackness. Then, after some time, he brought up the reasons for the trip. 'I've been here a lot in the last few days, making some observations. As you can see on the radar, the two satellites are going to collide.'

Quantum physics means light comes in bundles of energy called quanta.

'Hi guys, here is a space junk cloud briefing.'

The first satellite in space was the Russian Sputnik I in 1957.

Of 7,000 satellites, about 1,200 are still working, mainly for science and spying.

The junk includes old satellites and rocket parts, including astronauts' rubbish.

1979 Skylab, the first American space station, fell to the Earth in thousands of pieces. Since 1959 over 6,000 pieces of 'space junk' have hit earth.

Junk travels at up to 28,000 kilometres per hour, about 20 times faster than a bullet.

There are more than 300 million pieces of space junk larger than 1 millimetre in orbit.

Orbital decay is when space junk and friction cause low orbit junk to fall to Earth.

Junk orbiting at above 1,000 kilometres circles the Earth for a century or more.

Most of the junk is in low Earth orbit, from 850 kilometres to around 2,000 kilometres. If it is under 600 kilometres it will fall within several years.

There are estimated to be 500,000 pieces larger than 1 centimetre in low Earth orbit. STRATCOM monitors about 20,000 dangerous objects.

Satellites and debris pass within 10 kilometres of each other 1,000 times a day.

A 1 millimetre piece of junk could kill an astronaut.

'A United States Iridium communications satellite will collide with a now-defunct Russian satellite in less than two days—in fact, in 47 hours and 35 minutes—above northern Siberia. The random wreckage and cargo will create further hazards and a series of events resulting in numerous other collision risks.'

Newts interjected, as though there had never been any doubt about the event. 'The International Space Station, however, should not be threatened by the debris and it is currently the only manned craft.'

'Whoa, everyone, Newton's in the building! Thanks, Newts—sorry, *Sir* Newts,' GG added facetiously. 'So, we are all good regarding the calculations?'

Newts didn't reply, but may have pouted ever so slightly.

Tom still wasn't sure exactly what was happening with the satellites, but he got the feeling something very bad was in store for them. Matters weren't helped by all the to-ing and fro-ing of the Qbits, who all thought independently, which added a delightful element of chaos and cross-purpose to their chatter.

'Let's finish this discussion in the Great Hall. Shall we?' said GG.

Before he had time to respond, Tom found himself sitting back at the table in the Great Hall, the images from the space station now vanished.

Tom sank into his chair as GG took a seemingly unruffled sip of his macchiato. 'Spectacular coffee,' he said, smacking his lips together.

'Good God, GG—it's not real,' Alby scoffed, his face in his palm. He was not one for making a fuss of well-made virtual coffee. Once he had subdued his frustration, he looked up at the others. 'Can we continue?'

'Um, I wouldn't say no to another cup,' Tom said sheepishly. Newts obliged, producing this time a cappuccino supremely endowed with towering froth and a generous sprinkling of chocolate powder.

'This will only take a second,' Alby said, one eye bulging as it lingered on the cappuccino tower and the other trying vainly to maintain focus on the issue at hand.

'This coffee is something else,' Tom beamed, dipping his finger into the top of the froth and withdrawing it, dragging a huge trail of froth and chocolate with it. 'Thanks, Newts.'

GG couldn't help but nod in agreement; Newts did make the best coffee.

'My pleasure,' Newts said, successfully concealing his pleasure entirely, as he watched Tom spoon mounds of froth into his mouth.

Newts moved his handsome head slightly towards Mac to his right, who was stirring sugar into her latte and smiling smugly.

'What?' Tom asked suspiciously, eyeing the smug smile.

'It's nothing,' Mac smiled benignly, obviously pleased. She nibbled her wafer.

'You spiked my drink?'

'I simply used it to release some endomorphines, paracetamol and codeine to make you feel better. Works instantly.'

'That's amazing.' Tom took another teetering pile of drug-and-hormone-laced froth. 'Thank you, Mac.'

'It is my absolute pleasure.'

Now driven almost to utter distraction by the constant drivel, and visibly aching with impatience, Alby paced back and forth alongside the table like an impatient ringmaster in a circus.

'We have a situation here!' Alby barked. He knew that the serving of coffee and refreshments was all very civil, but he had greater considerations. GG jerked his head and rolled his eyes, while punching out small decisive steps: three one way, then three back.

After 11 such moves, GG was ready to resume.

'What do scientists do when they enter quantum time?' GG asked as he scraped the froth of his macchiato from the edge of the tiny glass and discarded it on the table before him. 'Retire?' It was obvious GG loved to lecture. 'Of course not. I've been researching space junk. There are quarry loads of debris out there. Cities of junk. Five and a half million kilos of man-made trash. Thousands of defunct space satellites. Many satellites have fallen back to Earth, but most of the junk is a long way out there—scattered far and wide.'

Alby's lips were knit together in clear irritation.

'After take-off, rockets jettison stages in order to save weight. The spent stages, along with adaptor linkages and the exploding bolts used in all this, are simply let go.'

'Dumped, in other words.' Newts shook his head in disapproval. In his day, high-shock-resistant heat-resistant lithium panelling had been an extremely valuable commodity. 'And gravity will do its work—it will all fall to Earth.'

'So, there is all this deadly hypersonic shrapnel, otherwise known as space junk, circling around the planet,' finished GG.

'There's nothing new in that.' Tom was not going to be persuaded by a bit of overblown anecdotal speculation. 'We all know there is a lot of stuff out there.'

'True,' GG conceded snarkily. 'This is one point. However, what we have here with these two satellites is something else again. It's the Kessler Syndrome.'

'Yes, but most of it stays up there, doesn't it?'

'Only if its geostationary orbit is around 35,000 kilometres,' Mac reminded him.

'You are gonna have to help me here, Mac,' Tom admitted.

Mac explained. 'That is where the speed of the satellite equals the rotation of the Earth, so it appears to stay in the same place. Most, however, are in orbit 100 to 1,500 kilometres away,' she explained. 'I too have been researching it.'

The Kessler Syndrome was proposed by NASA's Donald Kessler in 1978. He proposed that collisions compound—each collision generates debris, increasing the likelihood of more.

As an expert on the solar system, GG took the floor once more. 'Kessler says the more collisions there are, the more junk there is, and the more collisions, and so on. The orbit determines how long it will take to fall to Earth. This means that if a satellite is 200 kilometres above us, it could take 30 days to hit the Earth. The satellites at 35,000 kilometres are in geostationary orbit and could take about 1 million years, so there's no danger there. Most satellites that fall to Earth burn up on re-entry due to the extreme friction and heat.'

'Right, ok,' Tom said, his mind finally on the job.

Alby nodded, whereupon a picture of satellites whizzing around Earth appeared on the screen.

There was silence as they all gazed at the image, until GG again spoke.

'Looks like a rubbish dump with flies buzzing rotting scraps.'

'Hmmmpft.' Tom gazed in wonderment.

'Forty years of not cleaning up your mess,' Newts explained.

'Bit like your room, Tom,' Mac offered with a smile.

'There are derelict spacecraft, stages of launch vehicles, collision debris—all sorts of stuff—whizzing around Earth much faster than bullets,' GG elaborated. 'One astronaut even lost his camera while taking a photo—it's now flying above your head every day.'

GG emphasised this point by tossing his handkerchief in a little ball so that it flew past Tom's left ear and skidded across the table to halt in front of an unimpressed Mac.

'Due to friction, a lot of the space junk doesn't survive re-entry into the atmosphere and much of it falls into the oceans or unpopulated areas. However, in the last few years, with the huge increase in junk every day, several significant pieces have hit the Earth.' Not one to shy away from theatrics, GG threw his half-eaten macaroon at Tom's belly, where it left a tiny ganache-smeared impact crater on Tom's shirt.

A light year is the distance light travels in a year = 9,460,730,472,581, that's 9.5 trillion kilometres.

At last, Alby was satisfied; there was order at the meeting, they were all focused on the probabilistic equations, and GG had finished throwing improvised props. On the screen a series of clear formulae appeared, showing the rogue satellite.

'Ok, Watto, show GG's calculations for the collision—the kinetic energy is simply huge at that speed,' Alby explained.

# Great Tapestry

**Projected Collision Path**

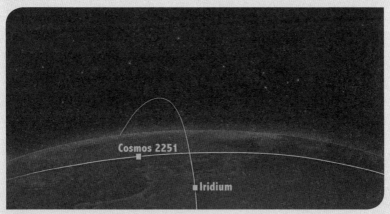

**Probabilistic Collision Impact Location: Siberia**

Collision altitude above Earth: 790 kilometres.

American Iridium X56 communications satellite—fully operational.

Russian Cosmos R78 satellite launched 1978—decommissioned in the 1990s.

Weight of iridium satellite: 500 kilograms.

Weight of Russian Cosmos: 750 kilograms.

Velocity at impact: 40,000 kilometres per hour.

Kinetic energy of impact: $Ek = \frac{1}{2}\,mv^2$.

New space debris scattered: 735 pieces above 1 centimetre—some up to 1 metre.

'Yes, while the object is small, the impact is huge,' added Newts. 'Classical physics I invented. Even something small, say 0.5 centimetres, can impact the space shuttle if it is travelling at 20,000 kilometres per hour.' Shy as he was, Newts wasn't going to be ignored. Besides, he loved mechanical or classical physics. (He had after all discovered much of it.) And so he loved to use equations to work out facts. 'Of course, Heisenberg's Uncertainty Principle does not apply here.'

'Thanks, egghead.' GG was not going to be sidelined by Newts' characteristic overemphasis on details and formulae. He dismissed it with a wave of his hand. 'The evidence speaks for itself.'

'When does all this occur?' asked Tom, eager to find any reason to leave.

'Watto, show him the countdown clock.'

On the Tapestry a clock appeared. Slightly discomfited, Tom had been expecting a longer time to think the matter through.

Collision Countdown Clock: 47 hours + 26 minutes + 51 seconds

There was an awkward silence and a moment of realisation; it gave them years to act in Qbits time but not very long in the real world. They had less than two days to stop the satellites colliding.

Unfazed, GG went on. 'The more precisely we measure the position, the less accurately we are able to gauge its momentum. The more we try, the less accurate we are. We need to guess, to use probabilities, in order to be accurate. Heisenberg Uncertainty Principle.'

'Guess? What time travel juice are you on?' scoffed Newts. 'And you don't know how fast it's going!'

Due to all the jumping from scientist to scientist, Tom was struggling to make sense of it all. He wished there was some way to combine all their quirky brilliant minds into one coherent creature, instead of having to put up with all their irritatingly human qualities too.

'These are too big,' GG explained. 'This is the current orbit. The collision will occur in less than two days. The 750 kilogram Russian dead satellite will collide with this active 500 kilogram American communications satellite at 30,000 kilometres per hour at a distance of 800 kilometres. Debris will scatter hundreds of kilometres on impact.'

'But Watto said both NASA and the European Space Agency monitor satellite orbits and space junk,' said Tom. 'They would be aware of this, and would have predictive models, wouldn't they?'

'Yes, but they assume nothing changes orbit—they just watch and don't forecast orbital shifts caused by gravity over time. They haven't taken into account the unexpected, improbable orbit moves we believe will occur. In a word, HUP matters here. Unfortunately we can't know both where it is and how fast it's going, so we use probability. Yup, we use HUP and then we guess a bit. Works in here because randomness prevails here.' GG looked incredulous, as if it absolutely befuddled him as to how such a simple detail could have been overlooked.

> Heisenberg Uncertainty Principle (HUP) by Werner Heisenberg in 1927, means the more precisely momentum of an object is measured the less precisely the location can be measured!

'Huh, HUP ? But the screen says ...' Tom didn't want to just go along with these experts. He felt it was important to challenge everything.

'However, *we* can forecast anything we damn well please.

The impact will probably totally destroy both the satellites because they are so heavy. I had a look at what the 750 kilogram 40-year-old Russian spy satellite did. I crosschecked and the Russian plans reveal nothing special, just the usual photographs, observations, and so on.' GG was now rummaging in his inner pocket for supposed notes of such research. He found a paper napkin with notes on it but dismissed it as some other subject and put it back. Of course, they were all in his wine-riddled head, but accurate to the finest detail.

Now Alby looked puzzled. 'Wow, 750 kilograms is heavy, isn't it? They don't minimise launch weight to get it up in orbit?' he mused.

'So, in summary, GG believes,' Mac explained, trying to install order and perhaps end the discussion, 'there is likely to be a hypervelocity impact, despite all the government monitoring suggesting otherwise. GG has calculated using Heisenberg that due to all the space debris the orbit will change and if the Russian orbit deteriorates slightly the two satellites will collide. NASA has overlooked that probabilistic change.'

Tom sensed closure had been reached. 'So, keep me posted. I'm going back to sleep now. Thanks for the hangover cure, Mac. Guys, let's keep a low profile, ok?'

Tom clattered his cup on its saucer as if making an attempt to clear up after himself, only semi-cognisant of the futility of clearing away virtual dishes. He wished they would all just learn to relax a bit. They were the most highly strung beings he had ever encountered. They made him nervous. They were four of the most famous free thinkers of all time, with a very different understanding of interpreting rules. Science was, after all, as Alby always stated, based on curiosity; questioning the way things were.

The scientists all nodded in agreement.

GG cleared his throat and leaned toward Tom theatrically. 'If I may have a quiet word with you first, Tom?'

Tom rolled his eyes. 'GG, we've just had thousands of not so quiet words. I'm outta here—it can wait till I'm awake.' And with that, Tom was gone.

Quantum physics may lead to multi-worlds existing = quantum weirdness.

Back in his bed, Tom fell asleep almost instantly, as he had only been away a few moments. Then, feeling as though he had only slept a few seconds more, there was a thump on the door. He rolled over and yelled, 'Guys, stop bothering me. Recheck all calculations.'

# Chapter 6

## Tom's Room

1 March 2015

11.03 am + 34 seconds

'What did you say?' came a familiar voice through the door.

Only half-awake, Tom realised he had been talking out loud and must have sounded like an utter lunatic. The voice on the other side of his door belonged to Tom's best friend and flatmate, Scott Maddocks, otherwise known as 'Mad Dog', or sometimes simply 'Dog', if one's laziness so

We are moving at huge speed around the Earth, Sun and the Universe.
The Sun and Earth are moving at about 70,000 kilometres per hour towards the star Vega.
As the Sun and galaxy are moving, we are always travelling at over 2 million kilometres per hour!

demanded it. He was called this not only because it was a contraction of his name, but because of his wild and unpredictable character.

'Mate, you're gibbering, you must still be drunk. Let's get some breakfast,' Mad Dog chuckled through the door. 'Harry's for a Tiger?' The door rattled on its hinges as Mad Dog seemingly tried to pull it off.

'Huh? Oh, yes, mate. Come in, for God's sake!' Tom yelled before Mad Dog really did rip the door out of the wall. He was a fairly solid fellow, after all.

'What's the time?' asked Tom when he saw Mad Dog's wild grin.

'Eleven am—brekky time. I need caffeine.'

'Oh hell, I need to be at Mum's by 1.00 pm. Yeah, let's do it. See you in 15—shower and Harry's.'

Tom lay on his bed figuring out how best to tell Mad Dog. What to tell Mad Dog? Like most of the human race, Tom worried about what others thought. Mad Dog was his best friend, and although he trusted him completely he did not know how to tell him there were four famous scientists performing a weird circus act inside his head! Well, technically they were in a quantum world entangled with the real world, but from where he stood they were inside his head. Like actors in a sitcom, people playing the roles of Galileo Galilei, Sir Isaac Newton, Marie Curie and Albert Einstein were in constant communication with him. Then there was this gibbering character Watto, forever rattling off useless information. Watto was the portal key to the entire Qbit entanglement.

Tom might as well tell his friend he had become engaged to Queen Elizabeth I or claim Neil Armstrong was his personal trainer. But Mad Dog was the one guy Tom trusted most in the whole world.

Tom and Mad Dog didn't look like brothers, but they were just as inseparable. Tom was fair-skinned, tall and lanky with thick brown curly hair, while Mad Dog was shorter and muscular with blonde hair and a tan. He looked about as unlike a mathematician as Tom looked like a physicist. Tom and Mad Dog had been best mates since high school and had lived together since they both started teaching at Sydney Uni. Tom taught first-year physics and Mad Dog taught engineering maths. Students loved them because they were young and energetic and both played rugby for the B grade. Tom was the coach, Mad Dog the captain. The students also knew the pair often held large wild parties which garnered them great respect.

Tom hoisted himself to his feet and trotted off to the bathroom. *Music, please, Watto—some of my favourites.* He started singing along in the shower as Watto pumped out some tunes.

Mad Dog chuckled as he waited in the kitchen; Tom had been like an mp3 player stuck on shuffle lately, breaking into song at every opportunity. House life with Tom was like a law of physics; all things went from order to disorder—entropy, the third law of thermodynamics, no matter what Mad Dog did to try to maintain order. And there was no point fighting a law of science. Tom just didn't care if things were a mess. And, as Mad Dog was a manic clean freak, the general cleanliness of the house tended toward an average of being essentially liveable.

Humans share about 98% of their DNA with chimps and 70% with slugs.

Once Tom had showered and dressed, there was yet more pounding at his door. 'Let's go!' He opened the door to find Mad Dog with an outstretched hand, proffering two paracetamol tablets.

'No, actually, I'm good,' Tom smiled, thinking of the miracle cure bestowed on him by the Qbits.

Tom thought back to the accident, coincidentally, Mad Dog had been there at the very beginning, when this whole Qbit entanglement had happened. While Tom's discovery was no mean feat, it hadn't happened exactly the way Tom had dreamt of discovering uses for graphene and atomic-level storage, or 'atto' storage.

Mad Dog had insisted they start riding bikes everywhere they went—to uni, to training, to the shops, to the pub. You name it, and according to Mad Dog, it could be comfortably cycled to. Even in a downpour or gale-force winds.

'We're scientists,' Mad Dog had said. 'We know what will happen to the Earth if global warming is allowed to continue. Everyone has to do their bit.'

Tom's excuse of 'I'm a physicist' had not allayed the appeal.

Together, as usual, Mad Dog and he had been riding home from footy, through the killer inner city traffic. Angry grey clouds textured like huge smothering cushions and exactly as in the paintings of Peter Paul Rubens, a contemporary of Galileo, hung low in the sky. In the distance, across the highway beyond the trees and the park and following the animal growls of thunder booming, lightning flashed. A storm was imminent. The energy and impending madness of riding on the storm had affected Mad Dog, who at this point seemed more wacky than usual.

Mad Dog had been riding along ahead of Tom, yee-hawing and yelling. Their team, the so-called Black Swans, had thrashed Western Suburbs, and although he had been happy, as the rain poured and lightning flashed and the sky darkened further, Tom wasn't over the moon about being on a bike.

As he and Mad Dog cycled through the park, only part of his attention was on Mad Dog's replay of the game.

'The back line worked like a well-oiled machine: Jake—great

game in the centre and Meyer on the wing was on fire. Wests' forwards just couldn't break through.'

'Yeah, great.' He was thinking about his science project, wondering if the download had worked. He couldn't wait to get home and test whether the saved data was retrievable and organised. Tom had engineered a mass storage device and had decided to call it the 'Watto'. It was his new design and he had tested it that day. It was a storage and Internet device that could be worn on the finger like a ring, which meant data could be with you always. It could provide almost unlimited data storage, using nanotechnology to increase storage space on the scale of individual atoms—the new field of 'atto' physics.

As a last-minute trial he had decided to see how much he could download and then retrieve at home. The Watto was made from tungsten, whose chemical symbol is W, with the extremely high melting point of over 3,000 °C. Watto was going to make Tom rich and famous when he sold it to a big company. He had used a new substance, graphene, to enhance the speed and battery life.

The ring had contained a trillion terabytes of information, but the issue was whether it would be retrievable or just a jumbled mess. To see if it worked, he had downloaded all of the information on the four scientists he would be teaching his class about in the next few weeks—Galileo Galilei, Sir Isaac Newton, Albert Einstein and Marie Curie, all saved in abbreviated subdirectories named GG, Newts, Alby and Mac.

Tom had always loved making stuff, which was why he was chosen when he was 5 years old to inherit the Meccano set stowed decades earlier in the roof storage of his great-great uncle. He started by constructing a facsimile of the Sydney Harbour Bridge, upon which his mother, doting as mothers often are, had considered him a prodigy. Of course, he wasn't. Even so, he pulled his first computer apart in his teens and rebuilt it almost perfectly.

Mad Dog was still talking, now describing the winning pass in the final minute of the game and as Mad Dog always pleaded his 'Law of Unintended Consequences had Kicked-in', or 'LUCK' as he always liked to call it, and it could be good or bad LUCK when with Mad Dog as he always took things one step too far.

Mad Dog screeched with excitement as lightning, transporting hundreds of millions of volts and currents in tens of thousands of amperes, boomed through the airwaves. At that juncture the highest point on the landscape was a light pole.

The lightning struck it, sparking an arc of electricity that zipped through the driving rain and zapped Tom's handlebar. The bike skidded across the asphalt into the kerb and crashed. Watto had taken a direct hit. Constructed from an alloy that could withstand enormous heat, the tungsten and graphene ring had become supercharged with the extreme voltage. Watto simply melted into Tom's finger, and Tom lay on the side of the road, dead to the world.

Three days later, Tom awoke in hospital.

'The doctor said the ring you were wearing probably absorbed the impact of the strike and may have saved your life!' sobbed Tom's mum. 'The lightning apparently was absorbed by super-heating the atoms and electrons on that ring you were wearing. Thank God it was made of whatever it was. Where did you get it? You could have died.'

Watto had saved his life so it was hard to hate him. Only now Watto was a random creature, a likeness of

Tungsten's chemical symbol is W, element number 74 and it's melting point 3,422 °C Atto is $10^{-18}$ = 0.000 000 000 000 000 001. Now that's a small! W-Atto.

Schrödinger's cat, constantly sending random information to Tom day and night, trying to please him. He was annoying as hell.

Tom was relieved to discover that Mad Dog was ok, too. He had a minor concussion and some guilt.

As the pair recovered from the accident, no one was the wiser that in addition to saving Tom's life, the ring had transformed; the electrons and information had somehow become super excited and mutated the data into a quantum state, creating—or awakening—four quantum beings, who resided in an alternative reality. The Qbits.

Gradually, Tom began to realise that he was no longer alone. He had become entangled with the random and chaotic quantum reality of the Qbits.

Back in the present, Tom and Mad Dog were ambling down the road to the strip of local shops—a bakery, chemist, newsagent and Harry's Cafe de Wheels.

Watto piped up inside Tom's head. 'We are travelling at 5 kilometres per hour in a northwest direction, with an estimated time of arrival of 2 minutes 35 seconds at current speed.' He was like an inbuilt personal navigation system that was impossible to switch off and never seemed to run out of batteries. But Tom was almost used to it by now. As a compromise, he would just instruct Watto to play music and keep him quiet that way.

They strolled across the road to the harbour side, with Tom's world bombarded with a classic AC/DC hit that GG had insisted Watto 'turn it up', and greeted Harry, who was busy yelling at the guy operating the deep fryer. Harry's Cafe de Wheels was a renowned institution and had been offering Harry's famous pies since 1938, with the requirement that each subsequent owner had to be called Harry. Tom wasn't sure how this provision had escaped the various anti-discrimination legislations over the years, and then thanked his lucky stars he was a scientist, not a lawyer.

'Mad King Harry III and Crazy Chin!' drawled Mad Dog as they approached the cart. This was the third Harry they had known since their uni days. Dave 'Harry' Taylor was the ninth Harry in total, a 55-year-old retired banker. Crazy Chin was his barista.

Harry's Café de Wheels was old school. A long-time witness to the ups and downs of Woolloomooloo, it had been there at the end of the Great Depression in the late 1930s to look upon the after-dark goings-on of sailors, soldiers, policemen and the bohemian set. And it was still pumping at 11.00 am with taxi drivers using it as a morning tea spot.

And of course, there was also the food, which was perfect 'day after the night before' sustenance. Cut potatoes hissed as they hit the boiling oil, warm kitchen smells of green peas sitting in boiled water swirled around them, and the whoof, gurgle and slap of the espresso machine was music to their ears.

Over the years, there had been laws restricting Harry 'Tiger' Edwards' use of the harbourside patch of concrete his pie cart occupied, requiring him to move his food caravan at least 30 centimetres a day to circumvent some archaic law about being non-permanent. Now the caravan was an international icon frequented by all the visiting celebrities—and best of all, it didn't have to move so much as an inch per year.

The side of Harry's caravan was plastered with pictures of all the celebrities who had popped in to enjoy one of Harry's offerings, including Elton John and nearby resident Russell Crowe. Tom found it difficult to imagine Elton John demolishing a meat pie topped with mushy peas and gravy, but the pictures were there to prove it. There were only a few makeshift tables scattered about beside the cart. Harry made cappuccinos for the locals to sit on the wharf wall and watch the world go by. Empty plastic milk crates made for extra seats if required.

Tom and Mad Dog sat and gazed out at the steely smooth harbour as their coffees appeared on the table, with a greasy bacon sandwich for Tom and vegemite toast for Mad Dog.

'Good night last night, gentlemen?' Harry stumped up a stray milk crate and plonked his buttocks onto the scratched plastic.

'Yeah, Harry—a little birthday celebration,' chirped Mad Dog, lowering his sunglasses to reveal his bloodshot eyes.

The speed of light 'c' is exactly 299,792,458 metres per second and it is considered the Universe's cosmic speed limit!

Harry smirked as he hoisted himself back to his feet. 'Well you two are probably best left to your own pathetic company today. I'm off.' And with that he strode back to the cart to resume his yelling.

Tom wasn't listening, he had that glazed over look again. Mad Dog thought he seemed like that often these days—a bit vague, like he wasn't fully there.

Mad Dog sat for a few moments contemplating Tom. 'Ok, so what's up?'

# Chapter 7

## Great Hall

### 1 March 2015
### 11.28 am + 45 seconds

Tom wasn't listening to Mad Dog because he was at that very moment pacing the floor of the Great Hall, yelling.

The Qbits had disregarded all the rules again.

'I was a bloody idiot trusting you guys. What do you think is going to happen now? They will find us. The FBI and Homeland Security will find us! And then there's the CIA, they'll be after us too.

> Any square piece of paper cannot be folded in half more than 7 times.

Those space cadets don't even know where space is, let alone why two satellites, on a probabilistic set of assumptions, might collide ... '

'He was nicer than the Russian,' interjected GG.

'Aha of course, so you're the ring leader of this circus?' Tom stopped in his tracks. 'What Russian?' Tom developed a heavy feeling in his stomach as it dawned on him what GG had done.

'Come and sit down, Tom,' suggested Mac, unruffleable as always.

'No, I don't want another of your or Newt's voodoo drinks or coffees. I'm supposed to be going to Mum's for lunch— I'll be lucky if I'm not arrested before then.' Tom huffed and puffed before continuing abruptly. 'And stop that. What are you doing?'

'Seeing if I can fold this paper in half more than seven times,' replied GG.

'Why?'

'Because Watto said you can't,' he replied.

'What?'

'Watto,' said GG.

Tom glared at GG, who gazed back innocently, before saying, 'It's all, as you say, water under the bridge now. Are you guys going or staying? I've got work to do.' He had folded it four times and it was already getting rather thick and difficult to manoeuvre.

The moon orbits every 27.3 days and is 27% the size of the Earth. When the moon is overhead you weigh less due to its gravity pulling on you.

'Not very happy with yourself today?' Newts asked with a frown, leaning forward to inspect Tom's eyes more closely.

'I'm fine. We've got two days, didn't you say? I'm having my coffee and hanging out with Mad Dog and watching boats sail by. And then I'm going to go and have some bloody roast lamb!'

52

'Pull yourself together, Tom,' Newts reprimanded. 'We need to fill you in on what has been happening.'

Qbits, satellites colliding ... Tom felt he already knew quite enough as it was. And he was certainly already angry. He really didn't need to hear any more of this foolishness.

'If you hadn't e-mailed, you damn idiot ...' Newts glared at his disgraceful companion. As former Master of the English Mint, he was used to things being managed correctly, and certainly in accordance with the law.

'Don't be such a cyberchrondriac. He had to be told.' GG was as independent and wilful as ever.

'Who are we talking about here? Who was nicer than the Russian?' Tom was trying to calm down as he asked.

'The President of the United States, my carefree young friend. Would you care for a glass of this excellent grape?' GG asked, almost serious for a moment. He inserted the elbow of the arm holding the goblet inside his stained and voluminous surcoat to reveal a wine bottle nestled in a pocket within. 'You insightful Australians refer to it as "hair of the dog".'

Newts shook his head in disbelief. Mac's eyes were cast toward the floor. Alby was tight-lipped as ever, and Tom simply glared at GG.

In 1687 Newton's Universal Law of Gravitation stated that all objects are attracted to one another. We are all attracted to the Earth and to each other. Gravity is the glue that holds the Universe together.

'You were all ignoring me,' GG slurred. 'Someone had to act!'

'Yes, someone had to act,' began Tom. 'But did you really have to e-mail the President of the United States of America?'

# Chapter 8

## THE WHITE HOUSE
### WASHINGTON

28 February 2015
9.05 pm + 49 seconds

It was disappointing, but President Robert 'Bob' Neil simply could not leave the function. Snow had been falling for days, blocking access roads and grounding all flights into and out of the international and domestic airports. None of the guests or staff would be in a rush to leave the party. And that meant he had to stay too.

Nevertheless, nothing could spoil the Disneyesque wonder of a President's 60th birthday party, celebrated with a White House Ball—the first he had enjoyed as the President of the United States of America. Soon the band would strike the opening notes to *Happy Birthday*, with the guest singer leading the tune. The Vice President would then propose a toast to Bob, followed by three loud cheers. When the song and toast had finished, he would cut the cake and with the band still playing, he intended to retire for the evening, without even so much as the company of Marilyn Monroe.

Some of the guests and even some heads of state had already drunk too much and were falling about—one man required an escort to his taxi, his partner snivelling beside him. Even so, it was hard to believe the world wasn't one big beautiful garden party, with all its inhabitants equally happy at this single moment.

The President's iPhone 8 had no messages from his daughter Kellie. He had been checking it every 5 minutes—he was a father like any other. She was late, due to a prior engagement at her boyfriend's, but had promised she would be at the party by 9.00 pm at the latest. The President would wait for them both to show up, even though they had missed the dinner and were now pushing back his bedtime indefinitely. *Hmpf—kids.*

For the hundredth time he checked his phone, however, there was an e-mail from a certain 'GG'. He snuck into the men's room and opened the e-mail, sniffing defiantly. Only one new message; and it was his birthday and everything.

THE WHITE HOUSE
WASHINGTON

**From:** GG@Qbits.me
**To:** RNeil@presidentusa.com
**Sent:** 28 February 2015 8.55 pm
**Subject:** Satellite collision in 44 hours 33 minutes

Mr President (Bob?),

Forgive me for intruding on your birthday party—it seems to be going well; however, the matter is urgent. An old Russian Cosmos R78 satellite, so named because it was launched in 1978 and lost power in the 1990s, by my calculation will collide with an American Iridium X56 communications satellite at 5.28 pm on 2nd March.

The Russian satellite will not survive the collision and I believe there is every possibility pieces of debris will re-enter orbit. Unfortunately, the satellite was once part of an early initiative by USSR to use nuclear fuel systems (despite the treaty banning them from doing so).

The fuel rod is well protected but if it doesn't burn up upon re-entry it may behave like a 'dirty bomb' when it smashes into Earth.

Regrettably, NASA and CIA are unaware of this and the Russians will probably deny it. I respectfully suggest that you act to prevent this and destroy the defunct Russian satellite prior to collision, using the newly tested nuclear weapons on board the International Space Station.

Yours faithfully

GG

PS: Sorry about the drone the other day.

Who was this GG? Bob had received so few unofficial e-mails since becoming President, he wondered how GG had come to have his secure personal e-mail address. And how could he know about the drone? And how could such a message bypass security and get through the system? There were techsperts, cyber mechanics who took care of such things. And why was he referring to him in such irreverent terms? He was the President of the United States, ferchrissakes!

This intrusion constituted a breach of national security at the highest level and could not be ignored. Within this secure world he needed to communicate with the inner circle of his machine: FBI, Homeland Security, and the recalcitrant CIA. This wasn't the time to entertain the whims of some hacker, some kid barely in high school, some nerd showing off his skills. In many ways, kids were smarter these days. But—alas!—the youth were now as troublesome as young people ever were. Here he was, President of the United States, worrying about his daughter.

Despite Bob Neil being a maths major, he was neither space nor cyberspace aware, and so it took some time for the contents of this extraordinary e-mail to sink in. GG was no high school nerd gone bad. He was either an utter nutter or someone who was about to save the world. Either way, Bob didn't like the chances of this guy remaining free for too much longer. Two satellites, Old Russia (that was the USSR), a nuclear fuel rod and an e-mail sent to and received by him without being filtered out. This was a high-tech prank at a minimum, and at

worst a terrorist threat to thousands, maybe millions of innocent people. But how?

Bob sidled over to the Vice President and Chief of Staff and
softly, almost whispering, asked them to attend a security meeting at 7.00 am. When he had finished breathing out his calm
instructions, he continued moving toward the rear entrance
and ducked out of the party. The President needed no excuse
to go anywhere.

He slipped into his office and forwarded the e-mail to the
heads of security for CIA, Homeland Security, NASA and the
FBI, just for starters. He simply wrote:

**From:**     RNeil@presidentusa.com

**To:**       Chiefs@presidentusa.com

**Sent:**     28 February 2015 9.30 pm

**Subject:**  Satellite collision in 44 hours

Refer attached e-mail, it is self-explanatory. I have had no contact—received tonight around 9.00 pm. Find this man.

I want an update on the Everest drone incident.

Meet in my office at 7.00 am.

Attachment 1 GG e-mail.

R Neil
**President**

# Chapter 9

## Great Hall

### 1 March 2015
### 11.38 am + 43 seconds

GG dismissed Tom's panic with a graceful wave of his hand.

'No need to worry, my righteous friend. The only connection to us is the Qbits site.'

Alby cleared his throat. 'I think United States security is going to try,' Alby paused as he thought this through, 'to find the source.'

> The Big Bang began the Universe about 14 billion years ago. After the Big Bang the Universe was hotter than the Sun. At $10^{-38}$ seconds after the Big Bang you were all quarks. And 12.5 billion years ago, you were carbon. Then 4.5 billion years ago you were all tar. Eventually at 3.8 billion years ago, you were all bacteria.

'Oh bloody hell,' was all Tom could muster exasperated and scared.

'Even so,' Alby continued, determined to make his point, 'A few minutes ago the CIA sent an Internet Trojan to search the Qbits website looking for GG@Qbits.me, trying to source the e-mail.'

'What the hell?' By now Tom had his head in his hands, elbows on the table. His mother would never have approved. 'For real? The CIA? Like in the movies?'

'The very same.'

'I'm so dead,' moaned Tom. 'But, how—'

'Speak to your friend, here.' Newts sneered across at GG.

Tom looked up to meet GG's fuzzy gaze. Seated in the large swivel chair, still attached to the goblet nuzzling into his linen shirt, GG looked like a scorned puppy.

Mac and Alby remained silent, while Newts managed to look even more melancholy, as if this was positive proof of his unhappy view of the world.

While GG appeared somewhat subdued, 5 cents to a phial of plutonium his mind was working on something.

Tom shook his head in disbelief. 'I am totally and utterly done for. When the CIA or one of those American no-rules-except-ours departments finds me ...' He slouched further into his chair. 'I may as well head down to Long Bay Prison and check in to maximum security right now.'

'Don't be ridiculous—it would be Guantanamo, wouldn't it?' GG commented without thinking.

For a quantum nanosecond, which is not very long, the Great Hall was quiet.

'So, seriously, what caused you geniuses to e-mail the President of the United States of America?' Tom asked. His mocha vienna coffee was giving off an irresistible aroma as he inhaled.

'How did you even know his e-mail address? Which is—' Tom took a sip of the rich coffee mocha before continuing, 'I've gotta admit, kinda cool.'

Alby smiled. 'We have an access-all-areas pass on the information superhighway. We can e-mail anyone anywhere and make sure they get the e-mail. No server or firewall exists for us. Watto is a key to the electronic universe.'

Watto displayed a huge smile on the Great Tapestry.

'And?' Tom glanced distractedly at the beaming grin.

'I think I can say President Neil was surprised to receive our e-mail. He called a security meeting for tomorrow morning, US time.'

'What a drama queen,' scolded GG. 'I texted him to say he didn't need to bother with all that! Just NASA is required.' There was another silence.

'I once met President Roosevelt ...' began Alby.

'Sorry, guys.' Tom shut them down. 'If I hear another word out of this troll I am going to scream and hit somebody. No contact, ok? No e-mail, SMS, YouTube, or *anything*, without express approval!' There was an uneasy silence; Tom had never threatened violence before.

'You were out of orbit yourself, Tom, last night at 3.00 am, jumping about to that—what was that? It was scarcely *music* ... what was that?' GG had grown up in a musical family and was genuinely interested.

'That's quite enough,' snapped Tom. 'You just leave the President alone, do you hear?'

There was a tight German harrumphing coming from the end of the table. 'Much as I enjoy a chat, for goodness sake,' Alby never lost focus, 'can we continue?'

'Thank you, Alby. You yourself play a fine violin.' GG turned back to Tom. 'Maybe we could make one? After this,' he waved his arms demonstratively. Tom sat stony still. He suddenly remembered that sometimes GG could be quite childish.

'I'm listening.' Tom directed this at Mac.

'There are two large satellites, one Russian and one American, and in ...'

'That is two satellites,' Alby emphasised. 'And in less than two days.'

'Yes, yes, I know about two satellites in two days, but what's this talk about nuclear-powered satellites? Nobody used, or was allowed to use, nuclear fuel rods in the 1970s—that's just weird,' Tom went on.

'Speculation,' stated Alby snootily, 'based on some file note GG found on an old computer system in Russia. He used it to get their attention'.

'Everything here is weird,' stated Tom pointedly.

'Yes, well, what if it's true?' asked GG.

'Discuss tomorrow.' Tom tried to systematise his thoughts into questions. Alby was about to answer when GG intervened. An unwritten law in science says that whoever discovers something should be the first to reveal it: a law the others had forgotten and GG was determined to uphold.

GG made a show of ignoring the look of incredulity on Tom's face. 'The Cosmos satellite seemed so much larger than the other satellites of that time.' He waited while Tom took this in. 'And, my young friend, this is what I discovered. There is a small but powerful nuclear engine on board. This little messenger is left over from the Cold War. The Russians—goddamn them, as the Yanks say—don't even know if the control systems on board function.'

It was all getting too much for GG, who flopped down into his chair. Then, with a thespian flourish, he downed a mouthful of his cherished wine.

'It's true,' Newts backed him up. 'I've just hacked into the Russian computer on board. At least that still works.'

'GG believes,' Mac continued, 'there is every chance there will be a hypervelocity impact despite all the NASA monitoring suggesting otherwise.'

'As I've been saying, I have calculated that due to Heisenberg's Uncertainty Principle,' GG explained, 'I have guesstimated that the orbit of the Cosmos will slowly deteriorate. And I have guessed it exactly. And when the Cosmos falls to a height of 600 kilometres, it will, unless the American communications satellite changes orbit, collide with the Russian satellite, releasing a frigate container of debris that will cause immeasurable damage ...' He pulled at the grubby cuffs on his shirt. 'It's a lay-down misère ...'

'And you have warned them?' It was Tom's turn to get excited. 'And the Russians?'

'Yes, young Tom. Finally some action!' GG leaned toward the table and gently nudged the bottle of wine, causing it to glide gracefully across the wooden surface. 'Would you care to celebrate with me?' He looked about. 'Anyone? Ok, then I'm going back to the Space Station. It calms me.'

Tom was increasingly feeling alone, burdened now with responsibility that a young physicist should not ever be confronted with. The Qbits were getting bolder and more determined to 'help'.

There are about 1.5 trillion bacteria on the surface of the body. That is, there are more living organisms on your skin than there are people on Earth.

# Chapter 10

## THE WHITE HOUSE
### WASHINGTON

1 March 2015
7.05 am + 47 seconds

The American President was a man unaccustomed to feeling confused, concerned and nervous; he was precise, logical, and a mathematician by training. He was briefed, and decisions were made. Things were dealt with in an orderly fashion. How had this GG person thought to send him an e-mail telling him these bewildering things when NASA knew absolutely nothing about any of it? And damn it, the drone?

All the various chiefs of staff received the e-mail overnight. That single e-mail had disrupted a plethora of routine meetings and caused these powerful men to convene urgently in the Oval Office—the President, Vice President, Chief of Staff and Defence, heads of NASA, CIA, Homeland Security

In 1946 the first computer ENIAC (Electronic Numerical Integrator and Calculator) was created. A Quantum computer will calculate at a trillion times the speed of current super computers. Qbits world operates at quantum speed.

and the FBI—before they had even had their breakfast. And all because the information contained in the e-mail 'might be true'. However, as each man quieted his grumbling tummy and strode manfully through the imposing hallways of the White House, the same thought occurred to everyone: *it can't be true or we would know about it. Just a hoax—an annoying hoax.* The one consoling aspect, they thought, as the Oval Office door swung open to reveal that the meeting had not been catered, was that someone would be held accountable and put in prison for this irresponsible and un-American hoax. And they would be the saviours of American morality yet again.

Terrorism alerts from the CIA, covert operations, all sorts of mind-numbingly convoluted orchestrations, were all part of the job, but they only came to the President to sign off on their various frolics—they never came to him for decisions. And not once since Bob Neil had taken office had he been the actual recipient of an event alert. It was simply unheard of! General practice was that the President knew of things not only on a 'need to know' basis, but on a 'can't be prevented from knowing' basis. Put simply, things ran more smoothly when the President didn't have these sorts of things to worry about. His job was to butter up the American people so they would vote for him, and more importantly, the eight power-ful men at the meeting would keep their jobs—for the next presidential term.

It was niggling away at Bob as he sat at his desk gazing blankly at the hungry faces before him; he knew that in theory less than a hundred people knew of the missile defence system on the International Space Station, which had only recently become operational and was indeed highly sensitive informa-tion. Who was this GG fella? And what did he know of dead Russian nuclear satellites potentially colliding with American communications systems? Furthermore, how did he know about the drone battle?

The President's series of internal rhetorical questions was interrupted by his Chief of Staff, who spoke respectfully to open the meeting.

'Mr President, we have checked and are still checking the origin of the e-mail and how it got through the secure firewall. We cannot yet verify the source.' His eyes flashed with desperation as he admitted this to the President. He was unused to admitting that basically he had not made any progress whatsoever—and had no way to spin it so that it even sounded like he had made any progress.

The NASA Chief spoke. 'There is indeed a non-operational Russian Cosmos R78 satellite in orbit but we are advised it is in a graveyard orbit, and it is very unlikely to collide with any monitored satellites and debris, according to our observations.' A distinct sense of calm immediately descended upon the meeting.

'Unlikely to collide ...' restated the President. '*Hmpf*—can't find the source?'

The Chief of Staff, Eric P Lowe, nodded and mouthed, 'That is correct, Mr President,' but no sound would come out. His clipboard slid an inch or two sideways on his lap as he tried to regain his composure.

The NASA Chief continued. 'NASA's Space Surveillance Network constantly monitors many defunct pieces of equipment and junk. We are in constant daily communication with the International Space Station. Just last week the crew of the Space Station had to enter the emergency pod, as a potential near-collision alert had been activated by a 1 centimetre piece of debris we tracked changing orbit—even a centimetre of debris travelling at a high speed can be fatal. However, our calculations and models show Cosmos R78 is not predicted to move orbit.

As for nuclear materials, there was certainly no record of nuclear fuel systems being on satellites—that would be a breach of the nonproliferation treaty we signed in the 1970s. We monitor all debris and, quite frankly, the chances of such an event occurring are estimated at millions to one.'

The Secretary of Defence and the Head of the CIA listened with an element of obvious concern. How could an e-mail get directly to the President? And why should they trust this NASA nerd? He looked like he had been growing his own drugs on a commune during the 1970s, not concerning himself with the ratification of the nuclear nonproliferation treaty.

The President spoke. 'So, let me understand this—I receive an e-mail from a random untraceable source called GG and so far we have established that there is in fact a defunct Russian satellite in orbit, and he claims there are nuclear systems on board, which we can't seem to 100% confirm nor deny from our intelligence. And how could he know about the Everest drone incident?'

He may as well have asked them to do their best impression of a stunned jack rabbit, for all the reaction he got.

'Ok, first let's find GG and bring him in. We reconvene at 5.00 pm today. Meanwhile, I will reply to the e-mail and see what we can learn.'

The Head of the CIA skilfully concealed a rising panic. 'Mr President, I'm not sure you should communicate directly until we know who and what we are dealing with. We should wait and see if they make any demands. It could still be a terrorist or blackmail attempt.' George O'Brien was a short bald man, aged in his sixties, who still kept fit. In his time he had been the best field agent in the CIA. A few years back he had retired and quit the firm, as it was called, only to be rehired to clean up the CIA and make it more accountable and effective—that is, less like a government service. The firm was now very well regarded and Bob was very good at getting the right intelligence to make the right decisions.

The President's eyelids fluttered briefly as he enjoyed his moment of control and decisiveness. 'George, George, I understand completely. But I am going to reply and I will simply ask for further information and background. I am deeply concerned that these people have hacked into purportedly the most secure office on this planet.'

A collective gulp could be heard by all of them around the table. But none dared to speak up to ask if he could at least draft the President's e-mail. They looked like a small herd of deer caught in the President's headlights. This was his moment.

'Any updates on the drone incident?'

This was going to be George O'Brien's moment. 'Actually, Mr President ... ah no.' He didn't want any further leaks.

The President clapped his hands together in closure. 'Ok, good. Dismissed, gentlemen,' he added. 'Thank you—this is Priority 1, need-to-know basis only.'

The most powerful men in America all departed from the Oval Office, suddenly frantic in their negotiation of who would do what; mobile phones were out; meetings were to be held at the most senior levels in all departments. The giant US intelligence machine was now in full search-and-destroy mode.

The President sat at his keyboard, delighted to be the first President to convince security that he be able to use e-mail freely. Nevertheless, his brow felt a little damp as he clicked on 'reply'. What to say to this loon? He resolved that as soon as he had got this one out of the way, he would e-mail his daughter and her new boyfriend—he wanted to catch up for a coffee.

THE WHITE HOUSE
WASHINGTON

**From:** RNeil@presidentusa.com
**To:** GG@Qbits.me
**Sent:** 1 March 2015 8.10 am
**Subject:** Satellite collision

Dear GG,

Can you give me more specific information about you and the situation?

R Neil
**President**

The President had barely hit 'send' when GG's long reply arrived. Bob was absolutely dumbfounded—how could he have replied so quickly? Bob slumped back in his chair and inside his head uttered the words, *what the heck? I'll be ...!*

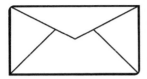

**From:** GG@Qbits.me
**To:** RNeil@presidentusa.com
**Sent:** 1 March 2015 8.11 am
**Subject:** Satellite collision in 34 hours 18 minutes

Hi Bob,

Hope you don't mind if I call you Bob. Firstly, I'm known as GG and I'm a scientist. Think of Galileo, and suppose that I have a modernised version of his DNA. However, we call ourselves Qbits and live in a quantum universe entangled with your world.

My friends are Alby (Qbit of Albert Einstein—he is very serious), Newts (Qbit of Sir Isaac Newton—very English) and Mac (Qbit of Marie Curie—delightful person). I was born in Pisa, Italy, in 1564 and I now live in this parallel electronic world, making me 451 years old.

When I was 46 years old I built the first telescope that could see the planets, and I made many discoveries. I still love astronomy. In fact, after I died they named the moons of Jupiter after me, which is pretty cool. I discovered the first 4 of them.

Before I made the telescope, everyone thought the Earth was the centre of the Universe, and didn't realise the moon was not a smooth round ball but had a mountainous surface like the Earth. Seems like the kind of stuff fifth graders know now!

I was amongst the first to support Copernicus in his

proposition that the Earth was not the centre of the Universe but the Sun was. In 1614, the Roman Catholic Church accused me of heresy for this! Then in 1632, I was condemned after an inquisition in Rome and was convicted and sentenced to life imprisonment. Later they reduced it to permanent house arrest at my villa in Arcetri, south of Florence (beautiful area—have you been?). But my goodness—I was just a scientist! These days I would've got a Nobel Prize like Alby and Mac did!

Turns out I was right—those churchy no-hopers have a lot to answer for. You should look at the Pope's secret files—they make your CIA files, even your Area 51, look like Christmas cards. They knew hundreds of years earlier that I was right, but they locked me up regardless.

Oh, and a warning re the Russian Cosmos satellite—I've attached the mathematical orbit analysis for the NASA guys you just met with to plug into their primitive mathematical model. Newts checked the calculations.

The collision will happen tomorrow. You need to take action!

Regards

GG

Collision Countdown Clock: 34 hours 18 minutes + 2 seconds

President Robert Neil just forwarded the e-mail.

**From:**     RNeil@presidentusa.com
**To:**        Chiefs@presidentusa.com
**Sent:**     1 March 2015 8.15 am
**Subject:**  Satellite collision

Bring this guy in and verify. Today.
Meet when GG is located, or evidence of threat confirmed.

Attachment—GG reply.

R Neil
**President**

It had to be remembered that there were many ludicrous claims and outlandish threats made against the world's most powerful government on a daily basis, and it was no surprise that all departments were inclined to consider this latest one to be a mere prank. After all, what the hell was all that stuff about Galileo? Probably just another madman making deluded claims to bring down the USA. But Bob just had that niggling feeling that something wasn't right. *How did he get my e-mail address? And the speed of that reply ... no terrorist group has NASA satellite capability, surely? The drone?*

But the rhetorical questions, once again, were left unanswered.

# Chapter 11

## Great Hall

### 3 March 2015
### 7.28 am + 43 seconds

Tom sat nervously watching the Great Tapestry.

'They're leaving their run a bit late aren't they?' he muttered grumpily.

GG sighed. 'The road to hell is paved with good intentions, my dear Tom.'

As the countdown clock ticked down, all the Qbits watched the action unfolding on the Great Tapestry.

With 1 minute and 2 seconds to go, it dawned on them that the USA may not, in fact, intervene, and that the satellites might end up colliding after all.

# Chapter 12

## THE WHITE HOUSE
### WASHINGTON

2 March 2015
5.30 pm + 47 seconds

The President was sitting in his office preparing to deal with the day's news. There was yet another e-mail from this GG guy in his inbox. No one had reported back about bringing him in. The time limit GG had given had well and truly elapsed. Just another hoax. He opened the e-mail.

Collision Countdown Clock: 1 minute + 1 second

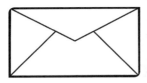

**From:** GG@Qbits.me

**To:** RNeil@presidentusa.com

**Sent:** 2 March 2015 5.30 pm

**Subject:** Satellite collision

Hi Bob,

Well, it happened. I was out by 1 minute, but given it was based on probability, using Heisenberg and predictive calculus, I'm claiming it as correct.

The important thing is—don't panic. I've attached a link to our website with the news alert we put out. I used the same words as in NASA's bulletin so as not to cause any issues with scaring the public. That said, you do need to take action to deal with the junk and debris, as it includes the Russian nuclear fuel system I mentioned.

This fuel rod is now in a deteriorating orbit and has commenced falling towards Earth. This will land like what you call a 'dirty bomb' if allowed to enter the atmosphere.

A former Kremlin scientist, a man called Vladimir Trakovic, seems to know about the use of nuclear power. He still lives in Moscow, but now works in their missile defence program. I'm working through options with the guys here to find the best way to deal with this new threat.

We set up a website so you can keep updated instantly
... might help your guys over there. Qbits' new motto is
'Anywhere, Anytime, Instantly'. Do you like it? You can
communicate with us on this site or via e-mail. Let us know
what you think about our website.

You have less than 40 hours, that is until 8.30 am Washington
time the day after tomorrow to deal with the nuclear fuel
rod before it enters low Earth orbit. The easiest and safest
solution is to use the International Space Station weapons
system that was trialled last month and nuke it.


Chat soon


GG
www.qbits.me/

The President swallowed. He wanted to hit 'forward' but was afraid he'd get into trouble. Was he condoning this mysterious crazy person's impersonation of NASA and its announcements? Well, he seemed to be doing the job NASA and all those other useless buffoons ought to be doing, so that was a plus. His brow dampened again. He hated when it did that—his forehead went all shiny and he looked like he had something to hide. He often did.

The phone rang.

'Mr President, it's Charlie Baxter on the line, he says it's an emergency.'

The President took the call. 'Charlie, I know what's happened. It's already on the web. I've just forwarded you the link to Qbits.'

The NASA Chief commenced his report regardless. 'Mr President, I have to report that two satellites have collided. We are currently assessing damage and debris. At this stage the International Space Station is not impacted. A report will be on your desk in 30 minutes.'

Bob rolled his eyes. 'As I just said, Charlie—I know this. In fact, I probably know more than you do. Forget the report—we meet in my office in an hour. Let's try not to make it into an international incident. For now it's just two satellites colliding in orbit—no nuclear, no Russia, no goddamn dirty bombs or heck darn Qbits!'

There was silence on the other end of the phone.

'Hello?'

'Yes, Mr President.'

'Sorry, it sounded like you had hung up—'

'No, I'm still here, Mr President.'

'Good. Ok. Contact the satellite company and explain the situation. Issue the alert immediately as it's already on the web. Find me your best quantum physicist. I want to be briefed on quantum entanglement.'

The President forwarded the e-mail to the Security Council, then sat in his chair staring blankly. Qbits, quantum world entanglement ... what on earth had happened? He had never before felt so exposed. Was it purely an accident or were these Qbits a new, more sophisticated form of terror? He longed for the days when he was in charge of nothing other than kissing babies and making rousing, meaningless speeches.

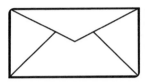

**From:** nasachief@presidentusa.com
**To:** chiefs@presidentusa.com
**Sent:** 2 March 2015 6.30 pm
**Subject:** NASA alert

At 5.30 pm a decommissioned Russian Cosmos R78 satellite collided with an American Iridium satellite. There is no danger to the International Space Station and the debris is being tracked in orbit.

Official press release:

It was reported overnight that the bright flash in the night sky over New York was a collision of two satellites. NASA is investigating and monitoring the space debris created by the event. Both were unmanned satellites, the Cosmos Russian satellite having been decommissioned many years ago and in a graveyard orbit. While the American Iridium communications satellite was still operational, all communications links have been forwarded to a back-up satellite. The crash occurred early this morning.

Further details to follow. NASA Communication Office. ENDS

Charlie clicked on 'send' and leaned back in his chair. Lying was far easier via e-mail. He loved technology.

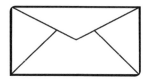

**From:**   nasachiefscientist@presidentusa.com
**To:**     RNeil@presidentusa.com
**Sent:**   2 March 2015 8.00 pm
**Subject:** Quantum briefing from Chief Scientist.

In summary, the key things to know are that quantum
physics is a fundamental theory of physics and in quantum
law energy can only change in small jumps called 'quanta' and
photons are a quantum bundle of energy.
We have research laboratories trying to build quantum
computers using qubits, which are the basic unit of quantum
information. Currently all conventional computers operate
using bits, with 1 or 0, and logic is processed one at a time.
If we can harness qubits then they can exist in both states
simultaneously.

The result would be that quantum computers calculate
equations at a trillion times the speed of current computers.

I would like to come over and run through this when you
have some time. It is an exciting field and with adequate
funding we would be global leaders in this development.

Regards
NASA

Bob didn't really understand what the e-mail was on about but
it sounded like someone just wanted money for faster laptops.
Not very useful.

# Chapter 13

## Great Hall

### 3 March 2015
### 7.35 am + 32 seconds

'Watto, check all e-mail traffic and summarise.'

Watto made a show of yawning awake on the Great Tapestry—as if he ever slept long enough not to constantly pester all those within his realm of influence.

'Sure, hi boss,' Watto chirped, flashing a huge grin.

Tom scanned the e-mails at light speed:

> We are about 150 million kilometres from the Sun, so if it takes a year to orbit the Sun, the Earth's average speed is 107,000 kilometres per hour.

**E-mail Summary**

President USA: The Qbits have suggested that we use nuclear weapons to destroy the nuclear fuel rod before it re-enters the atmosphere, as they don't believe it will burn up. They have set up a website—search it. FIND THEM.

NASA Chief: No record of any nuclear-powered satellites found.

CIA Chief: We haven't located the GG or Qbit website base, but we are tracking and using our leads and all our contacts. We are getting close. We have agents investigating drone signal lead—looks like it was from Sydney Australia.

GG to President: I'm sure, Bob, if your guys track down and speak to the former KGB agent Vladimir Trakovic, who now lives in Moscow, the CIA will be able to confirm experimental usage of nuclear power in the 1970s. The solution is simple; use the weapons on the International Space Station to blow up the nuclear fuel rod without delay.

Tom was furious. The Qbits sat in their seats looking at him sheepishly—even GG.

Tom shook his head. 'What *the* hell are you thinking? A website?' He looked around the table and then at Alby. 'Can't you control them?'

There was a puzzled shifting of their collective gaze, as if to question why Tom would think Alby was the head of the group.

Tom continued. 'Don't you guys watch TV? They will try to find us—you told the President that two satellites were going to crash and now that a dirty nuclear bomb is dropping to Earth. They will think we are terrorists! Then there's the CIA—they don't even know where space is. You *idiots*.' The word 'idiots' was a lot louder than any of the other words he had used, but his tone was generally rather matter-of-fact.

'Watto, bring up all the e-mails and the CIA network.'

GG's e-mails appeared on the screen. GG was completely sober now, and his wine glass was nowhere to be seen. He looked very concerned as he nervously spoke, attempting to defend his actions. He felt like not much had changed over the centuries, as he was again in trouble with the ruling authorities, who were just like the Catholic Church, trying to stop him making discoveries. He hated to be controlled.

His response was compliant but firm; he would not be told. 'Tom, I also e-mailed the Russian President, but I'm not sure I got the grammar right ... their reply was a bit short.'

'What?' said Tom, 'You e-mailed the Russian President? How, when, what were you thinking? And he replied?'

Mac spoke now, trying to calm the room. 'No one can track us, Tom. Put simply, we don't exist on the Internet—only on electrons. Current Internet and website technology relies on page traces or footprints; we exist at subatomic levels.

If a nucleus is a ball in a football stadium, then electrons are in the crowd.

It is impossible for anyone to ever track us, unless we leave a cookie trail, and to do that we would have to deliberately create it. We travel invisibly so it is impossible to find us.' And for some reason Tom trusted Mac—they all did.

'Impossible?'

'Quantum qubits—subatomic, untraceable, unstable and

based on impossibility,' stated Alby, trying to recover a little dignity after being accused of losing control of the unruly scientists. 'The CIA is just buying time with the President. The Universe will end before they find us.'

'We don't even exist in your universe,' clarified Newts, wanting that fact to be absolutely unequivocally clear.

'Impossible?' restated Tom. 'Ok, what did the Russians say, then?'

'We can translate and speak anything for you, Tom,' said Alby joyfully, pleased to see the tension level dropping. He didn't like all this conflict. 'The technical reply was to do with GG's mother along the lines of "go to hell, your mother is a trucker". Didn't really make much sense to me when I translated it. I think he was being nasty.'

This made Tom smile. 'CIA, Russia, Presidents—Qbits, you are out of control. I think it's time for me to talk to Mad Dog—he is the only one I can trust.'

There was an unaccepting silence; how could Tom not trust them? They were him and he was them, linked at the subatomic level. They shared DNA, or QED as Newts liked to call it—quantum electronic DNA.

'Meanwhile, keep a low profile, guys. It's a whole new ballgame now that we have both Cold War era superpowers involved. No more e-mails. Mac and Newts, you seem the most sensible—you are now in charge.'

Newts, as if to answer the call to arms as the leader, immediately took the floor; the debate was not over.

'Your maths is good, GG, but are you 110% certain? Maybe the nuclear rod burns up, disintegrates on re-entry?' Newts challenged.

GG's voice was even and cool. 'This time I am. As confident as one can be in the movement of the planets. The sun rising …'

'Crikey, GG, have you been drinking again?' asked Alby.

'I have not. But now that you mention it ...'

'Can we just get on with it?'

'No more messages to Bob Neil, NASA or anyone.' Tom did not feel like apologising, not yet.

'Get over yourself, Tom.' Alby was dismissive, as if to support GG. 'Remember the three laws—not the ones Newts invented, but the laws of the three R's: Respect for yourself, Respect for others, and Responsibility for all your actions. It's in your DNA.'

Tom settled in to be lectured by these past it has-beens.

'In this reality we have your moral values,' Alby explained. 'No one is doing harm, just warning your human race about potential danger. People may die. After all, we are part of you.'

'Part of me?' Tom asked.

'In a way, we are,' Mac nodded. 'In a quantum world, we can be everywhere. However, your atomic sense of right and kindness means none of us is a danger to anyone.'

'How does that figure?'

'It's in your genetic code—you and therefore our QED is full of random "righteous" ingredients baked into our crazy Qbit paella,' replied GG.

Tom looked at their faces and shrugged. No one said anything. Seemed like a typical GG weird but intuitive explanation.

'I need to talk to Mad Dog, I need to tell him.'

The atmosphere ends at about 500 kilometres above Earth and space begins.

'Well, meanwhile we are continuously watching the chatter—from NASA, the CIA, and anyone else with an Internet connection and a vested interest in keeping Americans alive,' said Mac in a tone that suggested she did not enjoy being part of that class of people.

'I need to let Mad Dog in on this. I need his help. He's still in the real world, unless you guys have forgotten.'

Alby huffed a German curse word. 'Stop going on about it and bring him to the next meeting, then!'

'What?'

'Bring him along. Build another ring and we can quantum teleport him in,' stated Alby slowly, as if instructing a child how to tie a shoelace.

'We can do that? Why hasn't anyone ever said so?'

'You never asked! Everything is possible—there is no unsolvable problem, only the wrong approach to the solution.'

'To the lab, Tom,' directed Newts. 'It'll take us 12 hours, maximum. It's a very simple construction.'

Tom was dressed and in the Uni physics lab in less than 30 minutes—this was his Priority 1. He needed to change the balance of power in Qbits.

In the lab, Tom found stowed in his work area the first prototype of the ring. It looked eerily similar; in fact, looking at it gave him a chill, a reminder of the day his life changed. But he needed Scott's help. His best mate might be radical, even illogical, but they had always been there for each other, like brothers. They had always said 'no secrets'. He had kept the Qbits from Scott for months since the accident at the end of rugby season.

As he held the piece of tungsten encased in graphene, he momentarily wished he had listened to his teacher and maybe become an accountant, working in an office. Just now he wished he had never heard of the Internet, cyberspace, portal, quantum physics and satellites crashing in orbit. Watto was meant to be a simple storage device but through an extremely improbable and chaotic turn of events it had created Qbits— an unstoppable electron universe. Watto himself was an uncontrollable icon.

Within an hour, with the assistance mainly of Newts, who seemed very mechanically minded, he had constructed a second Watto, capable not of creating a universe but of accessing it—a sophisticated quantum teleportation device. Mad Dog could now be transported or teleported into the Great Hall to meet with the Qbits.

Here is a palindromic number:
$111,111,111 \times 111,111,111 = 12,345,678,987,654,321$

Tom got back to the house late that night; it had taken time to test the frequency and teleport capability of Watto2, 'The sequel', as GG called it. As Tom entered the house he heard the rhythmic rattling of Mad Dog's snoring. In the kitchen he grabbed a pen and on the back of the envelope, in the order they occurred to him, he wrote a few starting points:

- US communications satellite

- Russian satellite

- President Bob

- cosmic collision

- nuclear engine

- dirty bomb

- NASA/CIA/Homeland Security/FBI

But this was the immediate problem. Selfish as it appeared, he could only do one thing at a time. He had to tell Mad Dog. Tomorrow, first thing.

Tom awoke early the next morning, no alarm clock needed. Tom banged on Mad Dog's door.

'Scott, are you awake? I have to tell you something.'

'What?'

'I have to tell you something.'

'What? Can't you tell me later?'

'I have a confession to make.'

'Well then, go to church.'

The only letter not appearing on the periodic table is the letter J.

'Scott, I need to talk to you. Something has come up.' Not for a very long time had Tom ever said this and he rarely called him Scott; he was Mad Dog to everyone.

This must have registered with Mad Dog on some level, because he rolled over and blurted, 'Breakfast?'

'Anything, Dog, as long as Harry's has it.'

'Fifteen minutes?'

'Ok, door in 15 and I'm buying.'

'Must be serious,' Mad Dog muttered.

Not much was said on the 10-minute walk down to the wharf, as they prepared themselves for the serious talk.

# Chapter 14

## Harry's Cafe de Wheels

4 March 2015

8.45 am + 27 seconds

The dockside streets of Woolloomooloo were resting—not a soldier, sailor or late-night reveller was in sight. Several stepped-on polystyrene food containers lay in the gutter beside a car, an empty pint glass sat precariously on a ledge and a bright green high-heeled sandal was posed suggestively in a doorway as evidence of the night before. Neither spoke. Tom and Mad Dog marched in stride along the footpath.

Mad Dog wasn't thinking too much; his head wouldn't let

Dangerous asteroids impact the Earth about every 100,000 years on average.

him. It was too early and he hadn't had coffee yet. However, at the back somewhere, in the part of the mind into which troubles and guilt are pushed, Mad Dog knew something wasn't quite right with Tom. Something was different, ever since he had been struck by lightning. But he just couldn't put his finger on it. Tom wasn't himself; he was always off somewhere, away with the fairies.

The visible galaxy is about 100 billion galaxies—each of which has about 100 billion stars.

He cast his thoughts back to Harry's, when they had come up with the Smarttek idea. The previous year, Tom and Mad Dog had decided to set up a business. It was called Smarttek and wasn't so much a business as a website they had whipped up one afternoon when bored. As such, the business model was rather broad, or perhaps non-existent. They had had business cards made up with their names prominently embossed and 'Director' printed authoritatively underneath, with a Smarttek logo emblazoned across the top. It was a research technology company intended to combine their respective skills of physics and engineering. But really the motivation had been to show their card to old school buddies they bumped into at parties, who were now working in the real world earning real money, as investment bankers or lawyers, and driving nice cars. They always seemed much more stressed out and grown up than Tom and Mad Dog, who now wanted to have a try at this adulthood lark.

It was to be an online help company for fixing uni students' laptops, clearing viruses, and entertaining science aficionados, geeks and anyone else who needed to find out something about physics, chemistry, mathematics and research technology. That day, over a cappuccino, Tom had also come up with the idea to develop the Watto—a high-capacity storage device for students and others wanting to download masses of information or just store songs, music—anything, really—but in a compressed format. 'Good luck' was all Mad Dog had said.

Smarttek was supposed to be a fun company. Tom was taking life far too seriously. Maybe that was it. What else was new? He was always like that. Tom would answer all the e-mail traffic, while he, his best friend and business partner, did other things. He felt bad, but he had other stuff to do. Next year's uni course outlines were overdue and he was responsible for marking the supplementary exam paper for Mathematics 1. If Tom was about to rip into him about Smarttek, well he was ready. And now he had this thumping headache—what was he doing out here in the heat?

At the T-intersection at the wharves, they turned right, passing one hotel and facing another. A boy riding a new-looking skateboard rocketed past. They watched forlornly.

'Let's sit on the wharf wall, out of the wind,' Tom said purposefully.

As cranky as a pair of old dogs who had missed out on dinner, they walked over to the counter of Harry's. They didn't need to look at the menu.

'Morning, boys. Up early?' asked Harry.

Like a couple of cowboys about to duel, they were tight-lipped.

'You boys are up so *early*! This is ridonculous!' This time it was Chin, who was making an extra large cappuccino for one of Harry's most regular customers. 'So, you uberbrains want two to go or are you walling it?'

'Business meeting,' said Tom. 'Walling it.'

'Alleyoop—gotcha,' nodded Chin knowingly.

Tom was having difficulty keeping up any kind of banter with Chin today. He was feeling a bit edgy. Tom knew he should have confided in Mad Dog right from the beginning.

He should have told him about the Qbits, and the voices in his head.

'On me,' Tom said, trying to alleviate the guilt by paying for the food. It was the best way.

'Tom, are you really paying?' Mad Dog asked incredulously, which only made Tom feel worse—was he really that stingy?

'Of course,' he said nonchalantly.

'Cool.' Mad Dog turned to Chin. 'Tiger with extra chips and a mega cappuccino, Chin.'

Tom's eyes bulged slightly, not expecting Mad Dog's order to be quite so extravagant at his expense.

'Just the Tiger for me, Chin, no chips and a ... um ... latte.'

Harry's signature dish, the Tiger, was named after its founder, and was a chunky beef pie served with bright green mushy peas, mash and gravy. It was awkward to eat on the wall, requiring a certain uncivilised skill, but it was worth every dollop of misplaced gravy.

Still not saying much, they sat on the edge of the harbour, dangling their legs above the various flotsam gently washing about below them.

Tom perched there, holding his left finger in his right hand, pie in his lap, coffee on the ground against the wall, protected from the wind.

Mad Dog was shoving bits of pastry into his mouth as if he had just returned from a survival camp.

'Mmmm ...' Tom was still looking at his pie like he had never seen a Tiger before.

'So, what's up?' Mad Dog finally asked.

Tom sat for a moment, then another, trying to get the words out.

'Remember the accident?' There was no need to wait for a

reply. 'Well, something happened. It was all right at first. The problem is they have let the cat out of the bag.'

Mad Dog paused with a pile of mash and mushy peas poised on the end of his plastic fork, threatening to overbalance and topple to the water below. 'Who?'

'The Qbits,' Tom held up his finger.

'Cat?'

'The Qbits! I want you on board.'

'The website?' asked Mad Dog.

'Not Smarttek, the Qbits. I'm entangled in a quantum world. I built a quantum universe by accident.'

Mad Dog set his Tiger down on the gravelly concrete. 'What are you banging on about? I cannot follow this. Does your head still hurt?'

'No,' Tom answered. 'Not on the outside.'

'*What are you on?*' Mad Dog must have raised his voice, because the entire cafe went quiet and everybody turned to watch.

One of the women sitting nearby whispered and stared.

Mad Dog waited for something to make sense. Nothing came.

The brain is about 2% of your body weight but uses some 20% of your energy.

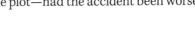

'I can teleport any time into their world,' Tom went on.

'Tom,' Mad Dog hesitated, as if approaching something fragile. 'I'm gonna ring someone.' He reached for the Velcro tab on the pocket in his shorts.

'Let me finish. I have unlimited access to the entire Internet and all online data and theories—anything, anywhere, anytime, instantly.'

But Mad Dog wasn't listening, instead he seemed concerned. His best mate was losing the plot—had the accident been worse than they had realised?

Suddenly Mad Dog's phone vibrated, saying he was receiving a call from Tom.

'What *the* hell? Did you lose your phone?'

Tom shook his head. 'I don't use a phone.'

Mad Dog's expression became a curious mixture of confusion, suspicion and intrigue.

'No need.' Tom opened his palms on his lap. 'I don't need a mobile phone to call you, or a computer to e-mail anyone. I can travel in the electronic world.' He smiled briefly and gazed into the distance at the yachts and carefree hobbyists. Then his shoulders slumped, his chin hitting his chest. 'Which won't do me much good when the CIA ...'

'Look, we can find someone you can talk to, Tom. Maybe your mother knows someone.' Mad Dog had genuine fear in his voice.

'You going to answer that?' asked Tom, nodding toward the phone in Mad Dog's now very tense hand.

'What?' asked Mad Dog. He looked down at it as if it were a spider and about to bite him. He pressed 'answer'.

'Hello? Look, whoever stole this phone ...'

'Mate, it's me.'

Mad Dog instantly knew the voice. He looked at his mate sitting next to him on the wall. Like a ventriloquist, his lips weren't moving.

'What the ...? How ...?'

'I know.'

Mad Dog wasn't sure whether to speak to Tom on the phone or just talk to him in person—he was sitting right there, after all. He decided to hang up.

'I want to give you something.' Tom shoved his hand into his zippered pocket. 'It's a device.' Tom took out the Watto2. The ring sat in an unfurled handkerchief in his hand.

'But it was destroyed—your finger ...' Mad Dog was now looking at the ring as if it were a snake.

'It's Version 2—well, Version 1 modified. Version 1.1.' The ring was no more than 2 millimetres wide, making it difficult to see when worn. Alby had insisted that it needed to be as discreet as physically possible.

'We built it—for you.' Tom recalled the accident. 'Scott, do you remember the day of the accident?'

Mad Dog took a sip of coffee. He didn't acknowledge anything Tom was saying, but Tom figured that was more because he was in a state of shock than him not making an effort to listen.

Tom went on. 'The Watto worked. That day before training I had saved all links and information on the life and times of Albert Einstein, Sir Isaac Newton, Galileo Galilei and Marie Curie. The Watto stored trillions of terabytes worth of data.'

Lightning flashes 'now', and then thunder is heard. You can count the seconds in between and divide by 3 to measure how many kilometres away the storm is.

Mad Dog jumped in. 'Hell, all I remember is that the storm clouds started building and then raced in from the east and we all bolted after the game. Next thing—*kapow.* Suddenly you had a deformed left-hand middle finger and a story to tell everyone.'

Tom grunted at the irony of it all.

'It was a close escape,' added Mad Dog, sincerely, deep in thought.

Tom took a big breath, straightened himself up, and yanked at the neck of his t-shirt. 'Mad Dog, you are going to think I'm crazy, but let me finish. I'm not dreaming, I'm not mad—but after the accident, when I woke up, something had changed. I kept thinking I was having dreams about talking to them. By "them" I mean my geniuses—the scientists. Watto wouldn't shut up—the four of them were chattering away in my head constantly. They still are.' Tom tapped his temple demonstratively.

He was nervous. 'At first it was like a dream, but over the last few weeks it has been as if the channel has tuned in and the clarity is like cable 3D TV. They exist in a quantum world. I go there, meet with them. They claim that we have built a quantum computer via the accident, we are entangled. And I am constantly quantum teleporting in and out of their world whenever I need to.'

Mad Dog's face had been frozen in a single disturbed expression for the entire monologue. But once the words had sunk in, he nearly spat out his mouthful of pie.

'You're still smashed, aren't you?' He was laughing out loud. 'This is ridiculous! Do you know what time it is? We need to sober you up.' He called out to Chin at the counter. 'We're going to need another couple of coffees over here, Chin!'

'Scott, I'm 100% serious. We seem to have unlimited access to all online data and theories—anywhere, anytime, instantly. I don't need a mobile phone or computer to e-mail anyone. I can just ... do it.'

Mad Dog was busy looking at his fingernails, as if inspecting some imaginary chip in non-existent nail polish.

'It gets worse—they say their names are GG, Newts, Alby and Mac. My subdirectories brought to life. A big bang, of sorts. And they call themselves the Qbits.' Tom picked up his coffee and took a warm loud slurp, more to gather his thoughts than out of a need to imbibe any further caffeine. The endless Qbit coffees had made him a little tense. His eyebrows were knit into a little pitched roof across his forehead and his eyes were as big and pitiful as they would go.

Mad Dog knew Tom was serious. He wasn't so sure about

the facial expression, but figured it could be due to his friend being about to totally and utterly snap.

'Sure, mate,' he said, as he accepted that something really was wrong.

Tom didn't miss a beat. 'The only way for you to help me is to meet them.'

'Meet, err, them?' Mad Dog frowned, suddenly nervous. Was this the same 'them' that were somewhere inside a little quantum world somewhere? He hoped they made house calls. His hopes were quickly dashed.

'Quantum teleportation,' stated Tom, handing him Watto2. 'Put it on your finger—please.' His mother had taught him that it is in our most trying times that it is most important to remember our good manners.

Mad Dog looked uncomfortable. 'It feels strange taking a ring from you and slipping it on my finger—it's almost romantic,' he began.

'*Put it on!*' Tom abandoned his mother's advice and decided politeness could wait until after they had saved the world.

'Quantum teleportation. This is a key to a door which we can unlock, but it's one way. And only Watto can let you in. You are about to enter the world of quantum magic. Don't touch it. The pin prick you will feel is a needle-like sensor—it needs to pierce through your outer skin to get to your nervous system for power and to access you.'

Mad Dog was clutching at his hand nervously. 'Tom, quantum teleportation is something science fiction writers invented. Doctor Who, Time Lords, Daleks—all that stuff. It doesn't exist.'

'Put the damn thing on now!' Tom thrust the slender ring onto Mad Dog's finger, the needle piercing through his flesh. Instantly, they were gone. Teleported.

# Chapter 15

## Great Hall

4 March 2015

8.55 am + 20 seconds

'I'm still hungry,' Mad Dog whined, tapping his belly. 'That Tiger wasn't enough.'

Tom couldn't help noticing how nervous Mad Dog seemed to become when faced with quantum teleportation.

'Still a little peckish, huh, after your Tiger? Do you want to stop and eat something, before the *world blows up*?' GG had lost it again. This was getting embarrassing.

If the sun stopped now, it would take 1 million years before we knew about it. Due to solar wind the sun loses billions of kilograms every second.

Tom had stopped talking, afraid of what would come out next.

Mad Dog looked around as if stunned. 'What *the* hell. Where is Harry's?'

'This is quantum reality, *Herr* Maddocks,' Alby jumped in. 'You are in quantum reality, Scott. Thank you for paying attention.' Alby loved to teach. 'The device on your finger has central wiring, a mechanism that entangles you with Qbits. The skin is broken ...'

'But how did I get here?'

'Quantum teleportation.' By the curt tone, it seemed Alby thought the process quite clear and requiring no further explanation. The confused expression on Mad Dog's face made it clear he needed to go on.

'Quantum teleportation, the principle of superposition. You are here and there simultaneously in two universes, one made of carbon atoms and one of electrons.'

'No joke—this is a quantum computer?' Mad Dog held up his left hand.

'That is correct. We like to think of it as a quantum universe.'

Mad Dog is made of $7.9 \times 10^{27} =$ 7,932,500,000,000,000,000,000,000,000 atoms.

'Mad Dog,' Tom explained. 'You, we, have quantum teleported into a quantum world. These guys are the Qbits.' Even now Tom could hardly believe this was happening.

Mad Dog stood speechless as three of the four figures seated at the table rose to greet him. All that came out was 'What *the* hell?' Tom smiled, that was his first ever reaction also.

Mac smiled, walking toward him, her pale face alert and welcoming. 'I'm Mac.' She held out her hand to Mad Dog. She looked attractive but familiar, so familiar ...

'These are the Qbits I was telling you about,' Tom explained again. Mad Dog was usually a lot sharper than this.

Mad Dog took her hand. 'Pleased to meet you, Mac.' He had already turned on the auto charm and was smiling broadly.

GG, still seated, hailed Mad Dog with his wine goblet. 'Come and join us, Mad Dog. Sit, please sit.'

'That might work.' Mad Dog grinned, spying the wine carafe. A little drink might assist him in making sense of all this.

Mac let go of his hand and went over to the table.

'Welcome to the Great Hall, Mr Maddocks,' Newts, as always, spoke formally. But he couldn't resist adding, 'We've been expecting you.'

'That's Newts,' Tom explained, a trifle nervously.

'Sir Isaac?' Mad Dog couldn't believe it. 'The man who ...' He wanted to jump up and down, high-five, and shout 'Whoopee'.

'Nearly the very same.' Tom knew exactly what was going through his friend's mind because he had been through this himself. And so he smiled. 'Mostly, we call him Newts.'

'Pleased to meet you, Sir.' Reluctantly, Newts took his hand. He was about to say something more, when Alby got in first.

'The father of mathematics has some reservations about bringing you here,' Alby noted sternly. 'Scott, in here, trust is everything,' he added.

'Nothing to do with mathematics, I'm afraid,' Newts sniffed, as if in the company of something unpleasant.

It would take 10 trillion protons laid side-by-side to span 1 centimetre.

Mad Dog's resistance was already weakening. 'Were there hallucinogenic drugs in our Tigers?'

'We need you to be careful of your behaviour,' Newts advised gruffly, now hoping to mask his shyness, but not quite succeeding. 'That is all. Please sit down.' Newts looked scornfully at his arch rival and best friend, GG. 'We already have one party boy on the team.'

'Leave the Dog alone, Newts,' GG laughed.

Scott was stunned that GG already knew his name.

'Meet GG.' Tom left it at that.

GG waved dismissively. 'Tom, can we discuss something please?'

Tom put up his hand. 'Yes, yes—later. Ok, background,' began Tom. 'Sir Isaac Newton died in 1727 aged 84, so he would be 372 if still alive. This is Newts, who is aged 25 and has Newton's QED and is famous for maths, inventing calculus and discovering the three laws of motion. He was the first scientist to be knighted, which occurred in 1705, under Queen Anne.

Next to you is GG. If Galileo Galilei were alive he would be 451, but GG is only 57. Galileo invented the telescope and was imprisoned for challenging the Catholic Church's belief that the Earth was the centre of the Universe. He remains a rebel but finally got his apology from the Church in 1992, over 350 years later—'

'Yeah!' interceded GG gleefully, raising his goblet. 'Worth waiting for!'

'Here GG really likes watching *Doctor Who* and sci-fi movies.'

'That makes me the oldest and wisest of the Qbits.' GG took a swig from his drink. 'Oh, and I love wine, it is God's gift—sunlight and water mixed to perfection. I also love action movies, especially *Terminator 7* and those X-Men freaks. Bit of a fan of *HitchHiker's Guide to the Galaxy* too.'

Immediately Mad Dog quipped, '42!'

'Don't panic, it's the answer to life, the Universe and everything,' replied GG.

Newts rolled his eyes as the pair high-fived.

Mac quickly obliged in relating her own history. 'I'm either

38 or maybe I'm 148, I'm not sure. I was born in 1867. I was 67 when I died in 1934. That's about it, I guess,' she said vaguely, clearly more humble than the others. 'Let's get to the current issue.'

When Mad Dog looked out of the window of the Great Hall into the real world, everything outside seemed to be stationary. He could see himself and Tom having a coffee at Harry's Cafe, with birds and clouds suspended stock still in midair.'

15 million blood cells are produced and destroyed in the human body every second.

Even tree branches had been blown sideways and stayed there, waiting a seeming eternity to spring back into place. Mad Dog didn't like the feeling.

His attention was quickly resumed by Mac, who spoke with a delightful French accent. 'Yes,' she was saying, 'in here things—everything happens at the speed of light. It will seem like you've been here for hours when it will in fact be seconds. So take a seat and relax, we have plenty of your time. To be precise, 1 second in your world is 53 minutes and 5 seconds in Qbits. We think and act at light speed.'

Mad Dog sat down next to Tom and Mac, suppressing a smirk at how cool it felt to think and act at the speed of light. The giddy power! He couldn't believe he was sitting in a room with some of the greatest scientists from throughout history. He couldn't think what to say; all that came out again was, 'What *the* hell?'

'Seems to be a common reaction to meeting us,' laughed Mac. Everyone else burst out laughing too. 'Tom said the same thing.'

'They must have received similarly lacking upbringings,' remarked Newts.

Mad Dog ignored him and instead said to Mac politely, 'Mac, I don't really know much about you—tell me about your life.'

Mac was chuffed, as no one ever asked about her. 'Scott, I was born in Poland and had four brothers and sisters. I was the youngest. I was studying physics and maths in Paris when I met my husband Pierre, also a scientist. We studied radioactivity.'

'And you got a Nobel Prize for discovering X-rays,' finished off Mad Dog.

'Here we go,' said Alby. 'She got two Nobel Prizes—in 1903 and again in 1911, but the first was a joint prize with someone else! And she is the only person ever to receive the prize in the fields of physics and chemistry.'

'You're just jealous because you only got one. And she could read at age four—impressive! So give her a break,' GG commanded with authority. He slipped in a wink at Mad Dog.

Mac had tears welling in her eyes as she continued. 'On April 19, 1906, my husband Pierre was killed in an accident. He was on his way to our publisher's office. It was raining heavily that night, just like it was when Tom had his accident, and he ran across—' she was choking up now 'he was struck by a horse-drawn vehicle and fell under its wheels, fracturing his skull. I was devastated.'

There was a brief respectful silence before she went on. 'My discovery eventually killed me. Working with radioactive materials, I developed leukaemia from radiation exposure—we didn't know then what we do today.'

Newts added, 'And they have named an element after her as well—number 96: curium.' He was quite taken with Mac, and her delightful French accent.

Then Alby spoke up like a spoilt kid, 'And for me there is einsteinium—element number 99, which was named after me when I died in 1955.'

Mac just smiled. 'That's about it. Oh, I've now found out that my eldest daughter Irene also won a Nobel Prize for chemistry in 1935 and my youngest daughter Eve Curie Labouisse wrote my biography after I died—isn't that so nice? I've been reading all her work, I'm so proud of her.' Now Mac had tears streaming down her face. 'She died in 2007 aged 102 years old. I just wish I could've contacted her.'

There was another silence, a little more awkward than respectful. No one knew how many relatives Mac had, and weren't particularly keen to go through them all.

Suddenly, GG banged his fists together and looked about to make sure he had everyone's attention: 'Two satellites!'

Tom was feeling the pressure. This banter was all so casual, but the CIA and whoever else could soon be knocking on his door. Suppose they could never return home? He watched as Mac handed Mad Dog a small tumbler of blue water.

'For your headache, Scott.'

Mad Dog looked at Tom questioningly.

'She's good,' was all he said. Mad Dog nodded.

'Normally I would have simply released the chemicals. I've used water because I think your body needs rehydrating.'

'Thank you, Mac.' He raised the glass. 'Matches your eyes.'

They all smiled, although Alby only smiled a little. He too was keen to forgo these pleasantries and get down to business.

Mad Dog, after emptying the glass, didn't know whether to enquire about the drink, the ring, this amazing room they called the Great Hall or the Great Tapestry showing a 3D view of them on the wall at Harry's. 'Am I missing something here? Where is this leading? How did we get here?'

'On your finger, Scott.' Tom felt like giving up. There was too much to explain. 'When I put the ring on you.'

Mad Dog held it aloft for everyone to see.

'How does it fit?' GG asked. 'We were a little worried about the size.'

'Snug.' Mad Dog inspected the device.

'Nice work, Tom.' Mac smiled.

'We all made it,' Tom said generously. 'Didn't we, Newts?' Tom's questions evaporated into cyberspace as he sat admiring the device. 'Newts did all the calculations, and GG's especially good at making things.'

All Mad Dog could manage was, 'Nice.'

'Looks pretty good,' complimented GG.

'Doesn't draw attention to itself,' said Alby.

'You could wear it anywhere,' said GG.

'Wear it with anything,' added Newts.

Alby had had enough. 'Perhaps we should get started.'

'Mad Dog,' Tom remembered his manners. 'Please allow me to introduce you to Alby.'

'Albert Einstein?' Mad Dog stood and extended his arm to the wild-haired man in the black jacket. The penny had finally dropped into the slot. 'You're kidding me. Marie Curie, Sir Isaac Newton, Galileo ...'

Alby spoke. 'They call me Alby now, my Qbit age is 42. I was born in 1879 and would be 136 if alive. I died in 1955 aged 76. Most people know I'm German. I—'

Mad Dog finished off the sentence, 'are known for $E = mc^2$, your photoelectric effect study in 1905, and your Theory of Relativity. You are very famous, Sir.'

'Nearly, but not quite,' interrupted Tom. 'Mac, Newts, Alby and of course GG share their DNA and are what we call Qbits. They are all mixed up with my DNA.'

'Talk, talk, talk.' Alby stepped back, and then attempted a joke. 'This is not a coffee shop.'

'Coffee?' GG's eyes lit up. 'What's it like at Harry's?'

Tom continued to try to explain. 'If the nucleus is the size of a golf ball then an electron is roaming around at a radius up to 1 kilometre, or could even have wandered 10 kilometres away on just that atom, but we can jump atoms instantaneously using quantum teleportation. So we have infinite space in our world for all of us, and we only need a single electron for transport!'

It is impossible to lick your elbow.

Mad Dog still looked overwhelmed.

GG looked at his left arm as if to consider trying.

Tom continued. 'It also means any electronic device is available via teleportation or quantum tunnelling—we can phone, e-mail, text, watch movies, listen to music—and we can pretty well be everywhere on Earth at once, as we move at light speed.'

GG put up his hand.

'Yes, yes, as GG will tell you, it takes 8 minutes for light to reach us from the sun, so it takes us 8 minutes to get there. Also, we are on the electron spin as in quantum physics, so there is, err, a certain randomness we rely on.'

'Our colleague Alby calls it "quantum magic". Newts believes we can understand it all, Mac is researching and GG doesn't care.'

'We are still working out how we seem to arrive at some places totally randomly.'

Mac then explained that it also meant that any lens was a window to the real world, so that was how, using Tom's retina, they could always see out. They could also use security cameras or any other mechanical device, but Tom was the only human that it worked on. They could watch the President in the Oval Office via electrons.

'You can hack anywhere?' Mad Dog looked excited. 'The CIA? You ... were ... hacking ...?'

'Nothing quite so barbaric,' Newts said. 'They were research access missions.'

'We don't have to hack or break into any system, remember?' Alby explained, happy as ever to instruct.

'We are everywhere, anywhere, instantly and yet nowhere,' Alby continued. 'We exist in random electrons in space–time. For us the Internet is not just a series of systems and doors to information. We don't go through official openings—we enter via quantum tunnelling. We can get in anywhere using quantum tunnelling, as it's impossible to go where we go. No one can trace us, because we can't possibly be there!'

Mad Dog's face said it all. *What the hell!?*

'Be that as it may ...' said Newts, clearing his throat. He sat pulling at the lace edging on his shirt cuffs. 'The Russian satellite has hit an American satellite, which is now, at this very moment ...' Carefully he extracted the loose thread from the linen, and then laid it carefully on the table before him. 'Watto, show us the instructional background info first.'

Mad Dog turned back to Alby. 'How can you access that here?'

'I was just on their system,' GG answered.

'Whose system? *NASA's?*'

Alby nodded distractedly.

Mad Dog was visibly shaken at the significance of this.

'Welcome to Mission Control, just like in the movies,' GG offered drolly.

'This is what I have been dealing with, Scott.' Tom sounded tired and worn out. 'We had rules and agreements. Unfortunately, there are people here,' Tom paused to glare miserably at GG, 'who behave as if the idea of freedom of information is an indiscriminate and universal right to all information, no matter how sensitive.'

Slowly, pausing between each word, not knowing whether to be impressed or scared, Mad Dog looked at GG and then at Tom.

'I have been worried about you, Tom. Vague, talking to yourself ...' Mad Dog looked to the others for support. 'And when you are out and about, instead of ... I don't know.' It was beyond expression. 'You're always walking about muttering to yourself.'

'Sorry about that.'

'I thought you had lost the plot!'

'In what way?' Tom asked.

Mad Dog scratched his head, searching for the correct expression.

'Absent-minded,' Mac helped him out.

'Vague?' Mad Dog laughed.

'Hopeless.'

'Couldn't run out of sight on a dark night.' He was enjoying this.

'I had stuff going on,' Tom protested.

Alby was again blunt. 'Can we return to the reason we are here?'

'Alby,' Mac said softly, 'we need to explain the how before we get caught up in the whys and wherefores.' She turned to Newts. 'You don't think you could make us one of your coffees, Newts?'

He thought about it.

'Just a little one? The boys would like a flat white and a long black.'

Alby leapt into the conversational crack. 'This may appear strange, but the observer plays a crucial role in bringing about the very situation she or he observes. Both a person's presence and their expectations physically alter what they see.'

'I know how that works,' Mad Dog nodded. 'But am I affecting what is happening here?'

'Remember, a quantum computer is based on randomness and we can be everywhere at once. Now you too are entangled.'

Mad Dog opened his mouth to speak.

'Scott, please allow me to finish.' Alby straightened his neck tie. 'Initially, the randomness of the lightning and the Internet caused Qbits to exist.'

'Watto, show Mad Dog the simple facts about lightning strikes.'

The Great Tapestry came to life instantly, with Watto's smiling face appearing in the corner. 'Okey-dokey,' it said.

'Watto?' asked Mad Dog.

'This is a random universe born in random moment, and Watto was the device and door.'

'Looks like the Cheshire cat with that smile,' observed Mad Dog.

'Actually, he is more like Schrödinger's cat, Mad Dog, but you know it is like falling down a rabbit hole in here,' teased Tom.

Gamma rays are really dangerous as they are very small with wavelengths less than $10^{-11}$ metres. The ozone layer averages about 3 millimetres thick and protects us from UV rays. A 10 second Gamma ray burst from a collapsing star could destroy the ozone layer.

# Chapter 16

## Great Hall

4 March 2015
8.57 am + 20 seconds

'We don't have time for this idle chitchat,' snapped Newts. 'We have plenty of time—this won't take a second.' Tom was in charge for a change. 'Ask Watto about lightning.'

But Mad Dog was unresponsive.

Tom sighed. 'Just say: Watto, tell Mad Dog about lightning.'

Immediately, the Great Tapestry flashed with a harrowing storm video and a list of facts about lightning, with the view of Harry's minimised in the corner.

Mad Dog just stared at Watto's smiling face as if it were a ghost.

**Lightning Strikes**

Thunder is sound so it travels at a speed of 343 metres per second.

Lightning is 'light' so it travels at 300,000,000 metres per second.

If you count the seconds from the flash of lightning until you hear thunder, then take that number and divide by 3 = storm distance away in kilometres.

When lightning strikes, run for cover, as it's 20,000 volts and could be lethal!

Voltage lethal at 200 volts if skin wet and 20,000 volts if dry.

The survivable limit is 27,000 volts for a large heart.

Only 10% strikes are fatal, most injuries are caused by the extreme heat.

The temperature of a lightning bolt is 5 times hotter than the surface of the Sun!

Around the Earth there are about 100 lightning strikes per second.

The fastest speed a falling raindrop can hit you is about 30 kilometres per hour.

Keep away from water and open spaces during a thunderstorm!

Supercharging Watto through the lightning strike merely provided the catalyst,' continued Alby, 'but concentrated super-charged data led to the universe being opened.' He turned to Mad Dog and the rest of the room.

'We'll leave that discussion there for now,' said Tom. He knew that some time in the future he and Alby would have to reason this through properly.

'The two worlds coming together,' Alby continued to instruct, 'the electrons and Internet a virtual soup of information. Of course, we were already there, in existence. We're not simply figments of Tom's imagination.' Mad Dog looked over to see what his friend was thinking. 'We simply couldn't access your reality. Atoms have memories, we think, so in your DNA everyone contains a percentage of everyone else, past and present. It's estimated that everyone has millions of atoms from all that came before. There are no new atoms in the Universe.'

The Body of Science:
TOE (Theory of Everything)
+ GUT (Grand Unified Theory)

GG was tired of being lectured to. 'We aren't talking about your big TOE here, Alby. Not in our random universe.'

'TOE?' asked Mad Dog.

'Alby believes there is a Theory of Everything,' replied Newts. The others all chuckled, even Tom. Alby had spent many of his final years trying to bring together a Theory of Everything, his big TOE, but had been unsuccessful to this day, undermined by the inherent randomness of the Universe and the law that GG believed in of 'unintended consequences' of events.

It was GG's turn to instruct. 'Cutting to the chase, in here, Mad Dog, we have access to every system, all the information on this Earth, everywhere an electron can travel to. Hell, we can hitch a ride to Mars via electromagnetic signals by riding electron waves, and plumb the minds of the entire history of mankind—one of whom, a genius, discovered the most important chemical formulation, that of sunlight and water into grape. Can I interest you in a drop of red? A shiraz, I believe, is your preferred poison?'

Mad Dog accepted the distraction gratefully. 'Thank you, Sir.'

'GG, please. One "Sir" is enough,' GG muttered, glancing at Newts.

'Thank you, GG.'

GG produced a twin to his own cutglass goblet and sloshed wine into it from the bottle. 'Anyone else?' There were various nods and shakes. Tom joined in.

Tom held his glass out to Mad Dog as if to say, 'Cheers, and welcome to my nightmare.' At last he had someone from his own world to help him navigate these hysterics.

One human hair can support 3 kilograms and a sneeze travels at about 160 kilometres per hour.

'But how did I get here?' Mad Dog wanted to know. 'Does it have anything to do with nuclear power?'

'Horse power, in Sir Isaac's case,' GG quipped.

'He should know,' Newts jibed. He held his right hand in front of him, as if holding reins. The other he swung as though wielding a riding crop. 'Giddy up, gee-gee,' he called, and then dropped his arm with mock dejection. 'It's a pity this GG isn't hoarse.'

GG flung his hands out in disgust. 'Watt a wit.'

'Joule be burning at the stake?' Mad Dog ventured.

GG patted his new ally and topped up his glass.

'Watch out for old killerwatt,' he gestured towards Newts. 'He burned 100 counterfeiters for King George I.'

Despite the hilarity, Alby would not be put off. Anyway, he'd never seen the appeal in puns. One of the difficult lessons Alby had learned was that not everyone was as quick or as intelligent as he, so he paused, giving Mad Dog and the others time to consider the information.

Soon the jokers had settled and were listening intently.

'This is why I have some concerns,' Newts replied. 'It is not my wish to play the brigand. We need to be responsible. No encryption or firewall can stop us. We must have boundaries.'

'It also means that as we live and travel on electrons every electronic device is available,' Mac explained, 'we can go any-where—do almost anything.'

'Any electron?' Mad Dog reached into his pocket to take out his phone.

'Yes, any electron—read as the entire Universe, Mad Dog.' Tom could barely contain himself. It was a relief to share all this.

'It's dead, anyway.' Mad Dog remembered the phone was out of credit.

'No mobile phone? Youth will wither and die,' Newts said morosely.

'We can watch movies.' GG assumed the posture of a kid at the movies—chin thrust forward and eyes wide open. Magically a jumbo bucket of popcorn appeared and he was stuffing it into his mouth. He passed the bucket to Mad Dog. 'Salviati?'

'Salviati?'

'You remind me of a character. Gifted and indolent.' GG was referring to his most famous book *Systema Cos-micum*, which had led to his arrest for heresy, as it recounted the story of three characters challenging the Catholic Church's view of cre-ation. Salviati was claimed to be Galileo in character, an intellectual searching for truth.

The Earth's temperature rises 20 °C for every kilometre underground, so it's about 5,000 °C at the Earth's centre.

'Well, thank you, GG.' Mad Dog started eating from the same bucket. 'I take that as a compliment.'

Tom was struck by how alike Mad Dog and GG were. Two

rebels in two universes; maybe Mad Dog had inherited too many of GG's atoms.

'Join us, Sagredo.'

'Sagredo?' Newts raised a smile at the implication, as Sagredo was the second of Galileo's characters—a noble man who was always seeking truth. Newts smiled at the implication.

GG leapt to his dainty feet and started whistling his favourite Monty Python tune 'Always look on the bright side of life' with his usual gusto, looking at Tom and calling out, 'C'mon, Tom, cheer up!'

Holding out one elegant arm, he gallantly swept Mac to her feet. The music changed and the Great Tapestry showed them attending a performance at the Tivoli Gardens, in wonderful, grand Copenhagen. A full orchestra played as they foxtrotted around the table, GG all the time laughing and singing; once again he was a conjurer working his tricks.

Tom and Mad Dog watched the dancing couple: Mac's skirt twirling and the tail of GG's coat, bright boardies and yellow crocs flashed around the room. The more conservative Newts and Alby averted their eyes; how could anyone take him seriously? They were jealous of GG's free spirit.

Although the music and steps were from the twentieth century, with GG and Mac gliding across the mirror polished floor of the Great Hall, with the great heavy overhead lights glittering like the Sydney Harbour Bridge on New Year's Eve alight with fireworks, there was something of the magic of sixteenth century Pisa and Florence, where GG had caroused the hours away.

'We move at the speed of light, Scott,' GG called as he sailed by. 'What's your friend's name? The one with the cabin at the lake you were at last week?'

'Sam?' Mad Dog answered, almost defensively. 'But how do you know we were at the cabin?'

When Mad Dog saw that Tom was laughing, he realised. 'You guys know everything?'

'Not quite,' GG puffed, as he fell into his chair. 'There's always more to know.'

Sound cannot travel through the vacuum of space because it needs a medium.

'Universes to conquer?' Mac teased. It really was like a movie trailer.

'Boldly go where no man has gone before,' GG joked. 'I've been meaning to watch that movie ...'

'Can we get back to this now, gentlemen?' Alby had started tapping his finger on the table, but not to the rhythm, which of course had now stopped. Beside him, holding a tray loaded with beverages was Newts. Alby moaned.

GG mumbled, barely audibly, 'Simplicio.'

There was an immediate chill in the air as the others wondered whether Alby would let this fly by. Simplicio was a serious insult; it was the third of Galileo's characters in his famous book—a simple-minded fellow whom Galileo had ridiculed by having him represent the pope's argument on the Earth's creation.

As if to distract them, Newts jumped in, placing beside Alby a tall glass brimming with vienna coffee, the thick cream seeping into the warm liquid lying below. 'I decided against the tea,' he added, then handed Mad Dog the nutbrown coffee, a chocolate bonbon from Belgium perched on the saucer.

'So it takes us around 8 minutes to get to the Sun,' GG repeated, still a little breathless. He peered at Newts' tray, checking to see if he had been catered for. 'Particularly if we stop off along the way,' he added mischievously, winking at his friend, who plonked a glass of water in front of him before turning away in disgust.

'Also,' Alby was not going to give up, 'we travel on the electron spin. In quantum physics there is a certain randomness available to us.' He looked about the table, daring anyone else to interrupt him. 'We don't actually understand this, not in the sense of something we can demonstrate and therefore prove scientifically. We don't rely on it, but we do make use of teleportation, or as I call it, quantum magic.'

'But doesn't using randomness,' Mad Dog began, 'mean that sometimes it doesn't work?' He then appealed to Tom. 'It couldn't be 100% accurate.'

'That's true,' Alby answered. 'And this was exactly how we were able to access Tom.'

It still wasn't clear.

'But what has this got to do with Tom?' By now they were all supported with drinks and tasty pastries.

'Any lens is a window,' Alby explained, perhaps unnecessarily, 'into your real world. And there's so much to do there.'

'Humans have made such a mess,' Mac said sadly. 'Not just your generation—all of us.'

'And we've been using Tom's retina ...'

'His retina?'

'Tom is like our—excuse the analogy—our puppet.'

'A puppet that is *in charge* here,' corrected Tom snarkily.

Alby looked apologetic. 'Tom is our hard-wire to the real world, a way we can see things, like watching 3D TRTV.'

'TRTV?' asked Mac.

'Tom retina television,' answered Alby, the master of acronyms.

Mad Dog thought this was a bit like someone telling Tom they were borrowing his bike, instead of asking. However, Alby was wearing his don't-think-about-interrupting-me look and so Mad Dog allowed him to continue.

'The retina is the innermost coat of the posterior part of the eyeball. It consists of a layer of light-sensitive cells that connects with the optic nerve by way of a layer of nerve cells, and in this way is able to receive the image.' Confident that everyone had understood this, although eyebrows were raised and small smiles were on view, Alby concluded, 'Using Tom's retina, we can always see out.'

'Really, Alby, you do go on.' Mac took a drink. 'Sometimes I think you're a walking, talking ...' The word would not come. Everyone searched their word stores.

'Lecturer.'

'Explainer.'

'Instructor.'

'Educator.'

'Googler!' GG declared. 'That's why he wears glasses.'

'For his Google eyes,' Mac declared. There was much laughing, sipping and nibbling.

The centre of the Milky Way is 240,000,000,000,000,000 kilometres from Earth.

'We were just joking, Alby,' Mac apologised, when she saw the hurt look on his face.

Alby responded with a little smile, then, determined as ever, continued. 'Some of us try to subdue our egos.' Of course, everyone knew that in Alby's case this was not true. Even so, they let it pass and he continued. 'We can also use security cameras or any other mechanical device. Tom is the only human it works on.'

Strangely enough, everyone began to relax a little, even Alby. He and Tom discussed the workings of a quantum reality with Mad Dog. Whenever Alby had a point to explain, he used diagrams and images on the Great Tapestry. Mac was able to explain some of the implications, particularly regarding the finite, painstaking and minute day-to-day checking and monitoring of their work. Time passed agreeably as they lost themselves in the maths and physics and gave themselves over to the wonder of it all.

Tom waited until Alby had answered all of Mad Dog's questions, as well as a few of his own. Then Tom and Alby continued discussing ways in which single photons of light are controlled and how they store information, all of which was vitally important to Tom's work to build a real-world quantum computer.

All the time, however, at the back of Tom's mind, he was aware there was still stuff he had to tell his friend. For Qbits did not consist solely of an august and solemn refectory with valuable furnishings and art. Outside the Great Hall were virtual corridors with doors that opened into wherever you wanted to go or places you'd do anything to avoid. Presidents' e-mails, CIA, British Intelligence, NASA, NATO —they were all there. Passwords didn't exist and you could get into it with just a thought.

Even so, it was important for Mad Dog to gain some understanding of Qbits before receiving the news he still had to deliver: that powerful and potentially dangerous agencies could view him as a security risk. There was also the immediate issue of the nuclear engine floating in a descending orbit. He and Mad Dog were on a high wire—and certainly were not looking down.

'I'll show Scott around,' Mac called from across the room. 'He's going to love snooping around here.'

'No good showing him the CIA,' GG stomped back in. 'Not worth looking at.' It seemed GG had left his good nature elsewhere. 'How can you run a security agency based on misinformation?' He flopped next to Alby. 'If you do not know what is true and correct, how can you keep it secret?'

'It's a mess out there—lies, misinformation and rubbish!'

'Space is becoming a cesspool.' Newts had slipped in quietly with GG. 'And what about the mess down here, and in Tom's room?' He busied himself with the plates and mugs. 'Communal living was not something we did in my day,' he muttered as he stretched across the table. 'And there was always someone to pick up after us. We need to clean this place before we start on the cosmic mess upstairs.'

They all sat down at the table and Tom took charge. The Great Hall seemed to transform into NASA's offices. The whole Qbit universe was, after all, an electron of virtual reality.

'Watto, take us into NASA and explain the current situation after the satellite collision. We need to move on.' Everyone nodded. 'Run the NASA collision footage and show the current situation with background on the shuttle.'

### NASA Update

NASA has announced its intention to clean up collision debris resulting from the collision of the Russian Cosmos and American Iridium satellites to ensure no fragments endanger other operational

satellites. NASA will next week send the recommissioned shuttle *Atlantis* on its first mission since 2011, to retrieve the large debris.

### Space Shuttle Program Background

The space shuttle is the most complex machine ever built by mankind.

In 1972 US President Nixon announced a plan to develop the first space shuttle.

In 1981 the Shuttle *Columbia* went on its first space mission.

The shuttle program was shutdown in 2011 after 135 flights.

Due to orbit speed, the Shuttle crew see a sunrise or sunset every 45 minutes.

Escape velocity is the speed required to escape the gravitational pull of Earth.

It takes 8 minutes for the space shuttle to accelerate to 28,000 kilometres per hour.

The space shuttle orbits the planet at about 28,000 kilometres per hour.

Shuttle fleet: *Enterprise, Columbia, Challenger, Discovery, Atlantis, Endeavour.*

Shuttle's hottest skin temperature on re-entry: 1,650 °C.

Mad Dog was stunned by the Great Tapestry's 3D imagery and speed. Tom continued as Watto kept information flowing almost unstoppably; he had nothing else to do.

'GG believes, or has pretty strong evidence, that one of the pieces of debris is a nuclear fuel rod from the satellite power system. NASA and CIA do not believe it exists, as they don't believe Russia had technology available to use nuclear fuel for small satellites in the seventies. We have access to the Kremlin database and historic information beyond what they know. Despite very clear instructions by me not to do so, GG has being trying to convince the President to destroy the nuclear engine, as it will re-enter orbit before the shuttle mission collects it and may well land as a dirty bomb.'

The mass of Earth is $6.0 \times 10^{24} =$ 6,000,000,000,000,000,000,000,000 kilograms and there is zero gravity at the centre of Earth.

'The?' Mad Dog hesitated. 'The President? The President of the United States?'

'Bob,' GG replied. 'Sounds more approachable.'

'Bob?' asked Mad Dog. 'How? Why?'

'Exactly what I said,' chimed in Tom. 'We are where we are, that's why I need you here. We need a rational debate.'

GG began, 'Because we need to hurry up and get this nuclear situation sorted out so we can start trying to fix—' but was cut off.

'GG and Newts want to get Bob to take out the nuclear power cell before it re-enters orbit. Alby and Mac aren't convinced— they hate nuclear weapons.'

'Nuke the nuke?' asked Mad Dog. GG and Newts nodded. 'Wow,' was all he could think to say.

'There must be something else we can do ... go to the media?' Mad Dog said, looking about in desperation. 'This isn't something we can just sit on our hands about.'

'That won't achieve anything other than scare the masses,' Newts added morosely.

No one mentioned that it was Alby splitting the atom during World War II that had led to the development of the deadly technology in the twentieth century.

'It needs to be taken out!' cried GG. 'And *soon!*' He looked as if he was about to start swinging punches.

GG strode suddenly from the Great Hall.

'Where's he gone?' asked Mad Dog.

'Searching the web—that door is like the Great Tapestry, it leads into the Qbit universe. It's chaos out there, like trying to find a planet to live on in our solar system. There is so much junk and misinformation in the virtual world, just like in space. You need to know where you're heading or I think it's a waste of time. In here, Watto is our tour guide and he verifies all the sources first. And he's hard enough to follow!'

Newts, who had been working at his screen, looked up. 'Everyone should stop worrying about their own skin. This is a *catastrophe.*' Newts used the ancient Greek word as if fully aware of its history. 'We are participating in a drama and this is the *denouement.*' Newts had not forgotten to mention he had once pierced his own eye with a needle and had also stared at the sun for days on end in the service of knowledge. 'Focus, people; we are witnessing the *upheaval of order!*'

Tom stood up abruptly. 'Time for real coffee, back soon.'

# Chapter 17

## Harry's Cafe de Wheels

### 4 March 2015
### 8.57 am + 24 seconds

In an instant they were back, as if they had never even left. Mad Dog had to double take, peering around suspiciously at his surroundings. He hadn't even put down the hand he had raised when he joked about the ring. He stared at his finger and the ring.

'That was 4 seconds,' said Tom. 'That equals about 4 hours in Qbit time. People just think you are daydreaming, not listening momentarily—kind of like that glazed over look I get a lot these days!'

Energy $= mc^2$. This means mass times the speed of light squared. So, as $c^2 = 90,000,000,000,000,000$; and if you split an atom that's a nuclear bomb—an enormous release of energy!

He looked out at the harbour and at Tom, bewildered. 'It wasn't a dream—we were just in a medieval hall talking to four legends of science. Collision of satellites, nuclear fuel rods ... tell me you know what I'm talking about.'

A piercing rallying cry interrupted the moment. 'Yo! Bada bing bada boom, coffee's up, get 'em while they're hot! Tom and Mad Dog, ready or not!' Chin leaned out the back door of Harry's Cafe.

'Got it. And yes, it all happened.' Tom got up.

Mad Dog looked at his watch: 8.57 am—it had felt like hours. Just as they had said, it was still the same time at Harry's.

'Takes a while to get used to it. Quantum time can make it feel like you have jet lag when you come out. Let's have this *real* coffee and then we will teleport you back in.'

'Sure, I guess,' replied an uncertain Mad Dog. 'Newts' coffee seemed as real as this, though.'

Tom laughed; they both did. Loudly. Old friends with new friends.

Then Tom filled Mad Dog in on some quirks of the Qbits as they went about finding alternative solutions, checking and rechecking calculations.

They looked out across the harbour from the wharf behind Harry's. It was hot and sunny and the harbour looked spectacular. Neither of them spoke. Living in two realities is something that requires some personal adjustment, as working out which reality you belong in is something not many of us have to worry about. At least the two best friends now had each other in both worlds—that was a great step forward for Tom, who had until now felt lost and alone, battling his own sanity, with one reality seemingly boundless, and the other with rules and consequences.

Atoms weigh $1.66 \times 10^{-27}$ kilograms = 0.000 000 000 000 000 000 000 000 001 66 kilograms.

Suddenly Tom got that faraway look in his eyes. 'They want us to run through the latest—are you up to it?' asked Tom.

Mad Dog just nodded; he knew his friend needed him and this was just what it now was—two worlds, two friends, and four complicated Qbits. They quickly downed their coffees and headed off back to Qbits.

When they arrived in the Great Hall, Newts was midway through proclaiming, 'We nuke it.'

Tom sat in his usual seat at the head of the table, while Mad Dog chose to sit on Tom's right-hand side next to Mac. The others took their places at the table.

Alby kicked off the briefing. 'The CIA has found the Russian scientist Vladimir Trakovic and he unofficially confirmed the use of nuclear power for their satellites, despite international agreement that it was too risky to use in space. The President now knows the debris includes a potential nuclear hazard but NASA still believes it can salvage and clean up the mess.'

Tom exhaled. This was big boy stuff. Just as well the United States was one of the key players.

'The argument is not about who to tell, but what to do about it.' Since residing in quantum space, Newts was quickly losing his tolerance for government enforcement systems. 'The Russians have admitted the satellite had a nuclear fuel source and it's now whizzing around the Earth at 30,000 kilometres per hour, with China or Washington DC in its sights. It was a violation of the treaty all right, but that's history. If it survives re-entry, which it was designed to do, then explodes on impact ...' His face was showing the strain of the dire implications of the information being conveyed. 'We can only imagine the outcome. Hiroshima might be an appropriate comparison.'

An adult has about 4 litres of blood and can lose 15% without any adverse effects.

Alby's eyes shifted warily around, but no one was paying him any attention.

'When the fuel cell re-enters, they'll only have 10 hours' notice from re-entry. That is not very many hours to relocate the population—how many people, do you think? Potentially millions of people if it hits a major city!'

'But we have just seen the e-mails from the KGB and the Russian military. The only way this could be averted is for the International Space Station to destroy it.'

Now Tom had had enough. He put up his hand like a traffic cop. 'What is it with you guys? You don't even exist in my world, and you think you are spies in a James Bond movie.'

Tom scanned the room; it was as if he was running a tutorial and none of the students had done the reading. All eyes were down, poring over hands, or picking fluff from a sleeve—no one was looking at Tom.

'Tom, with great power comes great responsibility,' stated GG wisely.

'Who said that?' asked Mad Dog. 'It sounds familiar ...'

'Ben Parker,' replied GG.

'Hmmm, no, don't know him.'

'Yes you do, he was Spiderman's uncle in the movie.' They all chuckled at GG like naughty school children.

Mac continued. 'But clearly the President is not getting the best available advice. Shouldn't we be telling him to nuke that thing right now?'

Despite her concerns, GG and Newts had made the necessary calculations. The debris was below the International Space Station orbit by 1 kilometre and would not be in the path of the nuclear fuel system. Newts believed there was a high probability, estimated at 95% probability, that the titanium casing would survive re-entry into the atmosphere.

Newts proudly continued. 'I, we, have calculated that with the velocity and weakening caused by re-entry, the fuel system would most likely explode on impact, releasing potential radioactive material over a 50 kilometre radius. And yes, I used Heisenberg.'

'Given the random decline of orbit, the highest probability is that it will hit a Chinese city, about 80%, as this is the likely re-entry point.' Tom slapped a lined map he had managed to conjure out of the quantum ether.

Mad Dog was stunned at the conversation but words just came out as if addressing the chairman of the meeting. 'Tom, that could be seen as an act of war by Russia with China.'

Silence. The magnitude of that statement hung in the air. They were just two guys sitting on a wall in Sydney having a coffee. What the hell was happening? Tom and Mad Dog looked at each other; the Qbits looked back and forth between them.

GG, who had been walking about restlessly, came to the table. 'I believe and agree with Newts that the solution is simple; the Americans must fire the missile defence system weapons and explode the canister in space, where the particles scatter into the depths of space. I will let Bob know. The public will not know. Or we warn the Chinese before the impact so they understand what happened.'

Warn the Chinese! Nuclear bombs in space! Fire nuclear weapons!

Tom was a research scientist, not an action hero. He belonged in the classroom or lab—where it was quiet and he could think. Rugby was his only real-life action. He was used to working with the tiniest units of measurement, trying to work out how to control mini micro particles: how to use them to store and transfer multiple data. This was his job and it was difficult enough. Everything had to be done very carefully and precisely. Yet Qbits were unstable, flighty and totally random. And the information they carried could be unreliable and therefore almost useless. Watto and these Qbits were taking over.

'The calculations are uncertain.'

Tom asked for more details. What were the altitudes of the debris? How many pieces were free-falling? He glanced at Mad Dog sitting beside him, still all ears, or both ears, listening to GG and Newts run through the calculations.

'We haven't told the President what he has to do yet,' Alby whispered. 'You sit tight.' Tom was still getting his head around this. 'The Americans—oh, and I guess the Russians now—are the only ones who know about it.'

'How long do we have before re-entry of the dirty bomb?' asked Mad Dog.

'Eleven hours.' GG wasn't his usual flippant self; he allowed the facts to be left just hanging out there.

'GG, e-mail the President. Tell him the facts. Give him 5 hours to confirm. We meet then. Meanwhile, that gives you all the equivalent of 18,000 seconds—the equivalent of 662 days in quantum time, to find a better solution. Drop everything else, check and recheck all data.' Tom was in charge.

The fastest human can run about 40 kilometres per hour based on 100 metres record of 9.74 seconds.

'We'll be at Harry's.' And with that, the pair disappeared, reappearing back at the harbourside almost instantly.

There was no shortage of conversation. They needed each other more than ever. Big decisions lay ahead in two worlds. Tom felt bad for involving Mad Dog, but what were friends for? Mad Dog, who was always bursting through boundaries, was plainly concerned but also excited about the future. Tom, ever sensible and perhaps more experienced with the Qbits' random behaviour, was more cautious.

'The President has replied,' Tom stated from out of nowhere.

'Huh, how do you know?'

'I'm online 24-7. They want to know if you're coming in.'

'Hell, yes!'

Hydrogen, oxygen and carbon make up 98% of humans—so you are all really just carbon atoms in water!

# Chapter 18

## Great Hall

4 March 2015
11.15 am + 25 seconds

Nuclear Fuel Rod re-entry in: 11 hours + 7 minutes + 2 seconds

The e-mail appeared on the Great Tapestry. GG was excited.
'He signed it "Bob"! Bob and I are like this.' He entwined
his two fingers and held them up to show how close they were.

Alby frowned; he didn't believe NASA had it under control, and therefore he didn't like their remaining options. He hated nuclear weapons—and it was his equation that in effect had created them. They all approached the table and sat down.

**From:** RNeil@presidentusa.com
**To:** GG@Qbits.me
**Sent:** 3 March 2015 9.15 pm
**Subject:** Satellite collision debris

Dear GG,

Thank you for all your help in this matter and all the information, which has helped us a great deal. NASA has commenced cleaning up collision debris and believes we have the situation under control.

We would like to meet you, perhaps for a coffee?

Regards

Bob

'Watto, tell us about the nuclear fuel rods and potential explosions—any relevant history,' instructed Tom.

They ran through various plans and probabilities of outcomes. Random, understanding totally random, was their core operation.

'So, after they try to retrieve it using the cargo shuttle on the International Space Station, in 3 hours they will realise that they cannot reach the nuclear cell—it will be below their orbit by 1,375 metres. But they should at least be able to see it ...' surmised Tom.

Newts continued. 'We can monitor it, as we have access to all networks everywhere, as you know. We will make sure their systems register the nuclear rod.'

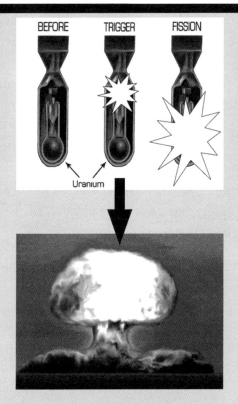

**Nuclear Explosions**

The first atomic bomb was used in World War II on 6 August 1945.

This was a uranium fission bomb called 'Little Boy' and was detonated over Hiroshima.

In this bomb a baseball size sphere of uranium was converted into energy killing about 130,000 people.

This is explained by Einstein's Special Theory of Relativity. E = mc² means 1 kilogram of matter converted into energy is equivalent to about 22 million tonnes of TNT.

The chain reaction only lasts a millionth of a second.

This extremely fast release gives off a very large amount of energy and causes temperatures to rise to tens of millions of degrees.

Tom took a deep breath. 'They will know they have missed it and will have time to use nuclear weapons if they are ready and have authority. GG, you need to let Bob know this is what they must do. From the time they realise they can't retrieve it they will probably have 5 minutes to launch the weapon before re-entry. They cannot hesitate or the fuel cell will commence re-entry. Send our projections.'

GG nodded in agreement. 'They have 11 hours and 6 minutes.'

GG started typing his e-mail, then stopped and looked up. 'We can do the launch for them,' he said, one eyebrow shooting conspiratorially to the top of his forehead.

Tom failed to register what he meant.

GG explained, 'We can do anything, anytime with electronics, including easily cracking the launch codes to every weapon on any electronic system anywhere, anytime. It's not a problem. Mac is very good at this. It'll take a while, but convert the time to Earth time, and we should be able to knock over the access codes if they are complex in about 1 second in your world.'

'And actually launch a nuclear missile? These are state-of-the-art security systems, surely?'

'Not a problem. It's very easy.'

Tom panicked. 'This is not something any one person should be able to ... you guys are all right—but not someone like me. What right have I to this power? This is not what I had in mind when I started designing things. It's too much; too much for me. Really, I should do the right thing by everyone.' The Great Hall was now filled with Tom's misery. 'I should cut off my finger—shut down Qbits.'

'You serious? For real? Youch!' GG said, waving his arms about, the sleeves of his surcoat flapping, unintentionally presenting a credible impersonation of the Grim Reaper. 'You really want to amputate?'

Tom knew he was being melodramatic; even so, he despaired.

Mac gently nodded her head disapprovingly. 'We exist everywhere now. It would just really hurt and achieve nothing.'

Awkward silence. Mad Dog interjected like the referee in a melee.

'Well, then it seems like the only solution is to nuke the nuke,' agreed Mad Dog, ignoring Tom's theatrics.

GG liked Mad Dog, a rebel with a cause.

'You want me to launch a missile? I'd rather launch myself,' Tom muttered, rising slowly to his feet. 'Everyone knows power corrupts, and this is what,' he paused, looking about in desperation, 'I have here.'

Mac moved to comfort him.

'Mad Dog, we are outta here!' Tom leapt at his friend. 'Teleport out. This has gone too far. What's your plan B? I want to hear it when I get back. A fallback plan. We will check back in 4 hours. Redo the calculations—and no nukes today. Find plan B.'

A galactic year is the time it takes the sun to orbit the centre of the Milky Way, and is about 225 million years. The Sun is about 20 galactic years old.

Suddenly Mad Dog and Tom were again going about their real-world day. It was now the afternoon, so they headed back to the house. Neither could help but occasionally glance skyward, as if to acknowledge all that lay above them, weighing on their shoulders. But who could they tell? They would be laughed at.

# Chapter 19

## Great Hall

4 March 2015

10.21 pm + 47 seconds

Newts, the most factually inclined of the four, began the report. 'They missed the fuel cell but collected into safe orbit some other dangerous pieces of new space junk. As predicted, the larger pieces, including the heavier nuclear canister, had drifted beyond the reach of the robot arm on the shuttle and will be soon hurtling towards Earth.'

There is a supermassive black hole in the middle of the Milky Way.

Mac leaned over and whispered to Tom. 'Newts and GG have been working on the launch direction and probability trajectories.'

'What about the Space Station crew—any fallout?'

'No, they will be holed up in the emergency pod after the missile is fired, SOP.'

'SOP?' asked Mad Dog.

'Standard operating procedure. They go there in emergencies like when random debris changes orbit.'

'That would be scary.'

'Terrifying.' They shared a micro moment thinking of the shuttle crew.

'What do we say to the President, Tom?'

'Nothing,' GG said. 'Not yet.'

'Any minute now and they'll know everything.' There were problems ahead and Tom could see them coming.

'You two need to keep quiet.' GG was being characteristically direct. 'We have to work through this—exact probabilistic launch coordinates.' The words 'exact' and 'probabilistic' hung uneasily in the electron ether.

Tom and Mad Dog exchanged glances that stood in for *bloody hell.*

'Listen, Tom, they have failed to act, so *we* must act. You have seen the data—you think as we do. Even Alby, who hates nuclear options, agrees.' GG was compelling. Alby nodded reluctantly.

All eyes were on Tom and Scott. They lived in the real world, it was their world.

'Ok, you two. Finish calculating the mathematical orbit while I confirm the trajectories.' Mac finished her coffee. 'And you, Alby?'

'I'll continue working through the strategy. That cliché ... what was it?'

'How are we supposed to know?' Already working, Newts did not welcome interruptions.

'Something about a square.' It was worrying Alby. Memories of past discoveries haunted him—weapons to match evil, nuclear bombs and the terror of holocausts; he was unsure of what good the science, his science, had brought to the world.

'Trafalgar Square?' Irritating as it was, Newts couldn't resist playing.

'For goodness sake!' It was Alby's turn to lose it. 'We're talking maths here.'

'Not Red Square?' That was Mac, mischievous as ever.

'Thinking!' Alby announced triumphantly. 'Thinking outside the square.'

'Oh, that passé cliché!' Newts didn't know whether he was more annoyed with Alby for starting this nonsense or himself for joining in.

'Not unlike yourself, Newts,' Alby sniped.

'Can we get on with this?' It was GG's turn to be irritated.

'You are a useless muon,' said Alby.

'You mean moron, moron,' snapped back GG.

'No, a "muon". It was discovered in 1936 and exists for only a millionth of a second before decaying into other particles. You are a decaying cretin.'

Alby cut off the discussion. 'There is only a 20% chance that it will hit an unpopulated area, and even less probability of it landing in the ocean. In both cases radiation may spread towards a populated area. Tom, we have your moral standing and values. We as a group would never use force to hurt anything—it's in your genetic code. We can be everywhere but your sense of right and kindness means none of us would deliberately do the wrong thing or pose a danger to anyone.

Lepton and quarks are elementary particles and fundamental constituents of matter. Muons are leptons.

And, ultimately, if you don't agree with any plan, we cannot implement it. You are the Qbits' on/off switch. If you ever say we must not do it, we will try to convince you, but we cannot act alone.'

The Moon's gravity is one-sixth of the Earth's, so you weigh less on the moon and you can jump much higher. The moon is moving away from the Earth at about 34 centimetres per year.

'What about all the e-mails you send?'

'That's just information, not action—big difference,' replied Alby.

'All this talk about ethics ... the house is on fire and we are arguing about who started it! Better to put the fire out first—what do you say? There has been a collision. We know there is a nuclear hazard about to enter orbit. No time to evacuate cities. We can supply them with the coordinates for the missile.' GG held up one finger. 'Exact coordinates.' Then a second finger. 'We can also tell them what is needed to destroy the missile before re-entry into the Earth's atmosphere—if we stop philosophising and talking,' he looked directly at the troublemakers, 'and start acting.'

Tom looked sceptical, and so did his friend.

'Guys,' Mac took control. 'We can continue this later.'

'When the fire is out.' Mad Dog said this as if he liked the analogy and could see the sense in it.

Tom nodded his consent.

'Where do we start?' Mad Dog asked. 'If you show me what you have managed ...'

'Does everyone agree with our plan?'

All heads were nodding in agreement.

Watto displayed the countdown clock.

Nuclear Fuel Rod re-entry in: 1 minute + 14 seconds

'Now,' urged GG. 'There is no plan B.'

'Now,' added the other Qbits in unison.

'The calculations have been verified, the coordinates entered into the missile system.'

Everyone looked to Tom. All he could say was the word they wanted. He knew they were right; he could see all the facts, the proof.

'Fire.'

And it was done. How easily a war could be started, with a single word controlling a launch system. Everyone was silent as they watched the sequence unfold.

On board the International Space Station, all hell broke loose. No one had communicated a launch initiation exercise, but there was no time to discuss it as they fled to the rescue pod to await instruction. They all moved quickly, assuming it was a drill to check if they were alert.

Unknown to the world below, the missile screamed through space. The nuclear explosion looked like a shooting star as it obliterated the fuel cell.

Chaos reigned at NASA Florida HQ, where the personnel assumed the President had taken over a launch initiation test.

The Whitehouse emergency nuclear missile line rang on the President's desk. It had never rung before. President Bob Neil warily picked it up as the security chiefs marched into his office, just as they had rehearsed so many times in drills, and took their seats opposite his desk.

> Black holes happen when a massive star collapses to a single pin point. Wormholes are believed to connect one side of a black hole to the other. The nearest known black hole is 1,600 light years or 16 quadrillion kilometres away.

'Hello?' he squeaked.

The President wasn't the only one trying to come to grips with the situation, it was only that morning that Scott 'Mad Dog' Maddocks had met the Qbits and he had already been involved in a nuclear incident.

# Chapter 20

## Great Hall

4 March 2015

11.15 pm + 47 seconds

'Hey, Tom, can I have a quiet word with you?' asked GG.

'Later,' insisted Tom. He had barely slept, as had been the case since the accident, and was therefore grumpy. GG, on the other hand, seemed chirpy and confident, having made his point that he would save millions of lives. 'So, Alby, how many millions of people have you saved so far?' He formed a zero with his fingers.

The Universe which includes our galaxy is still expanding—it is like a big balloon being inflated. Right now the edge is about 46 billion light years away.

'Same as you my old, fat, drunken friend.'

GG looked at him quizzically.

'None!' laughed Alby.

'Hey, Alby, last night I discovered the Grand Unified Theory, but I lost the piece of paper I wrote it on,' taunted GG.

'You're making that up.'

'Errr, well, yes. Anyway, apparently 40 % of all statistics are made up on the spot.' GG just continued to laugh as he walked off.

The NASA website appeared on the Great Tapestry and they reviewed the current news.

 ## Great Tapestry

**NASA Headline News**

**International Space Station tests Asteroid Missile Defence System**

The bright shooting starlike object over Asia last night was a test of NASA's new Asteroid Missile Defence System. NASA used the test to clean up collision debris resulting from collision of the Russian Cosmos and American Iridium satellite to ensure no fragments endanger other operational satellites. The International Space Station and Space Shuttle Atlantis also retrieved large debris from the collision. NASA indicated they were pleased with the test results and declined to comment further on the development, for national security reasons.

The President's fawning e-mail said it all; they were heroes.

**From:** RNeil@presidentusa.com
**To:** GG@Qbits.me
**Sent:** 4 March 2015 9.45 am
**Subject:** Satellite collision debris

Dear GG,

Thanks for all your help, you were right. Sorry we doubted you. The NASA mission news release is attached. We would like to meet you to thank you in person.

Kind regards

Bob

The Qbits laughed in self-satisfaction as they ate pizza and watched *CNN* news and amateur footage of the 'shooting star'. Crisis averted, the Chinese had thanked the Americans for shooting down the satellite, and it seemed the world was safe for the moment.

Tom looked at them all, proud of their achievements; no one was hurt and the never-to-be reported 'dirty bomb' had been destroyed.

Mad Dog was sharing a celebratory beer with GG. Newts was chatting to Mac in the corner of the room, leaving Alby and Tom at the table.

'Big risks were taken. Everything worked. Uncertainty and probability solved the issue,' reiterated Alby.

'Ok, guys, Mac, Dog—well done, I guess. So, everyone agrees now we go low profile. No more nuclear weapons, no more saving the world ...' Tom checked nervously. 'And let's try not to blow up anything for at least a week,' he joked.

'Um,' GG began, 'Tom? How about that quiet word?'

'Later, GG, much later. A lot has happened today.' Tom knew that whatever it was it could wait.

'Well, I think I'm going to turn in,' said Tom, 'but you should feel free to hang around. Just say "teleport" and Watto will arrange.'

Tom headed for bed, leaving the others to their own devices.

'Watto, can we take a look at the CIA and Area 51? I've always been curious. Can we get inside their files?' whispered Mad Dog.

GG smiled; Area 51 was one of the first places Tom had gone to as well.

Mad Dog commented on the door to the CIA—why did it have a steel vaultlike appearance? All the other doors were wooden and looked inviting, like the door to a house.

GG looked at Watto with a smile. 'Watto presents the door

as he sees fit—we can't control that, he is his own ... err ... Qbit, I guess. Hard bugger to control at times. Not always responsive, takes us all over the place when we are searching. It's the random thing.'

'How do we hack to get in?' asked Mad Dog.

Alby fielded this question. 'Quantum magic—we need no code or password. Our world is random, based on probability, so we instantly see the entry code. It's as though security doesn't exist.'

*Cool, way cool!* thought Mad Dog. 'So, we could, for example, gamble and always win?'

There was a hesitation; clearly this guy wasn't as pure as Tom, but he was a team member. Even GG hesitated.

Mad Dog sensed he had touched a nerve. They were just like Tom—conservative. 'I mean, if you were required to gamble to save a life, you could choose correctly.'

'Yes, of course. We are a living probability universe, an uncertainty event,' answered Mac.

Watto spoke. 'Right, we are in. Everything is sorted alphabetically.'

'Ok, ok, but what—' continued Mad Dog.

He was silenced by Newts whispering, 'The CIA has good listening devices; whilst they can't find us, we should be quiet so they don't shut down the library server. There will be no electrons to ride on if they shut it down. They can't find us but they can turn off the system—no electrons, no information to read.'

Mad Dog nodded in silence.

As the door opened, the Great Hall walls transformed into a library of files and books. It was the central storage facility of the CIA. The servers stored the files just like in a library and to the Qbits that was exactly what it was—an old-fashioned library sorted alphabetically by Watto.

'Where is Area 51?' asked Mad Dog.

'Filed under A for area—easy!' replied Watto.

'A for aliens?' asked Mad Dog.

And so, Mad Dog perused the most closely guarded files on the planet with a beer in hand. GG, Mac and Newts escorted him straight to the interesting stuff.

CIA Headquarters is in Langley but Area 51 is a secret base that doesn't officially exist. Some of its code names include Groom Lake, Dreamland and the Pig Farm. It has a multibillion dollar covert budget. There is a conspiracy theory that aliens crashed to Earth and the CIA has reverse engineered alien technology. At the entrance to Area 51 is a sign stating 'the use of deadly force is authorized'.

As they snooped, little envelopes whizzed around the room, which were e-mails from various senior people instructing covert operations all over the world.

Everyone was walking around in their own areas of particular interest, whether it was GG looking at the file held on the Catholic Church or Alby looking at secret nuclear research, Newts looking at the latest on the mathematics of the Theory of Everything and Mac investigating secret cancer research.

'Hang on, what's this?' exclaimed Mad Dog, as he stumbled across the Q section. There was a file on Qbits ranked second top priority, just below finding the head of the world's largest terrorist group.

Mad Dog read the file hungrily. CIA field agents were ready to be deployed to find this GG and his gang. They were ready; just a single thread of location was all they needed, and someone to interrogate. The Head of the CIA lived by the mantra that there is always someone willing to talk. They would find their man and bring him in; no matter what the cost.

Suddenly, there was a beeping noise and flashing lights as a security program swept by. Everyone stood still until the threat passed.

As the Qbits perused their own CIA file, Alby, Newts and Mac were a little disappointed, feeling like back-up singers in the Qbit band. Everything in the file referred to GG, who was far from being the head of the gang but had managed to get his name out there more than the others had. At that moment there could be nothing more random than the other Qbits being envious of GG's status as America's second most wanted.

'Watto, check and summarise e-mails,' instructed Mad Dog on a hunch.

 ## Great Tapestry

**E-mail Summary**

American President to CIA, FBI and Interpol: priority 1—find this GG and shut down Qbits operations. Bring them in for interrogation.

Department of Homeland Security: find location of GG and his operation.

CIA: shut down Qbits using whatever means. Bring in GG.

FSB—Russian Secret Service: what are Qbits?

MSS—China Secret Service: find someone who knows about this missile system.

MI6 London: detain any suspects with links to Qbits website.

O'Brien—CIA Chief to his wife: Honey, I'm taking a little 'vacation' to Australia. xxx.

The Qbits gulped.

'Delete the message before Tom sees it—best not to worry him,' suggested GG, who had become bored with the CIA files and was reading an old newspaper while lounging on a divan. 'They won't find us. Or, if they do, we will know before they do anything.' On this they all agreed.

'They can't find us unless we teleport them into our world,' Mac stated for what seemed like the gazillionth time.

GG stretched. 'Well, I guess there's nothing "we" need to worry about, then!' and snapped closed the paper.

'Where did that divan come from?' asked Newts to Mac; obviously he now wanted one too.

# Chapter 21

## Tom's Room

### 8 March 2015
### 9.45 am + 34 seconds

It was Sunday, it was summer, it was nearly the end of the university holidays. Life could be complicated but not in Sydney in summer.

Mad Dog selected an apple from the bowl and ignored Tom, who was sitting in the kitchen looking comatose. His eyes were focused on some unknown object a million miles beyond the kitchen table, and his mind attuned to other matters. Tom was listening to music and checking e-mails.

> The sun is 330,330 times larger than the Earth and continues to get brighter.
> In fact, it is about 40% brighter than when the Earth formed.
> Sunlight takes about 8 minutes to reach the Earth travelling at 300 million kilometres per hour.

Mad Dog grabbed a bottle of orange juice from the fridge. 'Want to have lunch in Bondi today? Leave in thirty?'

Tom nodded absently, and Mad Dog gave him a thumbs up as he slurped from the bottle and strolled back out to his room to put on his board shorts.

Suddenly, Mad Dog was in the Great Hall, with his juice in one hand and pants in the other.

'Whoa, don't I get a choice now?' Mad Dog joked.

GG, Mac and Tom all laughed at Mad Dog.

'Everyone take a day off and relax. We are going to the beach.' Tom beamed.

There was a shrill 'Yes!' from Mac, who loved being outdoors, even though they were really trapped in the Great Hall with a window to the world.

GG was ready to have fun too. 'I shall get changed and I will bring some chilled white wine, a 1985 Chateau Montelena,' he informed them.

'Nice. Good movie too,' responded Mad Dog.

'That's where our learned friend gets most of his knowledge,' sniped Newts, clearly not happy with the growing friendship of the rebels. Mac belonged with the more conservative and research-oriented Qbits.

'Off to the beach—nice day for it, too!' Mac wore a summer dress and a big floppy hat.

'Are you coming?' asked Mad Dog, unsure of how it all worked but excited at the prospect. He really liked Mac—she was very intelligent and pleasant.

'No choice. Well, I guess there is always a choice—Watto and Tom entangled together are our window to the real and electronic world, so when Tom goes places it just seems more real via his senses than just looking at the web. It's hard to explain, but even though it's all an electronic world, there is something more real about it when he is there.'

'Cool,' Mad Dog approved. 'Is time in here like relativity?' he said quietly, not wanting Alby to hear his ignorance. 'I mean, 1 second is like 53 minutes 'cos we see and think at the speed of light—right? So 27.17 seconds out there feels like a whole day in here?' he said pointing at the Great Tapestry portal.

GG answered. 'He won't admit it, but we can't yet prove the exact time dilation. We just worked out some basics. But by watching Tom listen to a song outside and through what Alby called *gedanken*, or thought experiments, we worked out more and more precisely the effective time. It's experimentally proven but not yet proved.'

'I heard that,' yelled Alby across the room. 'I'm working on it. There are no unsolvable problems, only the wrong approach to the solution.'

'Tom, before we go, we should really discuss something—it's getting slightly urgent now,' stated GG as everyone busied themselves for the beach excursion.

The blue colour of the sky is due to a Rayleigh scattering of light and 30% of all sunlight is reflected by the atmosphere back into space.

'GG, it's your day off! It's *my* day off! Let's talk about it when we get back from the beach. I promise,' Tom assured him.

'Promise?' asked GG again.

Tom had never heard him sound so needy. 'Yes, yes. Now I need to get to the beach!'

With that, Tom and Mad Dog zipped back to their place and headed off in the car to Bondi Beach.

'Turn left at the next intersection, second exit on the right.'

'Watto, I know where we are, no more need for GPS. It'd be more useful if you could find me a parking space, there are never any here.'

'In 1 minute and 25 seconds you will reach your destination.'

'Thanks, Watto.'

'Oh, and there is a parking space in Hall St. I just checked the satellite feed and in 500 metres a car space will open up just after the next intersection,' said Watto.

'Now that's what I'm talking about! Satellite? Which one?' asked Tom.

'The CIA has plenty of spare viewing capacity.'

Tom raised his eyebrows.

As they parked the car, Tom made his instructions clear; a day off, time to relax and enjoy themselves. Unless it was an emergency, the Qbits were instructed not to contact him. The blue sky and waves made for a perfect day and already Bondi was busy with a throng of locals, families, and tourists. The beach had security and wave cameras at many points so the Qbits could decide where and what they watched.

Water covers over 70% of the Earth: 97% sea water + 3% fresh water.

Lying on the beach, Tom closed his eyes. 'Watto, let's listen to *Tomorrow FM*. Thanks.' Tom chuckled to himself at the politeness of his request, as if Watto were real. Immediately, the music started playing in Tom's head. Mac started quietly singing along and Tom smiled to himself. Could be worse, could be GG belting out AC/DC's 'You shook me all night long'.

When the next song started, GG ran over and grabbed Mac's hand, whisking her to the floor space at the end of the table.

Tom wasn't in the Great Hall but could see everything. *Where did he learn to dance like that?*

Not a single thought was ever left unanswered now; he could hear Mac telepathically telling him they could do and learn anything, and that was how GG could dance. He decided to join them in the Great Hall.

He looked over at Mad Dog and gave him the thumbs up signal to come in.

The Great Hall looked like a scene from *Bondi Rescue*, with the walls and Great Tapestry adorned in a beach theme, the cameras from the beach projecting onto the walls in full 3D quality. It was almost like being there, with the sound of the waves rushing back and forth. Mac was a little embarrassed to be caught dancing in her summer dress.

'I have invited Mad Dog over,' said Tom.

GG was happy about this. 'Fancy a beer, my good friends?'

'A beer? Is the Pope Catholic?' replied Mad Dog.

'He is indeed but I really don't like him—at all,' GG retorted sharply.

Tom just shrugged in acceptance.

'Don't stop dancing on our account, we just came over to say hi and join the party. You guys are great dancers, enjoy,' said Mad Dog.

GG tipped his head as if to say, 'Of course.'

'Self-taught,' replied Mac. 'We watched some movies, *Dirty Dancing* and *Grease*, which helped.'

As if on request, GG grabbed Mac and got up close and personal in one swift move. Mad Dog began tapping and then singing along to the tune, as Tom sat there, stunned. What followed was so far the most bizarre Qbit event he had witnessed, seeing a 57-year-old chubby Italian dressed in board shorts and beach yellow crocs and formal shirt ripping across the dance floor to a tune from the 1980s. The act was almost a perfect rendition of the movie scene as he pranced about, but for his overweight puffing.

Tom was virtually speechless. 'How did he learn that?'

'We can learn anything pretty well as soon as we read it,' replied Mac.

'Huh?'

Mad Dog was still stuck on the movie theme. 'So, is it like in *The Matrix* movie—we can learn jujitsu?'

'Sure—kung fu, taekwondo, karate, jujitsu, kendo—in here everything is possible,' began Mac.

'Wait, stop. I get it. So, in here we can—I get it,' mumbled Tom hesitantly.

Mac continued. 'In here we are everything and anything. And I've been thinking; there is no reason that as we are you and you us that we can't reprogram your motor skills and fitness to learn it in both worlds. Unfortunately, we can't do that for Scott, as he isn't hard-wired to us.'

Mad Dog gave an understanding shrug; he was only a guest, after all.

'You can learn in here, where time runs slower. What would take you years in the real world, we can achieve in minutes, just like in *The Matrix* movie, which is, I hate to admit, where I got the idea. You can then use your new skills in the real world, and the extra benefit is that you get fit in both worlds. Want to try?' She changed instantly into a white robe and Tom moved to a blue fight mat Watto had created at the end of the table. GG and Mad Dog took their beers to the other end of the room to watch a movie. The entire exercise only took the equivalent of 2–3 seconds in the real world.

'Fortunately, unlike in *The Matrix*, we can only do real moves, and you won't die or anything.'

'Cool,' said Tom.

'And unlike in *The Matrix*, you won't have your brain plugged into a machine and be a battery-farmed human!' called GG from the divan he and Mad Dog were lounging on.

'He liked that concept, for some unholy reason,' remarked Mac, as she assumed a fighting stance.

Tom felt awkward fighting a woman—and one of the most famous scientists ever known to man. You would think by now he would have come to terms with the fact that all his thoughts were linked to theirs. As if in reply to his misgivings, Mac glided over and adroitly flipped him onto his back.

Tom groaned, 'Oh hell, what the ...? I thought you said it couldn't hurt me!'

Mac replied, 'No, I said it can't *kill* you.' With that, she launched a vertical kick at his ribs. He moved to avoid contact and block the kick but it glanced off his ribs, causing GG and Mad Dog to flinch in sympathy and give a 'that's gonna hurt in the morning' look. Tom dropped to one knee on the mat.

GG and Mad Dog started chanting, 'Fight, fight, fight.'

'$100 says Mac wins.'

'Done,' agreed Mad Dog as they clinked their glasses together.

Mac and Tom, arms raised at the ready, circled each other on the mat, trying to get into a position to make the next move. Tom was using the stalking time to play catch up, reading and watching *How to Jujitsu* on Watto, and requesting subconsciously to download from Watto all the information on martial arts.

Although Tom thought Mac was delightful, she was really starting to irritate him. He couldn't believe he was getting his butt kicked by a scientist. Enough was enough. He stood up in the *Karate Kid* 'crane kick' position. GG and Mad Dog just about choked on their beers with laughter. Tom knew exactly what he was doing; while Mac had read every textbook on every martial art, he figured she would be totally unprepared for his next move. It might just work. Focus. He didn't need to run the scene with Watto; he knew exactly what he had to do. Concentrate, wait for the moment, don't flinch, watch her.

Mac moved stealthily toward him like a cat ready to pounce. Perfect, thought Tom, she hasn't seen this move. She moved slightly to his left, he rotated the kick and locked her eyes with his. This was it. Ready for the killer blow, woman or not, he would take her down. And now.

He initiated the famous crane kick, aiming for her chin. The kick was right on line, perfect. At light speed, he launched. *Take that!* he thought, just before Mac leaned back far enough to avoid the blow. But how could her back arch so far? The next thing he saw was a sliding foot approaching his stomach—but no, wait, she would miss. Just at that instant, the kick hit its target. The fight was over as her foot slid into his groin. In less than a split second in Qbit world, or any world, the blow registered and Tom was down and out.

'Great film, that,' was all Mac said.

GG and Mad Dog stood and applauded, as Tom collected himself and stood up, puffing. It had been quite a lesson.

'Your turn, Mad Dog,' Tom yelped.

They all broke into laughter.

Mac and Tom went and flopped onto a couch Watto conjured up for them to take a well-earned rest.

Newts and Alby were sitting very quietly at the other end of the Great Hall.

The rest of the day at Bondi was relatively uneventful. Sun, surf and sea, just what they all needed. It was all quiet on the Qbit front, which generally worried Tom, but today he was determined to relax.

They stayed down near the beachfront and sat outside a cafe as the sun set, having a beer. GG and Mac watched from the Great Hall with a glass of wine. Even Alby and Newts were relaxing with a drink.

Newts had taken to watching old episodes of *Dr Who* from the BBC archive and was pondering if it was possible for Time Lords to exist. Newts had symbolically started wearing a long winter coat and multicoloured woollen scarf to make his position clear. He wanted to be a Time Lord. Momentarily, there was harmony in both universes.

As the day slipped away into night, Tom decided to check in and see how they all were.

'Evening, Tom,' said GG glumly. 'Can you believe our galaxy contains billions of stars and our galaxy is only one of billions? And what's more, we live on a planet revolving at 1,600 kilometres per hour and moving across the Universe at 2 million kilometres per hour. I was right about some of this stuff, and now they even think the Universe is expanding in all directions like a party balloon inflating, and we are moving further away every second. I wonder if it will one day pop?' he asked, looking at Alby. 'And there is even a song by a scientific group called Monty Python about the Universe, a real toe tapper and totally mind blowing.'

UV light causes sunburn and its wavelength is only $10^{-7}$ to $10^{-8}$ metres.

Soon they were all laughing, even Tom. 'Monty Python aren't scientists or philosophers, GG, just very silly men. They were a comedy group from many years ago.'

There was a silence, then Mac said, 'It is a very complicated world these days.'

GG paused, contemplating. He did find the song rather amusing, but had presumed the scientists were men of his ilk; highly charismatic and humorous, as well as having brilliant minds. He cast a dark glance over at Newts as if to illustrate the contrast.

'Arghwha!' yawned Newts. 'I'm tired!' he explained.

'You can't be tired—you don't exist,' jibed Mac.

'Huh?'

Alby came into the hall. 'What's all the carry-on about?'

'Well, as we don't really exist, we can't be tired, so you might think you're tired but you're not,' stated Mac.

'Huh?' said Newts again. 'Ok, let me get back to you on that.

So I can't be tired but I feel tired. And I thought time travel was hard to work out. It's a bit Shakespeare-like, to be or not to be, that is the question.'

'Hey, here's another random thing—he was born the same year as me,' chirped GG.

'Who?' asked Tom.

'William Shakespeare, born 1564, same as me,' replied GG.

Alby stood there waiting for another opportunity to say 'Huh?', while Newts slumped in a chair like an old deflated football.

GG's eyes flared. 'What is it with you guys? There is so much to be done.'

Tom piped up, 'Well I'm real and I'm going to the pub whilst you idiots can argue.'

'Noooooo!' exclaimed GG. Everyone looked at him, bellowing with a glass of wine in hand.

In 1590, Galileo had gone to the top of the tower in Pisa and dropped two cannon balls to prove they fell at the same speed. Three hundred and seventy-two years later the same experiment was done on a moon landing in 1962 when David Scott finally proved experimentally beyond doubt that they hit the ground together in zero gravity. Galileo was the first man to look at the moon and Jupiter. You could say space was his 'thing'.

'Doesn't everyone want to know about this amazing thing I have discovered? Why won't anybody listen to me?' yelled GG forlornly.

'How long will it take?' answered Tom.

'How long have you got?'

'Let's say 3 seconds.'

'Done.'

# Chapter 22

## Great Hall

8 March 2015

9.30 pm + 22 seconds

'Based on my observations,' GG began, 'I think there might have been a major disturbance in the Perseids asteroid belt, caused by Jupiter some time ago. Once a disturbance occurs, orbits and trajectories change and the annual Perseids meteor shower looks bigger and earlier than normal—gravity doing its work.'

'Hang on, hang on,' interrupted Tom. 'First we need some background, Watto—Perseids meteor storm.'

GG was going to have his moment, but first Tom needed to know what the devil GG was on about.

**Space Station**

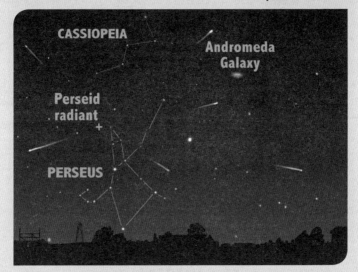

**The Perseids Meteor Shower**

The Perseids is the name of an annual meteor shower that usually starts in July.

The Perseids shower is caused by debris on the tail of the comet Swift-Tuttle.

The rate of meteors can reach 100 meteors per hour.

In 1833 a storm of 60,000 meteors an hour hit.

Particles are ejected by the comet as it travels on its 130-year orbit.

Comets are like dirty snowballs with dust and frozen gases.

Material hits our atmosphere at 240,000 kilometres per hour and disintegrates in flashes of light.

The point in the sky they appear to come from lies in the constellation Perseus.

The Perseids meteor shower has been observed for about 2,000 years.

The earliest recorded observation was in China in 36 AD.

Alby then spoke. 'It is far more likely that a person will be hit by a car than a meteorite. What is your point, GG?'

GG continued. 'Every day, thousands of meteors—hundreds every hour—small rocks and dust specks hit Earth from space, but only a few of those reach the ground as meteorites. Most are so tiny you can't even see them.'

'Ask the dinosaurs about major impact events,' added Mad Dog. 'Sixty-five million years ago a 10-kilometre-diameter asteroid, big enough to obliterate the whole of America, blocked out the sun and caused an ice age.'

Newts chimed in. 'Yes, Mr Maddocks, but NASA traces large asteroids for changes in orbits.'

Mac now chimed in. 'The Earth Impact Database has information on over 200 meteorite impact craters. Craters can be 300 kilometres wide—so it does happen. In fact, I remember in 1908 when I was 41 years old, the Tunguska asteroid hurtled toward Earth and exploded over Siberia, flattening 2,000 square kilometres of forest. No one knew what had happened.'

'Like the one in the movie *Armageddon*?' asked Mad Dog, with a degree of seriousness. 'I mean, could we divert an asteroid?'

GG was shaking his head in appreciation. 'Top movie—love that guy Bruce Willis. What a scientist!'

'Thanks GG and Mad Dog for your contribution—truly insightful,' grumbled Tom, now the chairman of another chaotic discussion. And Mad Dog was just as unpredictable as the Qbits.

Alby decided to weigh in again. 'If the meteorite weighs tonnes, it will pass through the atmosphere and will not be slowed down by the atmosphere. It would then hit at a speed of more than 40,000 kilometres per hour. The kinetic energy released would be huge due to the speed. $E_k = 1/2mv^2$.' He started scribbling formulae on the tapestry, when GG interrupted again.

'Bigger meteor, bigger bang!' He clanged his goblet against the tabletop for effect.

Mac liked to relate her science to real-life experiences. 'The impact is followed by a shock wave that is so strong it can flatten trees, like it did to the forests of Siberia in 1908. In fact, the study showed that if it had occurred a few hours later, it probably would have destroyed the city of St Petersburg in Russia.'

Mad Dog had studied the Ice Age and wasn't going to be left out of this one. 'The Ice Age was caused by the dust that is thrown up into the atmosphere from the impact blocking out the sun and cooling the planet.'

Tom needed to take control, as this was rapidly turning into a meandering lecture on meteors and galactic history.

'GG, what is your point in all this?' he sighed.

'I checked the AWS—the Advanced Warning System designed to track major meteors. The early warning system is showing "all clear" for any changes to orbits of meteorites. But it doesn't track the Swift-Tuttle comet, as it's so predictable—or it used to be.'

The Qbits were all peering at a view of the asteroid belt in the centre of Watto's Great Tapestry.

'So, what *the* hell is your point?' pleaded an impatient Alby, his moustache twitching strongly to the left.

'Indeed, get on with it,' urged Newts, his long tresses twitching to the left also.

GG, to dramatise his finding somewhat, blurted in a stage whisper, 'Qbits, as you know, the early Universe was bombarded by meteorites. There is evidence of craters all over every planet. What makes you think it is over? We still live on the same planet in the same solar system,' he stated emphatically.

'What are you talking about? Cut the melodramatic crap,

GG,' Tom scolded. He made moves to get up from the table and collect his things together.

GG would not give up. 'The majority of asteroids remain at great distances from the Earth and pose no danger to it. Guys, we have potential NEOs, which is not necessarily alarming but some might be big enough to make it through the atmosphere.

My guess is that a collision has changed the orbit of the comet. They are monitoring the wrong part of the sky. The other night, when they were asleep, I took over control of the Hubble Space Telescope and pointed it in a different direction.'

There was a brief silence as everyone digested the boldness of this move, and suppressed admiration for the ingenuity of the old lush.

'Watto, if you would please, some more on meteorites,' requested Tom.

**Space Station**

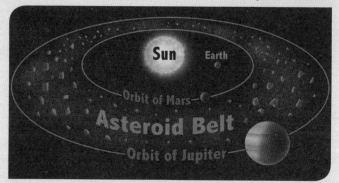

**Asteroid Belt and Meteorites**

The asteroid belt is located in the region roughly between Mars and Jupiter.

It has irregular-shaped bodies with some asteroids or minor planets.

4 largest objects: Ceres, 4 Vesta, 2 Pallas, and 10 Hygiea.

Ceres is a dwarf planet and is about 950 kilometres in diameter.

The size of the bodies can be as small as a dust particle.

Unmanned spacecraft have crossed it—it's not very dense.

Collisions between large asteroids do occur.

Every year about 100 million stones and 10,000 stones of 1 kg hit Earth, but almost none of them reach the surface.

Known as meteorites when they survive entry and impact with the ground.

About 10 stones of 1,000 kilogram or more reach the Earth each year.

As the Earth is 70% water, most stones land in the sea and unpopulated areas.

The one that killed the dinosaurs occurs about every 100 million years.

About 100,000 kilograms of cosmic dust shed by asteroids lands on Earth every day.

Before anyone could voice their complex reaction, Tom was moving right along to the important information. 'What are NEOs?'

Alby jumped in, 'Near Earth Objects. But there are thousands of asteroids, comets, spacecraft, and meteoroids that are big and being tracked by NASA. How would they miss any?' Alby was twirling the ends of his moustache now, and thinking about huge walls of ice hurtling toward tiny little Earth.

'Because, Alby, they monitor only the big kahunas like you, not a bunch of smaller ones or predictable regular comets like Swift-Tuttle. I have calculated that the Perseids meteor storm will hit Earth in about a week. I'm still working on where it will hit, when, and the intensity of the storm. I think this year's Perseids shower will start early and may well peak at nearly 100,000 an hour and may last for over an hour.'

Mac asked, 'Don't they have to be big enough to get through the atmosphere and not burn up?'

GG swallowed down some Italian insults as he drained his goblet. 'We are talking about the same people who didn't know about the two satellites colliding or Russian nuclear rubbish in space,' he said slowly and deliberately for effect.

Silence.

'Tom, if we can substantiate the claim, then we can't ignore the discovery. We are scientists—all of us. We must confirm and then take action. It's what we do.' GG was so serious that even Alby and Newts were almost unwillingly nodding in agreement.

Alby wanted to finish up. 'Gentlemen, we need to assess the accuracy of this claim. A 5-metre-diameter meteorite hitting Earth is like detonating a nuclear bomb.'

For a while, they were quiet. Tom paced the room, all the while wrestling with the usual question, *what do we do?* Tom shuddered. They had just averted one disaster and now another was looming! He was beginning to think the human race had notched up some pretty hideous karma to deserve all this. He was also starting to think the US Government was doing a pathetic job of 'monitoring' and 'investigating' things, from outer space to terrorist ePirate cells, if they had to rely on tiny little electron scientists in a quantum plane to keep stepping up to save their bare posteriors.

'First, we get some sleep. We will meet in the morning. Meantime, Newts and Alby can check GG's meteor storm, take control of Hubble and substantiate the claim, including developing models to predict the size, probability and likelihood of impact. Then call me and Mad Dog tomorrow and if all is correct give the information to NASA.'

The Qbits all nodded. GG punched the air.

'And once it's confirmed, you can alert the President *again* and brief him on the situation,' Tom added.

'Two–nil!' chanted GG. 'That's two–nil! What are you guys working on?' he taunted gleefully.

No one spoke.

Of course, Newts was feeling left out. How could this GG person keep making all these discoveries?

Tom and Mad Dog left. What had started as a fun day at the beach had ended up with the threat of Armageddon, leaving them wondering what the hell they were doing messing around with quantum physics.

A piece of a neutron star the size of a pin point would weigh 1 million tonnes. Space is not a complete vacuum: there are a few hydrogen atoms per cubic centimetre.

# Chapter 23

## THE WHITE HOUSE
### WASHINGTON

8 March 2015
7.32 am + 55 seconds

**From:** GG@Qbits.me
**To:** RNeil@presidentusa.com
**Sent:** 8 March 2015 7.33 am
**Subject:** Perseids meteor storm

Hi Bob,

We have heard on the grapevine that a young astronomer/
physicist has discovered a meteor storm approaching Earth.
Apparently, NASA did not see the anomaly that caused the
storm and with all your telescopes trained on big stuff, it was
an amateur's equipment that seems to have got the 'money shot',
as you call it. It was discovered by young Sydney University

physicist Tom Jackson and his colleague Scott Maddocks using the University's telescope last week. These guys are experts. We read their blog.

We took a look last night, it shows the storm location (we saved the exact location below so you can ask NASA to verify it).

We thought we had better let you know that we believe the meteor storm is going to hit the North Pole, inside the Arctic Circle, in 7 days.

We don't think it will result in too much damage but maybe you should warn Norway and especially the northernmost towns on Spitsbergen in the Svalbard islands. It would be a great opportunity to collect deep space meteor fragments and specimens.

Your early warning satellite needs to change direction by 1.4 degrees and view the Swift-Tuttle comet that causes the Perseids storm. Alby has e-mailed the NASA CEO and let him know.

As I live in an electronic universe unfortunately I can't meet for coffee, but I do fancy strong coffee like Harry makes.

Kind regards
GG

PS. If you don't reply in 24 hours we will e-mail the Norway Government, giving them time to evacuate.

Here is the link to the article posted in the local science site we found and checked out. These guys are good astronomers.

www.qbits.me/meteorstorm

It's funny the extent to which purely factual, helpful information can infuriate the receiver. When he cautiously opened the e-mail, the President was immediately furious. He picked up the phone to his head of security and took it all out on him.

'Call NASA and the CIA again. I want answers—who, where and what the hell is going on now? Who are these people and how do they get information and do things we can't seem to? Tell me this isn't true. Check whether this is a hoax. If it is, I want these folks caught and brought to justice. And get me NASA on the line and see if this early warning thing exists and what it's for. And if any of this is true, get our best scientific team out there—today!'

Once again, e-mails zipped around the planet to people having coffee, some at work, some asleep, and of course some on the toilet, though they'd deny it if you asked. This was how things got done—multi-tasking.

In very little time it had been established that NASA had again missed the data on the storm. An emergency response scientific team with security support was selected by NASA for immediate deployment. Although it was protocol to invite the people making the discovery, no one was comfortable with this, least of all the CIA, so they proposed to completely ignore Jackson and Maddocks, as it were.

The President clicked on the blog.

### SYDNEY ASTROPHYSICIST PREDICTS SPECTACULAR PERSEIDS METEOR STORM IN NORWAY

Two young Sydney scientists announced that the regular Perseids meteor shower will be a once-in-a-century storm and will be much more dramatic and intense than usual. It will be visible across the Northern Hemisphere starting on 16 March. The meteors should not be large enough to have a big impact but will be visible for thousands of kilometres in the night sky.

The scientists were doing some observations at Sydney University when they noticed some unusual data and a change in the Swift-Tuttle trajectory. They don't believe anyone is in imminent danger and intend to notify the authorities today.

The storm has not yet been confirmed by NASA or the European Space Agency but physics lecturer Tom Jackson and his colleague Scott Maddocks are credited with the discovery.

The President contacted the King of Norway and the Prime Minister, providing them with the data and information that NASA had received from Hubble, without mentioning the Australian discovery. The President had already sent a polite e-mail to the Qbits requesting them to remove the news post for international security and safety reasons, they didn't want people flocking to Svalbard. The blog post disappeared almost instantly.

# Chapter 24

## Great Hall

9 March 2015
11.35 am + 9 seconds

Perseids Meteor Storm in 168 hours + 30 minutes + 29 seconds

Tom woke the next day, immediately noticing his stomach muscles were aching. He felt like he had been through a heavy rugby session. He only had a few moments to ponder this sensation, however, as he was immediately whooshed into Qbits. He was greeted by Mac.

'Well, we *were* fighting for quite a while, and that training ...' she began.

'But you said I couldn't be hurt!' Tom insisted.

Mac rolled her eyes. 'I said you can't be *killed*, Tom! I wish you could take things a little more literally. You're a scientist, for God's sake! And it affects your muscle tissue because your DNA is linked to electrons, so the activity you do in Qbits will get you fit in the physical world.'

'Yes, yes,' said Tom. He was sick of having every little thing explained to him. 'But I don't understand.'

'Look, I can fix it, so relax. I will just release some endomorphines via the brain.' Mac crossed her arms, amused despite her irritation at this mollycoddled young man.

Tom patted his abdomen expectantly.

'Just a little tuning up,' Mac clarified. 'You really now only need 4 hours sleep and your stamina, reflexes and general body will be about 20% stronger if we keep training a few seconds a day. You won't be superhuman but you'll be good enough to match most you should meet. If you train you can probably get to 30%, which will put you in the fittest and strongest 2 to 5% of the population.'

'Wow, Mac, that's awesome!' Tom beamed, images of the Incredible Hulk lumbering through his mind.

'Morning, all,' Mad Dog croaked, his spirit slightly more willing than his flesh at this stage. 'What's new? Dare I ask?' Mad Dog was virtually sleep talking.

Tom raised his eyebrows. 'Watto, let's see Hubble's findings and e-mail traffic.'

# Great Tapestry

**E-mail Summary**

Bob Neil: Dear GG, Thank you for all your help, we have checked and your data again appears correct ... I really would like to meet you.

NASA: team established and ready for immediate departure to Svalbard. We await confirmation of external team members. No contact made with Australian scientists at this stage.

Norway Intelligence Agency: alert reimpending meteor storm, commence evacuation of Svalbard immediately. T–minus–7 days until forecast storm hits. All civilians must be evacuated.

CIA: Bios on Jackson and Maddocks, find their current location. Priority 1.

'GG, if you weren't already dead, I'd kill you with my own "top 2% of population in strength" hands.' Tom was still vainly dwelling on the elite physical condition Mac had bestowed upon him. 'Sanitise all information on us now, *right now!*' Tom yelled.

'Done,' GG responded proudly. 'All bases covered. I'm with the program, on the same page as you. The bios the CIA found are totally boring, you are just a couple of amateur enthusiasts with a telescope and access to university equipment.'

'Ok, then. Well done on implementing the response so quickly. But please don't make us famous and risk people finding us,' Tom chastised; even Mad Dog was nodding enthusiastically.

'Tom, Dog, there is no possible connection. We discussed this—they cannot trace or link us.'

Tom massaged his stomach absent-mindedly. 'Ok—all good. Well done, team.'

'And they haven't tried to contact us, so it looks good.'

And with that they left the Great Hall.

Watto alerted GG, who had requested an immediate alert for all R Neil e-mails. GG was as confident as ever they couldn't trace them. He Googled 'Harry's' and got hundreds of responses, he just fiddled with the order so that Harry's Woolloomooloo was about thirtieth on the list. He had to give it to Bob—he was smart and now paying attention to GG's every word. Respect at last.

George O'Brien had just landed in Australia to work under-cover with a younger colleague at Sydney University as visiting academics in the computing department. GG would watch his every electronic movement, no need to worry Tom or the others.

'Watto, just file in my Bob Neil follow up later file.'

**From:** RNeil@presidentusa.com
**To:** O'Brien@CIA.com
**Sent:** 8 March 2015 7.40 am
**Subject:** Lead

George

See GG's attached e-mail. Might be a lead—look for 'Harry's coffee'. Check any links to Sydney University, interview Jackson and Maddocks about this Perseids storm, see if GG contacted them. We need you back here—please get back to Washington as soon as possible.

Regards

Bob

# Chapter 25

## Harry's Cafe de Wheels

10 March 2015
10.30 am + 34 seconds

The coffee at Harry's was great, as always, and Chin was irritatingly chirpy.

'Morning, men, a couple of caps made by the Chinman? Hot, hot, hot and bodelicious, just like me!'

It was just what they needed. The sun was shining and the pair, for what seemed like the first time in a long time, relaxed. They perched on the harbour wall sipping and looking into the dazzling water, and couldn't help but laugh at the latest escapades of the Qbits.

Approximately 60% of the human body consists of water. There are about 37 litres in the body of an average adult. Brains are 75% water, bones are 25% water and blood is 83% water.

Mad Dog agreed the quantum beings were completely uncontrollable, but he could see they were trying to do good, so he thought it would be best for everyone if Tom just tried to ease up on the restrictions. Tom had to concede that despite their somewhat high-risk behaviour, so far they had actually helped the world.

Mad Dog shook his head and expelled a big sigh. 'No wonder you were going mad, Tommy. All that crap going on every day inside your head, where a second can take an hour! I'm surprised you are still sane.'

Reading the look on Tom's face, Mad Dog paused. 'Err, can they hear me now?'

Tom checked and shook his head. 'Hmm, let's see—GG is watching a movie, Mac is listening to music and Alby and Newts are working on some new theory. None are looking out through Watto.'

'Phew! Well, hell—that GG is a character and a half! And Alby and Newts, wow, they are some serious dudes. Just wanted to get that out there when they weren't listening.' Pausing again, he lowered his voice to a whisper, as if volume mattered, 'Oh—and I think Mac is kinda hot.'

In the Great Hall, Mac gave a little smirk.

And with that they burst out laughing. Tom was so relieved that he had someone to talk to about the random uncontrollable Qbit world. The only problem was that they could never tell anyone else. They agreed the real world wasn't as secure as the Qbit world, and they must never link themselves to the events or they would be hunted down, for real. It was clear to them both that they were in fact the weakest link in the system—they, after all, could be shut down.

They enjoyed the peace and quiet as they sat sipping. Even Mad Dog, for once, was happy to just meditate on his own thoughts for a few minutes. As they whiled away the moments, a dark car with tinted windows pulled up at Harry's. Nothing unusual about that—everyone liked to stop at Harry's. However, the two men who got out were rather intimidating with their dark glasses, suits, guns and swaggers, as they walked straight past the Harry's counter and made directly for Tom and Mad Dog, who were sitting innocently on the wall.

'Are you Scott Maddocks and Tom Jackson, lecturers at Sydney University?' asked the shorter of the men. The taller one, who was still very short if you thought about it, said nothing.

All Mad Dog could think about was how guilty one always feels when speaking to authority figures, if indeed that was what they were, even if they are just asking directions. He knew how this felt because one night Tom and he had been returning home from rugby practice late and a police car had pulled up beside them, giving a few honks on the siren for good measure. Mad Dog had wanted to jump into a bush but Tom had hauled him back by the shirt tail, wanting to hear what they had to say first.

'Is this Bayswater Road?' one had asked, sticking his head out of the window.

'I don't know,' Tom had replied cunningly. He knew he couldn't be questioned without a lawyer present.

'What's that sign there say?' asked the officer impatiently, craning his head to see the street sign.

'I repeat, I don't know,' Tom had responded, refusing to look at the sign and preparing to quote the *Law Enforcement (Powers and Responsibilities) Act 2002*.

'Must be Illiterate Moron Road,' quipped the other officer, putting his foot on the accelerator and speeding away.

'That's how you handle nosey policemen, Mad Dog—with dignity,' Tom had advised, and they had continued walking unharried by the authorities.

But not this time. Tom's throat was frozen in fear, and Mad Dog had nowhere to jump other than into the harbour, and he wasn't that fast a swimmer. Everyone at Harry's was now focused on them.

'Yes,' they replied instead, swallowing lumps the size of thumb drives.

'We have an urgent communication from the Australian Prime Minister.' The taller one flicked an envelope against his palm absent-mindedly, as if trying to remember what he had been asked to do with it.

'We have been instructed to pick you up on 13 March at 0700 hours to take you to the airport. Any questions, call the number on the letter or call us on 0415 137 007. We will answer 24/7. Any questions?'

Tom and Mad Dog didn't say anything.

'Any questions?' he said again.

'Err, you said if we had questions we had to ring that number or ring you,' stuttered Mad Dog.

'Yes, yes I did. But do you have any questions now?' huffed the taller one. Why in God's name would the Prime Minister want to communicate with these half-witted yobbos?

'We don't know if we have any questions now—you haven't let us read the communication yet ...' began Tom, trying to explain the conundrum.

'Give him the letter—and let's go get a Tiger,' muttered the shorter one to the taller short one, before stomping off toward Harry's counter.

Tom and Mad Dog nodded in acknowledgement as the taller short one handed them the letter before heading off to the counter also. Chin eyed them suspiciously, not particularly wanting to serve a couple of spooks who had been roughing up some of his favourite customers. Chin had an active imagination. The short one stared at the menu and the taller one stared at Chin, wanting to give his order.

Tom and Mad Dog slunk away from Harry's, not wanting to open the letter within view of the Feds.

10 March 2015

Urgent communiqué from the Prime Minister of Australia.

Attention: Tom Jackson and Scott Maddocks

The President of the United States has urgently requested your assistance in Svalbard at the NASA Perseids meteor field study from 13 March until the study is complete. A research fee, as well as all expenses and travel arrangements, will be paid at the expense of the US Government. The Department of Physics at the University of Sydney has been notified and is fully supportive.

This is not compulsory but you will be doing your country a great service and we would encourage you to take this opportunity to assist the Perseids project.

If you choose to take up this opportunity and I know you will, the briefing will be on board the flight on 13 March to Norway. If you wish to discuss, please feel free to call me on the below number.

Yours Sincerely

Mavis Kelly

Prime Minister of Australia

+61 111 111 111

Tom was flabbergasted. He looked first at Mad Dog and then at the Federal Police, who were now sitting in their vehicle digging into a steaming pile of mash and mushy peas to find the pie beneath.

'Watto! Teleport now!'

'What does this mean?' Tom asked Mac when they zipped into Qbits a nanosecond later. 'How has it happened?'

'The Americans are pragmatists. There is a situation and they need to deal with it,' responded Mac calmly.

'Still ...'

'NASA really can't ignore that you discovered the storm now—it was a mistake telling them,' Alby noted.

GG sipped from his wine goblet as he tried to hide. He didn't see the problem; in fact, in his mind this was a great outcome. He would get to be there, literally, in the proverbial eye of the storm.

'NASA thinks we are astrophysicists. We are first-year physics and maths lecturers! There's been some mistake. If they ever figure out ...' Tom appealed to the others. Newts and GG exchanged glances.

'Alby,' Tom implored, searching for an ally, 'you know I'm not up for this.'

Alby shook his head, but was smiling nonetheless.

'You forget you can ask Qbits anything—you and your good friend Mr Dog are far more than just first-year lecturers. Each of us can solve any problem and answer everything, instantly,' Newts reassured him.

'We can't go! How can we go? I—we—just don't have the knowledge. They will find us out!' Tom screeched. 'And semester is meant to start next week! We need to be there!'

GG put down his goblet and rolled his eyes. Tom was panicking again. This act was getting old. 'The Dean of Studies has insisted you go, as it is a prestigious opportunity that will cast a favourable light on the esteemed institution,' remarked GG drolly, quoting the Dean's e-mail he had seen verbatim.

'We won't leave you, Tom—and Scott will be there to help,' cooed Mac encouragingly. Tom's eyes opened wide; was that meant to be reassuring?

By contrast, nothing ever seemed to scare Mad Dog. In fact, he had a look of 'hell yeah!' plastered all over his silly face.

'There is nothing to fear at all,' stated Alby slowly. 'They cannot find us.'

'They won't need to "find us"—we will be right there in front of them!'

'No matter what they try, we will know about it before they can do anything,' emphasised Mac.

The Qbits were now unified and determined to see the meteor storm first hand and for Mad Dog it was a free holiday. A vote was not going to be required on this.

GG was pounding on the table with a curled fist. 'We discovered it! We should be there to see it!'

Mac was slightly more circumspect. 'It could be dangerous—these things are unpredictable.'

Newts and Alby were busy searching NASA's e-mail server. 'It seems that NASA is sending a small expert team to Svalbard and evacuating the town, so no civilians will be left. It also states they have accredited Tom and Scott with the discovery.'

'There is a memo debating whether or not to invite you both to join the research team, as the President didn't want to upset US-Australian relations by not inviting you—seems like the President is an honourable man,' added Newts, impressed.

GG muttered, 'An honourable horse's arse, I'll bet.'

The die was cast. They packed up every warm piece of clothing that Australian beach bum university lecturers could own (i.e., a jumper, a pair of jeans, and a scarf each), and hoped some good woollens would be provided.

Mac reckoned that in March the temperature in Norway was a big minus number that was just barely survivable. Tom's cousins had once gone skiing, so he popped round to their place in Maroubra and asked to borrow a polar fleece jacket. They couldn't begin to understand why he would need it in the middle of summer, probably some fancy dress party they figured.

# Chapter 26

## Harry's Cafe de Wheels

13 March 2015
6.03 am + 11 seconds

Tom and Mad Dog waited in front of Harry's on the warm sunny footpath. At the tail end of the Australian summer, there was already breaking daylight by 6.00 am and it was 25 °C. The pair were feeling quite toasty dressed in jeans and shirts, each with a ski jacket tucked under an arm.

The typical size of a meteor is about the size of a sugar cube but they can also be massive: an asteroid impact killed the dinosaurs 65 million years ago and the crater was 56 kilometres deep.

In a couple of hours real time they would leave Sydney and head to London, transfer to go on to Oslo and then fly a further 3 hours due north towards the North Pole to Spitsbergen, Svalbard, just inside the Arctic Circle. Watto calculated a total of 30 hours' travel time including stopovers. Plenty of time for in-flight entertainment and watching movies if they wanted to, or in Qbit time they could spend nearly 11 years in total in the Great Hall thinking, talking, and planning at light speed.

Mad Dog knew exactly the option he would take. In the Great Hall he would get no hangover, could hang out with GG and Mac, could research whatever he liked, watch movies, trek into space, and solve cyber crimes—and these were just all the things he had done in there so far. Hell, he could even fly the plane, GG had told him, if they took over autopilot. But he had a feeling Tom wouldn't be too pleased with that idea. Tom needed to lighten up.

They were both embarrassingly excited, as neither of them had been to Europe, so despite the uncontrollable outcome that loomed over their heads, they were feeling chipper enough.

Mad Dog genuinely did not know exactly where Norway was, and wasn't sure how to pronounce Svalbard. And while they both felt quite important, they were unable to tell friends or relatives where they were going or why. This was NASA protocol to stop 'storm seekers' following them, especially as Svalbard was being evacuated.

The Federal Police vehicle arrived right on time and the officers even jumped out and opened the door for them. These guys were important international scientists, the police had been instructed. They were to treat the mission as a diplomatic priority. That meant the siren en route to Sydney International Airport and all the bells and whistles of a police escort.

They received a quick security briefing in the car on the way to the airport, and were once again told not to

A car travelling at 80 kilometres per hour uses half its fuel to overcome wind resistance.

mention the trip to anyone. Tom assured the policeman that they were very reliable in terms of 'confidentiality' and that Australia and the US and indeed Norway could count on the muckabout scientists to keep a secret. The policeman simply replied that their phones and e-mails were being monitored and the consequences of breach would be serious. Tom had looked at the policeman's large twitching moustache and gulped fearfully.

When they got to the check-in counter they were handed first-class tickets and ushered away from the crowds to a VIP lounge, a glass of wine slipped into their hands. Maybe this wasn't going to be such a chore after all. Mad Dog now wasn't sure whether he would prefer to be pampered and sucked up to for 30 hours or play hackers and crime fighters for over a decade with the Qbits.

GG had already decided on behalf of Mad Dog that it was time for a long party and he had asked Tom to teleport him over after they took off.

As they boarded the flight Tom teleported in to see how the team was preparing for the trip. Tom was checking personal e-mails with Watto when he noticed a stray e-mail in the spam folder. Curious, he asked Watto to open it.

By the time Tom had finished reading, he was absolutely furious. Who had done this! What exactly had been going on behind his back?

'What the hell? Qbits, we need to talk *now*.'

They looked at each other. Newts was about to admit liability for whatever it was he was accused of, Alby didn't really care, and Mac was a bit worried she had overstepped her authority with her recent work and e-mails to her old university in Paris. Only GG seemed very nervous.

'Does anyone have anything to tell me?' Tom asked.

Alby, Mac and Newts looked varying degrees of impatient. GG's eyes shifted around tellingly.

'GG?' Tom asked again.

'Nothing special,' GG responded.

'If I were to find a deleted e-mail that appeared to incriminate you, would you have any idea what it was about?'

GG shook his head absent-mindedly, pretending to think really hard. A bead of sweat trickled down his forehead.

Tom cut to the chase. 'Which one of you *muons* entered the lottery?' he yelled.

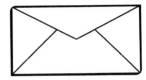

**From:** lotterieswin@lotteries.com
**To:** TomJackson@smarttek.me
**Sent:** 13 March 2015 9.15 am
**Subject:** You have won a major prize

Dear Tom,

Congratulations on winning $10,000 last night. You got 4 numbers.

If you contact me at the below number and provide identification we can deposit the money today.

Kind regards
Cathy Hampton
05 9973 1333
Lotteries Commission of Australia

Alby and Newts just shook their heads and shrugged their shoulders. Mac looked blank, not exactly sure what the lottery was. GG and Mad Dog didn't move.

Mad Dog considered his position, coming to the conclusion that attack was the best form of defence. 'We thought we might need a bit of spending money. I wasn't sure it would work, anyway. Tom, as I always say it's just the Dog's law—plain old good LUCK.'

GG smiled in relief.

'Random number generator. Apparently in here we can win anything we choose to—quantum magic!' added Mad Dog.

'Told you it would work,' gloated GG proudly.

'Told you Tom would be furious.' Newts was pleased with himself. This GG was just too much to manage and now with Mad Dog running around they were like modern day Robin Hoods.

'You're all jealous it worked. And what would you know, Alby, you're only 136 years old, Mac you're only 148 and Isaac you're only 372 years old. Me, I'm 451 years old. That makes me wiser than any of you. Like Yoda.' GG was on the attack, wine glass in hand.

'You talk such garbage. Look at you—you're old and fat. We are much younger and understanding of modern attitudes. We are more cosmopolitan,' retaliated Newts.

'Hey, at least I've got a personality.'

Tom held up his hand to GG. 'Stop, stop. The more you say, the stupider you sound.'

Mad Dog elbowed GG. 'What's the problem, Tom? We didn't go for the big prize—just four numbers. GG reckons that because we are random we can get all six and win the big prize if we choose to.'

The other Qbits were intrigued by the mathematical

implication of using their randomness to guess lottery numbers. They had a certain respect for GG and Mad Dog's obscure thinking—was it cheating or legitimate if you could do it?

'We can't return it, it's not like we can say, sorry, we didn't mean to pick those numbers, have it back.'

Tom knew it wasn't a king's ransom but if he didn't deal with it immediately, where would it end? Clearly they could win every lottery. They could easily steal all the money in any bank, as money was mostly electronic these days. They were all making up the rules as they went along; do-gooders with control of nuclear weapons, and now it was clear they could also control any amount of money; anywhere. The CIA would surely detect them.

'Watto, reply with our account details and donate the whole lot to a charity of Mac's choice.'

Fortunately for Mad Dog at that moment, the real world air steward interrupted to offer them things to make them more comfortable during the journey. And all Mad Dog could think or say was 'Y-E-S!' Yes to a pre-flight drink, yes to a towel to wipe his hands and face, yes to a newspaper, yes to pyjamas and slippers, yes to a blanket, and yes to another pre-flight drink.

All Tom could think was what the hell were they doing? Recruited by NASA, hunted by the CIA, and a gathering list of other enemies and frenemies. And now lotteries. Alby and Newts advised Tom that the scientific group had a security escort comprised of CIA agents, who were already based at Svalbard, which seemed odd to Alby and Newts, who didn't trust the US much and trusted the CIA even less. This time Tom agreed with the Qbits and instructed them to ferret around to see if they could explain the development.

The speed of sound in air is 340 metres per second or 1,224 kilometres per hour.

He quoted the Art of War which surprised all the Qbits. 'Ok find everything about the CIA based there. We must know all potential threats. Sun Tzu.'

He also instructed them to find out about the others they would be working with, as the only international project they had found in the area was the Svalbard International Seed Vault, and he was not sure why they would be involved with that.

As they were taxiing on the tarmac, Tom's mum phoned and he virtually had to hang up on her. 'I will e-mail you, Mum—promise!' he insisted.

'Aunt Narelle said you went over there looking for fleecy jackets! What is going on, Tom? Are you ill? Is Scott all right?' Tom's mother worried.

'Mum—I can't talk. I'll e-mail you!' Tom said again, trying to suppress the urgency in his voice. Truth be told, he was already a little tipsy from the pre-flight drinks and was starting to find the whole exchange rather amusing. 'Love you, and yes I am perfectly warm. Feeling great. Scott's great too. Ok—bye!'

Security protocol. He couldn't say where he was going. Why did everyone always worry about Mad Dog? He was a grown man, for goodness sake!

As the flight hit cruising altitude, and the seatbelt signs flicked off, Tom tapped his friend on the shoulder, ready to teleport him.

The aircraft is travelling at 825 kilometres an hour. If you jump out though, the terminal velocity for any skydiver is 120 kilometres per hour—you will not fall any faster.

Issuing the customary greetings all round, Tom and Mad Dog hesitated when they came to GG, who was dressed in ski gear like it was minus 20 °C.

'What?' GG asked defensively. 'My motto is be prepared.'

'Oh, I hadn't realised you were in the Scouts, GG. Are you any good at tying knots?' asked Tom facetiously.

Newts laughed. 'It's the best he can do just to get his shoe-laces tied correctly!'

GG looked genuinely offended.

'For God's sake—he never even wears shoes with laces,' cried Tom dismissively, pointing at his crocs.

'So you think I'm stupid too, Tom?'

'No, all I said was ...' he tried to clarify.

'I might be a little vague at times, Newts, but you're butt-ugly, dressed in short eighteenth-century socks and frills and poncy artifice. Get with the twenty-first century, you dweeb.'

It had been coming for a long while; GG and Newts started wrestling like school kids.

The others were silent. Sometimes the randomness of the Qbits' human-like behaviour just took your breath away. This world was as real to them as the first-class cabin of the aircraft was to Tom and Mad Dog.

Eventually Alby broke up the fight with a few well-timed throat clearings and a couple of German hurrumphs. 'Can we focus on the briefing?' he asked calmly.

'Ok, Watto, let's have a briefing on what Alby and Newts have on the team we are meeting with, and then Svalbard. Keep it brief. We can read the details later.

## NASA Perseids Project Science Team

### Tyler Maddalena. Head scientist. Age 55
Background: physicist, mathematician, studied at Harvard and Cambridge.

Career: at NASA, responsible for all science and satellite research and field missions.

Personal file: married, 2 children, pet dog, lives 20 minutes drive from NASA, suffers from asthma. In last staff appraisal by NASA director seen as tough and not interested in promotion.

### Doctor Emma Scobie. Astrophysicist and meteor expert. Age 33
Background: NASA 5 years. Wrote thesis on predicting meteor storms/mineralogy.

Personal file: single, no pets, works long hours according to review.

### Jake Whittaker. Mineralogy expert. Age 30
Background: PhD in determining mineralogical content of extraterrestrial material.

Personal file: studied same university as Maddalena.

## CIA Agents

Seems there are 15 agents based here. Six have been assigned to remain, the rest are evacuating. Do you want all their names and profiles?

Memo says NASA had to leave behind 2 other research team members, as you guys took their spots. You won't be popular with these guys!

'This is *so* embarrassing,' Tom huffed, once Watto had finished reminding them how underqualified they were for the mission. 'We are like preschoolers compared to these guys. What were we thinking!' He could sense he was no longer relaxed in his woolly slip-ons and complimentary eye mask, and his bum was starting to ache.

'Embarrassing for them?' asked Newts rhetorically.

'What? Look at their qualifications! We teach first-year physics and maths!'

'But we are experts at it,' laughed Mad Dog. GG clinked glasses with him.

'I'm with Newts,' replied Alby. 'How embarrassed would you feel if you spent billions of dollars and studied for years researching such an event and some amateur, non-expert, humble, barely educated young Australians from the other side of the world e-mailed the President, who then calls your boss, to let him know the event you are paid to monitor will happen in a week and you had absolutely no idea?'

'Ouch,' observed Mac. 'I don't think they are going to be pleased to see you guys,' she said softly.

'What the hell—I wish I had never got involved in this thing,' muttered Tom under his breath. This whole Qbits fiasco was starting to feel like a runaway train—from the day he had been struck by lightning to the day he was stuck in a plane and shot off to Norway to be made a fool of. This was Scott's preferred way of doing things—events just happening, rolling with the punches, taking the path of least resistance. Tom, however, was logical, planned, conservative. He did not like surprises.

Watto continued jumping around to various pieces of information, as others updated themselves, some on their personal virtual screens and some on the Great Tapestry. Watto had turned the Great Hall into the image of an aircraft first-class cabin so they could all be in the moment. He was now serving a cocktail.

Newts and Alby had a personal screen open and were typing feverishly.

Tom wandered over. 'Guys, what's going on? What are you reading?'

GG seized the opportunity to be the teacher's pet for a change. 'They are … err … on Facebook. We set it up yesterday and linked our profiles to the Qbits homepage,' GG began. 'And Newts is angry with Alby because he won't accept him as a friend, mainly because Newts reckons Alby shouldn't be using online dating, as he can never actually meet the people he is chatting to.'

Mac piped up. 'Facebook is great—I've found and been chatting to my grandkids. I've told them I'm alive in cyberspace.'

'But you are all dead. What are you all thinking? You don't exist!'

'I *told* them that. Immature, unethical, uncontrollable,' stated GG, tsking and shaking his head, arms folded, with his beer bottle still dangling from two fingers.

'You're all dead. Even *you*.' He pointed at Alby and Newts. 'Alby—online dating? What are you thinking?'

Alby was embarrassed. 'No, no, I'm merely communicating with a woman with a strong intellect about science matters.'

'Where? Sorry … *how* did you find her?' asked GG.

'Not at all relevant,' replied Alby.

'Why won't you accept my friend request?' chipped in Newts, clearly quite hurt by his main Qbit ally isolating him.

'Am I your friend, Alby?' asked Mac.

Alby nodded politely. 'I'm not adding GG either,' he added, only fuelling the situation.

'Ok, I'm not sure about the whole Facebook thing,' started Tom.

'But you guys use it all the time! By the way, why haven't you accepted me as your friend?' asked Newts, getting very tense.

'Newts, I haven't logged on in a while,' replied Tom.

Watto immediately put Tom's Facebook page up on the screen, as if requested to. Tom now felt as though his privacy was being violated, with everyone having open access to all his stuff. And the profile photo was very unflattering—it was his university gym membership ID photo.

'First things first,' he instructed, 'Watto, accept all Qbits as friends.' That dealt with Newts. Now the ethical issue. *Be rational in this irrational, random world, control what you can.* 'Ok, Alby and Mac, you shouldn't really lead them on in the real world—no more chatting to women and long-lost relatives.'

'But I think I'm falling in love with her,' pleaded Alby.

'Did you tell her you are high maintenance?' quipped GG.

But Tom controlled access, and it was hard to argue with what he said. They all knew that the risk was unmanageable.

All nodded, but Alby continued. 'But we can use it whenever we like?'

'Ok, yes,' Tom huffed. 'But no traces—security between the worlds can never be compromised.' All agreed with Tom's logic, but still the worlds drifted ever closer together.

'Good, because I've invited Bob to be my friend and so has Alby,' piped up GG.

'Bob?'

'Bob Neil, you know, the ...'

'Oh my God! Quick! Everyone unfriend me and Mad Dog, and anyone we know! The CIA will be sniffing around this in a flash!'

Tom was right. The four of them had screens in front of them instantly.

'Done.' They all replied.

Concerned, GG looked at Mad Dog and asked, 'But we are still mates?'

'Good mates,' replied Mad Dog.

'Get me a receptacle, I'm going to be sick,' said Newts.

'Watto, it's your job to monitor and ensure there are no linkages to me or Mad Dog on their Facebook pages. Ok?'

Watto winked his feline eye.

'I'm going back to sleep,' Tom grumbled.

*www.facebook.com/AlbyQbit*

## Facebook

### Alby

Updated on March 13, 2015 at 11.35 am.

Interested in Science, Art, Politics, Women.

### About me

Born 14 March 1879. Current age 136.

Working on Theory of Everything = TOE and GUT = Grand Unified Theory.

### Wall

### Recent Posts

My favourite sayings and science:

$E = mc^2$ and $c^2$ equals 90 quadrillion. Cosmic speed limit = c.

Gravity cannot be held responsible for people falling in love.

When you sit with a nice girl for 2 hours, it seems like 2 minutes. When you sit on a hot stove for 2 minutes, it seems like 2 hours— that's relativity.

Imagination is more important than knowledge.

I never think of the future. It comes soon enough.

Only 2 things are infinite, the Universe and human stupidity, and I'm not sure about the former.

I want to know God's thoughts when he invented light.

What also really interests me is whether God had any choice in the creation of the world.

### Alby's friends: 22

### Friends request sent

Bob Neil

Stephen Hawking

| Newts | Mac | GG |
|---|---|---|

**Facebook**

Newts

Updated on March 13, 2015 at 11.35 am.

Interested in Science, History, Art, Politics, Cricket.

**About me**

Born 25 December 1642. Current age 372.
I am a knight—Sir Newts.

**Wall**

**Recent Posts**

Favourite book *Principia Mathematica* written in 1867.

Member of Trinity College Cambridge.

Laws: energy can't be created or destroyed—it can only change form.

If I have seen further it is because I have stood on the shoulders of giants.

Objects accelerate if a force is applied, that's $F = ma$.

G-force is the force when you accelerate e.g. roller-coaster rides 5 x gravity on loops.

Earth's gravitational acceleration: $g = 9.8 \text{ m s}^{-2}$.

Energy must be conserved. It can never be destroyed or lost … so find it!!

Gravity is the force that draws objects toward each other.

Law of universal gravitation—we are all attracted to each other and everything!! $F = Gm1m^2/d^2$

| **Newt's friends: 3** | | | **Friends request sent** |
|---|---|---|---|
| Alby | Mac | GG | Elizabeth II |

*www.facebook.com/GGQbit*

## Facebook

### GG

Updated on March 13, 2015 at 11.35 am.

Interested in Life, Universe, Everything, Wine, Music, AC/DC.

### About me

Born 15 February 1564. Current age 451.
In 1609 I built the first telescope.

### Wall

### Recent Posts

Jupiter—318 x Earth, greater than sum of all other planets known.
I dropped 2 cannon balls from the top of Leaning Tower of Pisa in 1590.
Heavy items don't fall faster but at the same speed—in fact 372 years later in 1962 man landed on the moon where there is no gravity and David Scott the astronaut dropped a hammer and a feather—and proved it.
Favourite book: *Sidereus Nuncius and the Starry Messenger, Systema Cosmicum*.

### GG's friends: 75

**Friends request sent**

Bob Neil

| Alby | Newts | Mac | AC/DC |
|------|-------|-----|-------|

## Facebook

### Mac

Updated on March 13, 2015 at 11.35 am.

Interested in Science, Medicine, Environment, Fashion.

### About me

Born November 7 1867. Current age 148.

### Wall

### Recent Posts

Everyone should support cancer research and donate to Hôpital Claudius Régaud.

Happy Birthday, Amelie!

Favourite universities: Warsaw University of Technology, Lviv Polytechnic, Adam Mickiewicz University.

Nobel Prize winner in 1935 was my daughter Irene Joliot-Curie.

Favourite book 1937 biography by Eve Curie.

### Mac's friends: 15

**Friends request sent**

Jane Goodall

|  |  |  | James Watson |
|---|---|---|---|
| Alby | Newts | Mac | |

# Chapter 27

## Great Hall

### 13 March 2015
### 11.35 am + 55 seconds

Tom was awoken by the sound of someone trying to vomit.

'God, I hate flying! It's so unnatural,' whined Newts. 'Does anyone have anything for travel sickness?'

Alby was trying to convince him it wasn't possible for him to get travel sickness.

The Sun is just a star among hundreds of billions making up the Milky Way Galaxy. The estimated temperature at the centre of the sun is 15,000,000 °C.

'Well then, explain why I've been vomiting since we took off,' Newts snapped.

'Metaphysically impossible.' Alby was adamant, lips pursed.

'Get a life, Alby. I'm off to watch a movie,' said GG. As he turned to leave, the others' attention returned to the sickly Newts.

Mac was holding a glass of beige water for Newts. 'Try this.'

'What is in this potion?' asked a wary Newts, his face as white as a sheet. 'I'm not drinking it!' scolded Newts, mopping at his brow with a lace kerchief.

'Don't be ridiculous, it's perfectly safe,' insisted Mac.

'What formulation have you established that can reduce the symptoms, if I may be so bold as to ask?'

'GG's formulation—he read about it online, and I made it from an old recipe I found.'

'I'm not drinking anything that vagrant drinks!' Newts was behaving like a spoilt child asking about his first dose of cough mixture.

'Ginger beer. I've had some and I don't feel sick.'

'Ginger beer?'

'Yes, fresh ginger beer.'

The distance to the sun is 150 million kilometres = 1 astronomical unit = 1 AU. If you drove to the sun at 80 kilometres per hour it would take over 200 years!

Newts curtly took the glass and started sipping, hoping he wouldn't vomit as he drank it.

'I'm watching *Return to Avatar*—the first one was fantastic. Any takers?' GG was now holding a film canister, with a roll of celluloid inside, merely for effect. 'Hey Tom, ask Mad Dog if he wants to teleport over.'

Tom ignored GG; he wanted a nap. Mad Dog took up the offer.

Tom awoke with an elbow to the ribs as they commenced their descent into Svalbard. They had changed flights in Norway to a small local aircraft and were exhausted after nearly 24 hours flying.

'How do you sleep with all the noise and announcements and crap?' Mad Dog was grumpy and looked like he had been on a big night out.

'I was listening to Qmusic, so didn't hear anything.' He was rubbing his eyes like a young child woken but refreshed after a deep sleep. He looked around and smiled.

'Ladies and gentlemen, we have commenced our descent into Svalbard, the heart of the Arctic, and will land in 10 minutes.'

Mad Dog looked down the aisle; they were the only people on the 40-seat aircraft. 'Ladies and gentlemen?' he repeated sarcastically.

The Captain spoke again. 'Tom and Scott, we are landing on the largest island, called Spitsbergen which means "pointed peaks". Some of the largest glaciers in the world are found here. You can see the huge pointy snow-covered mountains on either side. Looks like we are landing on a beautiful evening.' The accent was heavy Northern European. 'The Svalbard Islands are very isolated, located far out in the ocean, about 1,000 kilometres from the North Pole.'

The conversation had become more personal after the pilot remembered they were the only passengers; he had come to the conclusion they must be important, as they were arriving when everyone else was leaving, so he decided to impress them with a geography lesson.

'In fact, here in Svalbard it's a special week, as it's Sunfest week. Today the sun sets at 4.00 pm but shortly there will be 24 hours of sunlight from the end of April until August. Then we will have 24 hours of darkness from October to February. So enjoy and celebrate Sunfest week. Please return to your seats and turn off all electronic devices and fasten your seatbelts for landing and welcome to my home. It's 5.45 pm and the outside temperature is minus 5 °C, with a wind chill taking it to minus 12 °C.'

'Great Hall?'

Mad Dog nodded.

'Watto, let's see some basic information on our destination—Svalbard,' said Tom.

 ## Great Tapestry

**Svalbard Key Facts**

Svalbard is an archipelago and literally means 'cold coast'.

Svalbard is close to the North Pole—60% land covered by glacial ice.

Svalbard has 10 large islands and the largest is Spitsbergen.

Longyearbyen is the main town on Spitsbergen with a population of over 2,000.

Discovered in 1596, when GG was 32 years old. It was mainly whaling until 1750.

In 1925 Norway was given sovereignty over Svalbard.

Everyone except for a few essential people have been evacuated.

Polar bears are the largest carnivore—Svalbard has more polar bears than people.

They are as tall as a man and twice as long, weighing in at around 500 kilograms.

In the summer months when the ice melts, they are ravenous.

Locals carry guns as polar bears enter towns looking for food in summer.

Temperature ranges from minus 20 °C during winter to 6 °C during summer.

Lowest temperature recorded in March 1986 at minus 46 °C.

Svalbard is home to the Global Seed Vault or as its known the Doomsday Vault.

'So, it's as cold as hell and we will be able to see the northern lights,' summarised Mad Dog.

'Hmm, looks like it. Looks pretty funky,' said GG. 'All the houses are different colours.'

'The so-called northern lights the aurora borealis phenomenon is caused by solar eruptions and solar winds,' continued Alby, 'and named after the Roman goddess of dawn, Aurora, and the Greek name for the north wind, Boreas, credited to Pierre Gassendi in 1621.' Alby sipped from his macchiato, the froth clinging to his moustache.

'Hey, I've heard of that guy. He was working on the same stuff as me in the 1600s. French guy? Never met him. Guess he's dead now—oh well, that's life,' GG reminisced.

Mac was characteristically introspective as she pondered the day's information. 'The Seed Vault seems like an interesting project,' she began. 'Shame the planet has come to that—creating a modern-day Noah's Ark to protect crop seeds in case of nuclear war. It has billions of seeds; everything from sunflowers to ancient rice seeds. I might go research that.' And with that, Mac abruptly moved from the table to a room she had created at the end of the Great Hall for some quiet time.

'Just another big fridge for food,' GG dismissed.

Tom and Mad Dog sat at the table, watching the Tapestry. The islands of Spitsbergen looked like you could walk up them, through the snow.

'Welcome to the world's refrigerator, cold some of the year, freezing the rest,' commented GG. They couldn't help but chuckle at this; even Newts smiled. Sometimes the obnoxious GG's simplifications were just right.

Alby read out some more facts about Svalbard from his personal screen. 'The main town we are flying into has 2,000 people. There are Russian and Polish research stations on various islands. Recently, the Americans established a research station on the main island to study polar bears and possible extinction but many of the locals who were used to having Europeans present were much more sceptical of the Americans—especially as the 15-person security contingent outnumbered the scientists by a ratio of 3-1. As we know, those security people are CIA agents.'

Mac joined in. 'I can confirm they are doing some research but most of it consists of researching what the Russians are doing and they have state-of-the-art listening equipment with unlimited satellite air time. They have been monitoring your phone calls to gather background on you both.'

'What the hell?' asked Mad Dog.

'Well, we are here to watch a meteor storm and collect some samples and get back to uni in Sydney in a week. There are only a few people in town and they are watching all of us. Got it, GG and Alby? Just drop it. Watch a movie or read a book, or I will put Newts in charge of everything.' Tom was sternly eyeballing everyone in the room.

There was silence. Whilst Newts was happy at the accolade, he was surprised—he had thought he *was* in charge.

Alby continued with a news search of Svalbard. 'It seems the town has been evacuated by NASA as a precaution ahead of the storm and only four locals remain. The Chief of Police and three hotel staff—the manager, a chef and a housekeeper to look after us. That makes five scientists, four locals and six CIA—it will feel like a ghost town with so few people around.'

'Great, there goes the wild Sunfest party I was going to.' Mad Dog looked dejected.

Alby looked slightly disappointed at the end of the meeting and went back to his Facebook page. Everyone noticed.

'What's with him?' asked GG. 'Grumpier than normal.'

As they dispersed, Mac winked at Tom, but no one else noticed.

Back on the plane, the seatbelt sign was on. Ready for landing. Tom handed a small note to Mad Dog, who smiled; he was now in on the plan.

When glass breaks, the cracks move at speeds of up to 4,800 kilometres per hour.

# Chapter 28

## Hotel—Spitsbergen, Svalbard

14 March 2015
8.32 pm + 19 seconds

Shortly after landing, Tom and Scott found themselves bumping along in a military Hummer on their way to the temporary NASA research facility, which had been set up in the main hotel in the town. They guessed it must be a CIA agent at the wheel, as it wasn't the Chief of Police or hotel staff, and he didn't seem evolved enough to be from NASA.

Panspermia is the hypothesis that life was and is distributed in the universe by meteors.

Once at the hotel, they were met by the NASA crew. 'Welcome to Spitsbergen,' said Tyler.

Tom and Mad Dog did their best to appear at ease in the marble, glass and stainless steel reception lobby.

'Please take a seat.'

There was a moment of unease as everyone waited for everyone else to sit down. When this mild chaos had passed, Tyler smiled pleasantly and then began. He had an air of authority; he was not a man to suffer fools or be crossed.

'I hope you had a good flight. Congratulations on your find, impressive work gentlemen. I'm sure you've worked out by now that I'm Tyler Maddalena, and this is Emma and Jake, who will be part of the team.' They had been given the team names on their itinerary. Qbits research was far more intrusive, by now they knew pretty much everything about them.

'My role is to ensure that this research project is focused and successful. To achieve that, we need to assign tasks and work together. We have set up a mobile lab in the hotel business centre and Emma will be in charge of assigning elements of the work to each of us.' There were little smiles and nods of acknowledgement.

'In a moment our security colleagues will run through some Internet protocols; as we are not authorised to publicly discuss our findings, for the next few days we are in a communications blackout.'

'No worries,' Mad Dog said. Tom nodded too—it didn't impact them in the slightest.

Each day the sun evaporates about 1 trillion tonnes of water from Earth.

'That said, please believe we want you to feel at home here.' Tyler gave a vague noncommittal smile as he concluded his little welcome speech.

'Thank you,' the boys said, shaking his hand and those of Jake and Emma.

All Mad Dog could think about was GG's blithe comment;

222

'Welcome to a cold isolated hell'. And the note Tom had handed him, it was now or never.

'Anyone fancy a refreshing beer at the bar? It's beer o'clock,' said Mad Dog, glancing at his watch demonstratively. Tom frowned at him, trying to be serious as they had agreed. 'It's always beer o'clock somewhere in the world,' Mad Dog clarified.

'A welcome drink—great idea, Scott,' Tyler assented, tempted to look at his watch upon hearing the odd terminology. 'It's important you speak your mind,' he said, smiling at them warmly. 'We Americans are very good at saying what we think.' He paused for a moment. 'Perhaps too good.'

Emma didn't say much; she just wanted to get to work, not sit around making chitchat with these useless amateurs. There was too much for her and Jake to do, and they needed to get started, get an early night, no alcohol should be consumed on missions. But at Tyler's instigation they made their way into the small hotel bar.

Tom then realised why Mad Dog had done this, it was going to be odd and they would probably think the two of them mad, but he realised Mad Dog had worked out the best way to do it.

'I'd like to propose a toast,' said Tom uncomfortably.

Jake and Emma exchanged a look of surprise, as Tom had certainly seemed like the quieter of the two.

'We meet here for scientific research and coincidentally today is a day which Scott and I celebrate every year with a toast. We'd like to recognise those who made all this possible. Please stand, everyone.'

All Emma could think was, *damn time wasters.*

In the Great Hall, Mac ensured everyone was watching the Great Tapestry events.

'I'd like to wish one of the greatest men and perhaps the greatest mind of all time a happy birthday. He changed the world, so here's to our good friend Albert Einstein—good old Alby.' Scott and Tom clinked glasses awkwardly.

Jake liked this touch and was first to clink glasses with the two, and Tyler followed with some gusto, thinking what nice guys they were, good fun. Emma just thought they were mad, but joined in anyway.

'He is 136 years old today,' continued Mad Dog. 'Happy birthday Alby.'

Instantly, in another world, Alby was mesmerised watching the screen. He had thought everyone had forgotten. He was dumbstruck at the gesture.

While Alby was caught in the moment watching the Tapestry, the group gave a shout of 'Surprise!' as Tom and Mad Dog appeared in the Great Hall.

'Here's to you, Alby—136 years old and looking no more than 42,' cheered Tom. GG popped the champagne and they all raised their glasses to toast Alby. The party had started.

Alby was touched.

Happy birthday Alby flashed like a big neon sign on the Great Tapestry.

Mac then produced a large birthday cake from the chair next to her, with $E = mc^2$ iced on it, with what looked like two and a half candles.

Champagne gets you drunk faster due to the bubbles.

There was a moment of hesitation as they tried to work out why only two and one half. *Got them*, thought Mac with satisfaction. *They can't work it out.* But it wasn't going to pass unnoticed—nothing went unsolved in Qbits.

As GG suddenly broke into a rousing chorus of 'Happy birthday', followed by three cheers led by Mad Dog, Alby couldn't help but think that they weren't such bad people, and perhaps that annoying GG was not a bad person either. *Must be Tom's*

*DNA*, he concluded, forever thinking, analysing. *I must see if I can prove if individual DNA when shared electronically can lead to conflicting individual personalities but team work when required.*

The cake was dutifully cut but not without the inevitable question. 'Ok, Mac, tell us the riddle.'

'Well, Alby, you are a theoretical physicist and probably best known for your Theory of Relativity and time dilation. Well, we know that 1 second in the real world is 53 minutes and 5 seconds in here.'

They all started laughing except Mad Dog. The joke evaded him; sure he could read at light speed in Qbits but he didn't have the shared DNA, which created a degree of the spontaneity they all had. Tom looked at him and said simply, as if to share with all of them, not just Mad Dog—136 years is 71.5 million minutes old. In Qbits that's equal to only 1.35 million minutes or 2.5 years old. Alby is but a toddler.'

'So, Alby, tell me about your life. You were so famous—what was it like? Were you rich?' asked Mad Dog.

Alby was absolutely overwhelmed that they had remembered. And now excited, Alby began. 'I always wanted to ride on a beam of light. Being a Qbit now is pretty close. I didn't do very well at school, I was said to be a bit disruptive, like our friend GG. My first job was at a patent office and I studied whilst working. I like using what we used to call *gedanken*. That translates as thought experiments, where you couldn't use experimentation but just your thoughts, like I used to imagine travelling on a light beam and try to work out if I could ever catch up,' said Alby. 'I got married to a fellow student but it didn't work out. The war started and with Nazis in control of Germany, I left and went to the US.

But much remains unsolved in our world, and none of my work would've been possible without those that went before. As stated by our friend Newts, if I have seen further than others, it is only because I stood on the shoulders of giants like our friends here. Without the rebellious determination of many before me, I would never have had the chance.'

'Hear, hear! Let's get back to party time.'

At that moment Tom cranked up the music and grabbed Mac and began to whisk her around the dance floor.

After several hours of frivolity in Qbits, Mad Dog and Tom were startled when Tyler stood up to leave.

'Scientists, the success of our mission depends on teamwork, precision and preparation,' he stated grandly. 'Until tomorrow, 6.30 am. Goodnight.'

'Ask not what your country can do for you,' joked Mad Dog as Tyler left.

Jake smiled but Emma was not amused; this was her opportunity.

Sound travels through water 3 times faster than through air.

'We have a colossal task ahead of us.' Smiles vanished. Emma and Jake were keen to get started. 'We must track the trajectories of major meteors so we can recover them. We have state-of-the-art tracking telescopes on the roof and access to satellite feed of incoming meteors for the next week.'

'Our tasks will be the same?' wondered Tom.

'Any major fragments that enter intact need to be tracked, location identified and collected for analysis. That is our mission—track, locate and analyse.'

'And Emma, what if some of the debris collides with another object—like a building. What's the safety plan?' asked Tom, wanting to show that he too could be thorough and analytical.

'Satellite feed and our analysis say they will break up, and large meteors are not expected to survive re-entry.'

226

'Is this the same satellite that gave you guys a heads up that a storm was happening?' questioned Mad Dog. There was instant tension. He had hit a nerve.

'Every large meteorite surviving re-entry will be tracked and collected.' Emma was firm; there would be no mistakes and no discussion of the failure of NASA to discover the storm. 'You guys will assist us in the monitoring, tracking and calculating of the trajectories.'

Emma and Jake rose. 'Goodnight, gentlemen. See you at 0630.' The tone suggested clearly that the evening was over.

# Chapter 29

## Hotel—Spitsbergen, Svalbard

15 March 2015

7.00 am + 31 seconds

Perseids Meteor Storm in 38 hours + 8 minutes + 41 seconds

Tyler tapped his watch as he walked past them in the temporary lab, indicating they were late. 'Storm at 9.08 pm tomorrow night, work to be done.'

'Hell, only by 30 minutes,' said Mad Dog defensively. 'It's 7.00 am.'

'Quick breakfast and then we must get started. Storm in plus 38 hours,' said Tom.

'Mate, can you smell that? I'm in heaven. Bacon, eggs—oh my God, French toast,' said Mad Dog, more like a university student than a lecturer. The hotel breakfast was a delight to behold. The hotel staff had been evacuated except for the manager Simone, chef Fred and a housekeeper.

'Oops, here comes the ice queen.' Emma was coming in to check up on them as the boys were working their way through a third plate of bacon and eggs.

She left them with the comment, 'See you in the business centre. If you ever finish.'

'First proper meal for days,' said Mad Dog in between mouthfuls.

The storm was due to hit in a little over 37 hours. The entire town had been airvacced via a combination of the Norwegian Government and NATO. They had taken a walk around the town late last night. It was a quaint place, with colourful cottage-like weatherboard buildings, which were now dark and deserted. It was eerie; not a single domestic animal, light or any sign of life. Shop windows had been hastily boarded up, doors padlocked to protect against no known life except them and the CIA and hungry polar bears. It was like being in a day after movie. Silent, dark and cold. Only the breeze made a noise to break the silence.

As they wandered into the office, Emma greeted them sternly.

'You're late. We have lots to set up and we need to agree on tasks.'

Although she seemed a bit preoccupied, Emma's smile was warm. But clearly the holiday was over. 'We need to work closely together as a team and we don't have long to set up.' They did seem intelligent, she thought, but far too easygoing. This was a mission, and potentially a promotion. If nothing else, it would redeem her team for having missed the storm origin.

'Jet lag,' offered Mad Dog. 'Sorry. I just need a bucket of coffee and I will be ready to go.'

Jake chuckled.

'You'll pick up the coffee over there.' Tyler indicated the large black airpot of coffee.

'Thanks, Tyler.'

Pushing his chair away from the desk, Tyler rose to his feet.

'You know where I am,' he boomed hospitably. 'Come and see me when you need to. We have to talk. This work is technical. It's also delicate. Emma has the task list, she is in charge. I have an 8.00 am link-up back to HQ in Florida. Back at 9.00 am to assist.'

'We are sure we can help make this a success,' said Mad Dog, pumping squirts of coffee from the thermos.

For once Tom appreciated his friend's confidence.

'It's great to be here,' Mad Dog reassured them.

'Scott, why don't you help Jake calibrate the lab equipment? Tom, you can help me with organising the known mineralogy of past meteorites so we have a reference scale, and set the telescopes to the predicted entry points to try to capture footage of the meteor entry trajectories.' Emma chose Tom as the obviously more sensible one, as the calibration was far more menial.

Jake indicated for Scott to follow him to the other room. The temporary lab had been set up inside the hotel's business centre, as this meant not travelling outside unnecessarily in the freezing conditions. The telescopes were on the three-storey hotel roof near the noisy air conditioning system, simply because it was a natural wind break and the generator was the warmest place outside, where it was minus 15 °C with the wind chill.

'You can use that terminal,' said Emma, indicating the screen on the long business centre desk next to her as she sat down. 'I'm just clearing my e-mails. Let's get all the data downloaded from NASA's database on meteorite composition. The system is online to NASA, so you have full access to the data library. I don't need to reinforce that everything you see is confidential.'

Tom just nodded, thinking, *if you only knew.*

'Please excuse me while I attend to my messages.' She tilted her head slightly, then began typing madly.

Tom stared at the screen, not quite sure where to start, so he took a long slurp on his coffee. 'Gah!' he blurted.

Emma's head shot up but she didn't show any further interest.

Upstairs, Mad Dog screwed up his face as he piled a little more sugar into his mug. *American filtered coffee!* He was missing Harry's already.

Jake was a lot more chatty away from his boss. 'It's pretty cool you discovered this storm. Really threw our guys, a couple of amateurs showing up billions of dollars of equipment and thousands of people.'

Clearly, they were all puzzled. 'Yeah, a fluke really. We were just looking for disturbances in the radio signals in that part of the sky and noticed something out of whack and—bingo.'

'Wow, lucky break—for all of us. And now we get to see it live. Unbelievable. Emma is good at what she does, you'll get used to her.'

'Lotsa security guys around,' Mad Dog observed awkwardly, trying to stop himself from making any personal comments about Emma.

Jake shrugged. 'We always have some, not usually these guys, but I guess as they were here anyway it was an easy option. No point moving them out and another lot in. Lots of valuable equipment and we are logged on to central NASA, so remote cyber terrorism is always a risk. NASA SOP.' Jake was starting to relax. 'Sorry, standard operating procedure. Our lives at NASA are full of acronyms. Just stop me and ask, if I slip into NASA speak.' Jake seemed like a good guy, despite the fact he did a lot of talking.

The conversation was cut short because Mad Dog was suddenly sucked into Qbits.

# Chapter 30

## Great Hall

15 March 2015
8.52 am + 46 seconds

Perseids Meteor Storm in 36 hours + 16 minutes + 41 seconds

Mac was unusually determined. 'Tom, if possible, I'd like to visit the Global Svalbard Seed Vault this afternoon. What an experiment! It houses nearly the entire planet's range of seeds in one location in case of a global disaster. It even has some extinct varieties—I've been reading about it overnight. I've looked into their systems and it is quite the scientific marvel. To see the history of the whole world's food supply in a single vault. Survival of the human race. Alby says he thinks he can access security codes so we can get in.' Mac was geeking out on them again.

'What? I'm not going all the way out there to look at some damn seeds. I'm staying here. I mean, could you think of a more boring thing to look at?' GG grumbled, then put his headphones back on and continued watching the Bruce Willis movie *Armageddon*—again.

Newts just shrugged his shoulders. 'No one knows the code to open the vault, it changes randomly daily. Only two people know how to access the code. Best of luck, Alby.'

'Hey, Newts, did you know you were born the year I died? Go figure!' yelled GG a little too loudly through the blasting volume of his headphones.

'What are you doing?' asked Alby, looking at Newts.

Newts was pounding up and down on a treadmill. 'I saw this on TV. It's great—it has multi levels and monitors your heart rate. I'm going to get fit.'

'You idiot—we're not real, and nor is that treadmill. Your heart rate can't go up, you can't get fit.' Alby was shaking his head whilst GG sipped on his wine, one earpiece set back on his head to expose one ear, like a DJ.

The nearest star is over 40 thousand billion kilometres away.

GG smacked his lips together as he thought about it. 'Well, this wine tastes good to me—very real. I say go for it, young man!'

Tom chuckled at the bizarre combination of activities.

'Go for it, Newts, maybe you can have my spot on the rugby

team,' Mad Dog quipped. They all laughed, and Alby shrugged his shoulders and went off to the far end of the room.

Easily distracted, Mad Dog turned to the treadmill and asked, 'Newts, how did you discover gravity?'

'Scott, I wanted to know why the planets didn't fall out of the sky onto us.' He gazed nobly into the distance as he spoke, still stomping away. Then he dropped his head. 'I was a bit of a loner and not that popular when I was young.'

Mad Dog's eyebrows furrowed for a second before he spoke. 'They say *Principia Mathematica*, the book you wrote, was the greatest science book ever written and that you invented calculus—did you have any help?' Mad Dog couldn't believe what all these guys had done in their lives. Here he was, in his twenties, playing rugby and drinking beer, when these guys had been hellbent on solving the riddles of the Universe at his age; and now they were his roommates.

'Do you really think my book was the most famous ever? You know, it just came to me when I was thinking. These days there are so many disturbances, how can anyone get time to quietly think?' Sir Isaac was serious, even as he pounded faster up and down on the treadmill.

'Anyhow,' said Tom emphatically. 'We have the afternoon free, so let's go take a look at the Seed Vault.' They could easily complete any of the required tasks by lunchtime and head over after that.

GG readjusted his headphones and picked up his glass of wine. 'Great, let's visit a fridge full of seeds. Should be riveting.' At that moment in the movie on the big screen Bruce Willis crash-landed on the asteroid. 'Now *that* is what I call riveting!' GG exclaimed.

The average distance between the Earth and the Moon is around 400,000 kilometres.

Newts, puffing on the treadmill, gave his now hourly

galactic weather report. 'The meteor storm starts in 36 hours. That's about 15 years time in here. It's looking like a beauty— lotsa activity out there.'

From the little three-storey hotel on the hill, they heard a deafening noise outside and could see what looked like a military helicopter from a movie.

Before Mad Dog even managed to open his mouth to comment, Alby piped up with, 'It's a twin-rotor Chinook. They have been out on morning patrol. No one is allowed to enter or leave Svalbard until the storm is over. Their base is at Ice Station Kroner, which has been locked down, with nine staff evacuated and six left here to help you guys.'

'Ok, Watto, give us some info on this Seed Vault before we go to work.'

# Great Tapestry

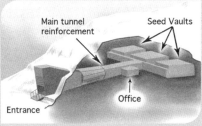

**Svalbard Seed Vault**

Known as the Ark of the Arctic or the Doomsday Vault, it opened in 2008.

The seeds stored here will remain frozen for up to 200 years.

The temperature inside the Svalbard Global Seed Vault is minus 18 °C.

The capacity of the vault is 2.25 billion seeds.

It is 130 metres above sea level.

There is a 120-metre tunnel into the mountain that leads to 3 seed chambers.

Each chamber is 20 metres deep, 10 metres wide and 6 metres high.

200 fibre-optic cables give off a turquoise light.

Vault is made of 1 metre steel reinforced concrete with 2 airlocks and blast-proof doors.

The outer half of the entrance tunnel is a steel pipe with a diameter of about 5 metres. It is all designed to withstand a nuclear explosion.

The tapestry showed the schematic of the vault and its main features. All were impressed.

GG quipped, 'Sounds like a Steven Spielberg film. Maybe they will do a sequel *Raiders of the Arctic* or *Doomsday Vault*.'

Mad Dog chuckled and joined in, 'Or *Snowmageddon*, or Arnie could come back as the Germinator.' They simultaneously high-fived to celebrate the winning combination.

Newts had been doing some research to show off for Mac. 'Svalbard, or Spitsbergen, was chosen due to its naturally cold climate; 2.25 billion individual seeds, 130 metres above ground, inside a mountain, to last for 200 years,' Newts continued.

'Definitely a sequel to be made here,' again quipped GG. 'Do I really have to come? I'd rather wait until the movie comes out ...'

'It's colder like space in there,' retorted Mac, knowing this was the only way to pique GG's interest.

He raised an eyebrow, refusing to commit to the discussion. 'Not nearly as cold as space, just a fridge with all salad and no beer,' he said drolly.

For this, Mad Dog high-fived him again, but when he saw Mac's look of disdain he dropped his head as if to say sorry for encouraging the old goat.

Alby had been closely monitoring the CIA. He just didn't trust it—or any secret service, for that matter. Too much history in the War; never trust the intelligence force. 'Seems the CIA has communicated to NASA that at midnight today the vault will go into "Doomsday mode", with no access in or out after that curfew.'

'This whole area is one big fridge,' restated GG, 'no need to close the door—it's freezing inside and out ...'

'How are we going to get there?' asked Tom, trying to stay on message.

'Snow scooters, it's just like riding a quad bike. And the locals leave their keys in them, the trusting souls.' This sounded like fun to Mad Dog.

'What is the name of the mountain housing the Seed Vault?' asked Tom.

'The mountain housing the Seed Vault is called Platåberget, or "plateau mountain" in English. The seeds are sealed in specially designed four-ply foil packages inside the vault. Steel-reinforced doors, multiple-locked chambers and a video-monitoring system supervised remotely from Oslo, Norway—plus, presumably, the polar bears—will further protect the vault.'

'And we need to take guns for protection from polar bears, right?' said Tom.

Watto nodded and smiled.

'Let me get this right—there is a vault with samples of the entire planet's seed varieties stored there in case of global disaster so we can re-start the planet, and it's in the Arctic, where a meteor storm is about to hit, and we are going there with guns?' said GG, wine glass in hand, smiling. 'Sounds like a movie to me. A pretty far-fetched one, at that.'

It is believed that the Universe is 95% dark matter and energy that we can't see.

# Chapter 31

 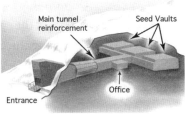

Main tunnel reinforcement    Seed Vaults

Entrance    Office

## Seed Vault Entrance

15 March 2015
1.45 pm + 26 seconds

Perseids Meteor Storm in 31 hours + 23 minutes + 41 seconds

Emma and Jake were a little perplexed about the boys' desire to check out the Seed Vault. Neither had ever been and they pretty much thought it would be a big fat waste of time, since the thing would be locked and it was pretty underwhelming from the outside.

Tom was secretly relieved, as it would mean neither of them would ask to come along.

'Ok, we have 2 hours until dark. If we take a snowmobile it's only 15 minutes to get there, look around for an hour or so, and head back before dark. Agreed?' Tom was concerned that the

CIA might follow them and they didn't want to show them they could access the secure vault, if indeed they could.

'We told them we were just going for a look, and not going inside, so we can't be away too long. They think we are just excited tourists taking photos of the sign—best we keep it that way. Alby is sure he can crack the codes.'

If you run in the opposite direction of the Earth's rotation then you are relatively going 1,600 kilometres per hour!

They put on the NASA issued jackets to keep out the wind chill. The hotel had a small fleet of snowmobiles. Rather than grabbing umbrellas, as hotels often provide when one ventures out in bad weather, they had been instructed by the Chief of Police to take his flare gun in case of a polar bear encounter. The instructions were clear; to fire into the air and get out of there—none of this 'standing still' nonsense.

The Chief of Police was relaxed, as during winter the bears should have been on the ice pack farther up north hunting and didn't usually come near the town. It was just a precaution more than anything. He couldn't understand why they would bother going to see the door to the Seed Vault, which was all that was really visible, but he was proud his town had a critical international asset in his patch, so was pleased they were making the effort.

The snow scooters were great, and there were no road rules to think about as they shot across the fields. Freezing as it was, it was a real adrenalin rush racing through open snow-covered fields at maximum speed. GG was enjoying the ride in the Great Hall, encouraging Tom to cut corners and whooping away as he egged Tom on to race Mad Dog. From the 3D Great Tapestry, it was like an arcade game, with Tom and Mad Dog as the characters.

They didn't need the GPS on board the scooters, as Alby

guided them to the location. They pulled up to what looked like a *Star Trek* set. It appeared particularly uninviting; a concrete mass protruding from an ice-covered hillside. There was a small bridge to the entrance with blue lights on the top section. The sign simply said, 'Svalbard Global Seed Vault. No entry permitted, property of Norwegian State.'

In the Great Hall, Alby had been diligently working with Newts to create an algorithm to open the door. The assigned task had taken them several minutes, or in Qbit time, days.

From the entrance they could just see the shoreline through the misty sleet. No one had followed them; the CIA was the only one who would bother but the Qbits had tracked them via their communications and they were all in the warm hotel monitoring the area from the comfort of their new luxurious HQ. Perfect.

As they walked up, Tom wondered how this was all going to work, and Mad Dog had absolutely no idea. 'Open sesame,' he joked.

'Ok, Alby, is this going to work?' asked Tom.

'We use the electric current as transport, plenty of electrons and then like "quantum magic" we are inside the Seed Vault mainframe. Then, using the algorithm, we set the pass code to 000000 and you punch that code in.'

'Quantum magic,' drawled Mad Dog.

'Let's keep moving.'

'Right. We are in and just changing code.'

'Try the door.'

On the Great Tapestry they waited what seemed like hours for Tom to punch in the codes to open the large doors. It had to be physically entered, as there were no electronics to do it from the mainframe. The door failed to open.

Back in the Great Hall, there was silence. Alby never got

this sort of thing wrong. The Qbits could crack any code—that was what quantum computers did. Alby's face contorted with a look of failure.

Everyone looked at Tom, waiting for someone to work out what to do now.

GG offered some advice, 'Let's go back and grab a beer.'

Mac was annoyed with GG's attitude, and wasn't sure why the code had failed. The silence continued to hang around like a lost neutrino. Alby and Newts were busy recalculating, looking at what had not worked.

On the screen, only a second had passed in the real world, almost an hour in Qbit time. In the Qbit world, just as Tom was thinking it had failed, there was a loud click as the vault door mechanism opened. There was a relieved cheer and then laughter—it had merely been an expectation time gap. The relative time in Qbits was so slow it had appeared not to work. The speed of transmission had given the impression of failure. Checking no one was around, they entered through the sensor door, which closed behind them after a minute.

So this was the Doomsday Vault designed to preserve the future of civilisation for generations to come, located 1,000 kilometres from the North Pole in an Arctic desert. Mac was singly impressed at man's capacity to build such a facility.

GG was far more sceptical about the need for it and the likelihood of its success. 'The vault is valuable if there is a war or major event but there are many ways the world can end. It could be through asteroid impact, which is about a one in a million chance, and no vault will help if there is an ice age.' He added, after a well-timed belch, 'If it's a supernova explosion there is nothing we can do, or if there is an unexpected gamma ray burst, which will happen any day in the next few billion years. And boyo—if it's a black hole, then hang onto your hats, as we just have absolutely no idea! And the chance of that happening is about one in a trillion.'

'Thanks for cheering us up. Don't forget the chance of an alien attack like in those ridiculous films you insist on watching, GG,' sniped Newts. They all laughed.

Inside the vault, Tom and Mad Dog moved along the eerily silent entrance tunnel for some 120 metres until they reached the three chambers.

'What if the people who survive don't know it's here, or can't get in?' asked Alby. Silence. No good answer to that one was forthcoming.

The tunnel entrance led to what looked like a small office with the sign 'Command centre' on the door and on to the main airlock. Another electronic door code was easily cracked. They quickly marched down the tunnel to the airlock doors. The schematic was up on the Great Tapestry. It was a simple design, like any warehouse, with racks and racks of seed packets organised by country.

The required fail-safe system was simply the cold environment and keeping out radiation in the event of a nuclear disaster. Inside the chambers were shelves with millions of seed packets deposited by each country in sections in sealed foil containers. It was up to each country to provide its unique agricultural collection. All were catalogued both electronically and manually in case of disaster.

As they walked around they saw ancient rice varieties from China and several hundred wheat varieties from Australia. Mac was overwhelmed at the scale of the venture. To get all the world's countries to cooperate and construct such a project was beyond Alby's comprehension, as he had grown up in a world at war. The Qbits were overwhelmed by the example of what humankind could achieve if it put science first. Even GG was awestruck by the clear cooperation to not only build such a bizarre construction at the end of the planet but to get everyone to participate. All agreed it was quite an outstanding engineering and science project, clever in location and simple in design.

Newts added, 'The one in Afghanistan was looted and destroyed during the war there in 2010 and the vault in the Philippines was scattered by a typhoon. This is designed to withstand both nature and man's stupidity.'

GG said, 'What the hell have they got broccoli seeds for—do they really think future generations want to rebroccolify fields everywhere? That will delight kids for eternity. A chance gone forever to get rid of broccoli.' Everybody ignored him.

'Wait, wait!' exclaimed GG. 'All of a sudden, nothing happened,' he quipped.

'Ok, time to go guys. Good idea Mac and well worth the trip,' Tom added. Mad Dog nodded in agreement.

An extremophile is an organism that thrives in areas that are detrimental to life.

The vault door opened and as they exited the tunnel the wind chill had increased to make it feel even colder than when they had entered. With heads down and scarves across their faces, they headed towards the snow scooters, dreading the ride back into the cold wind.

# Chapter 32

## Hotel—Spitsbergen, Svalbard

16 March 2015
8.02 am + 5 seconds

The next day started with another fantastic breakfast. It was the day of the storm and even Mad Dog wanted to be on top of his game, so he asked for a couple of cans of Red Bull to wash down his pancakes. It was going to be a long day waiting.

The crew busied themselves setting up the spreadsheets to record data and testing recording equipment, satellite links and back-up systems to ensure they were ready to track, document and retrieve the meteorites on impact.

Time is defined by science; the only reason for time is so that everything doesn't happen at once.

By now Emma had started to relax, as they were 'systems ready'. Jake was impressed; every task these guys had been asked to do was not only done with speed but they just got it right. They were sharp. The spreadsheets and downloaded data were perfectly organised and collated, and models were tested in quick time. These Aussies knew their stuff. Emma too was quietly impressed, especially as they weren't jeopardising her project and promotion, which was her main concern.

But this was not the time for philosophical and moral niceties. Newts had taken the lead in getting all the tasks done, with the help of Mac. The fact that a quantum computer can hold more than one value at a time meant that all research and testing could be done simultaneously at Qbit speed—Alby's quantum magic.

The CIA, who were bored with sitting around attempting to be involved, had been designated as what they called in their jargon the QRF, the Quick Response Force, and were happy that they were now 'active' and part of the main game.

During the storm, the scientists would take the coordinates reported and retrieve large meteorite fragments before they became buried in the light snow, if possible. That meant that those within a 5 kilometre radius must be followed as a priority and larger fragments documented for search over the next few days. Tom's role was to triangulate important trajectory analysis data captured to allow recovery.

The day dragged on in both the real and quantum worlds. It seemed like an eternity as they all sat watching the countdown timer on the Great Tapestry.

Perseids Meteor Storm in 36 minutes + 53 seconds

Finally they all thought.

They all had ringside seats to the upcoming galactic show. Most excited of all was GG, as this was something he would have lived for when he discovered the telescope in 1609, over 400 years earlier.

'Where is the clerk?' asked GG, referring to Alby's first job as a patent clerk.

'What's up with Alby?' asked Newts, who was working intently in the far corner.

'Alby, what are you doing?'

'Just researching an obscure communiqué I just picked up near Svalbard. Someone called Delta Force said, "Svalbard is clear and they are on their way." The CIA has six remaining operatives here. Delta Force aren't part of the CIA but a counterterrorist group, America's covert operations group. I'm just checking, as it seems odd timing, and I just wanted to ascertain whether the CIA knows about them being nearby.'

'Most likely SOP. None of them trust each other, CIA, Delta Force ... and the Doomsday Vault is internationally important. You know how paranoid the Americans are.' GG wasn't having Alby mess up the party.

Alby nodded, wanting to agree. The logic seemed robust, but there was just something about that message.

Inside the Great Hall the others were all watching the Great Tapestry portal showing the Hubble telescope's view of the incoming meteor storm in 3D, with random specks now darting about in the otherwise serene calmness of space.

Curiously, at the end of the table, GG seemed distracted and was not his excitable, boyish self. Less than 30 minutes to go. Then he put his wine glass down.

'*What have I done?*' he screamed suddenly, in the most serious tone they had ever heard from the flamboyant GG. 'I need all your help—*now*.' It wasn't a request, it was a command. He was yelling, utterly terrified.

Instantly they were all at the table. 'There is a miscalculation about the intensity and size and breakup on entry. Some of the meteorites are of a size that can cause serious, potentially cataclysmic damage to this area. I have miscalculated the average meteorite size and storm severity. Many of the meteors are huge. I can now see them on Hubble. I have risked Tom and Scott's lives!'

There was absolute quiet in the Great Hall. They all were aghast; they could see the view from Hubble of huge meteors hurtling towards Earth. Not small space rocks but giant boulders. The screen showed the recalculated probability and error in breakup assumptions. Watto clearly showed the large meteors which were big enough to survive re-entry and cause small nuclear bomb-like explosions.

'We will all be killed—we have less than 30 minutes until the impact of large meteorites in this area. We have no weapons that can be diverted in time.'

By now Tom and Scott were standing with the Qbits, gauging the danger. With no time to get to the aircraft and evacuate, a direct hit might kill them. And predicting exact ground impacts wasn't possible, even for them.

In less than 30 minutes the first large meteorite would hit the area. They needed to do something, anything, or they would be obliterated. The potential impact was that of a small nuclear detonation; a direct hit would wipe out half the town—hopefully the other half. They needed to do something, let everyone know—but how to convince them this late in the proceedings? Tom and Mad Dog slumped in their chairs, feeling helpless.

Mad Dog muttered under his breathe barely audible, 'Really *bad* LUCK.'

They had hours in here, but only minutes to act back in the real world.

'Okay, let's take another look.' Alby and Newts, given the perilous situation, calmly reviewed the calculations.

'I calculate this as a day's work to pinpoint impact sites—we have time, as that's only 27 seconds out there.'

'Might get lucky. Move to safe locations or hillsides to avoid impact,' said Newts sterilely.

'We need more than luck. These results: they're one in a thousand of a direct hit, but even with indirect hits the velocity will cause a huge bomb-like crater and explosion of rock and debris.' He thought for a moment. 'Ok, no time to recalculate. We had better play the odds. You Australians heard of Las Vegas?'

'Of course.'

'Ever thought of going there?' asked Alby, distracting himself momentarily.

'What? Is this relevant?' asked a terrified Tom.

'We need to randomise outcomes and find a lucky place and then get there asap. Newts, let's first calculate the odds of impact right here. Simulate the large meteors.'

'We need to calculate the trajectories and move to safe ground in the next 15 minutes.'

Not knowing what to do, Mad Dog jumped in. 'Guys, if ...'

Tom felt bad. He wondered how Mad Dog was handling all this. 'I'm sorry I got you into all this ...' he began.

In 1989 Arpanet commenced as the predecessor of the Internet.

'But Tom ...'

'My fault—trying to save the world and e-mailing everybody. If it wasn't for me we wouldn't be here,' confessed GG. No one denied it was his idea. There was no time for blame, though.

'What do you mean? We all know why we are here. We wanted to be,' said Mac firmly. 'Qbits, there are no unsolvable problems, only the wrong approach to the solution. Think laterally.'

Even so, Tom for one still felt bad. The discoveries were both his and Mad Dog's, and it was honestly impossible to untangle who had discovered and done what. And they had had help. Big help.

Suddenly a shout came from behind the Qbits huddled near the Great Tapestry, running emergency scenarios looking for potential safe locations in the mountains.

'Guys—will everyone just shut the hell up? Stop gibbering and *listen!*' Mad Dog was very angry. There was understandably silence. *Poor Scott—not handling recent events very well,* they all thought.

'The only safe place is the Seed Vault. It is designed to survive nuclear bombs. It should be able to withstand the impact of any meteorite forecast in this storm. It's built into the side of a mountain, for God's sake!'

The silence changed from one of pity to one of shock. How did a non-Qbit think of this brilliant idea? Of course that was the answer—a totally random solution. Newts spoke precisely as Watto cleared the screen of the many calculations and random data they had put up. 'It took you 17 minutes to get there yesterday, that gives you 15 minutes to convince everyone and leave for shelter. Achievable.'

GG gave his mate a huge pat on the back. Tom looked at him with relief. 'Thank God you are here, Dog.'

'We need to convince the NASA guys to follow us. We have 3 seconds to work up a plan and execute it in the next 10 minutes.' Tom was precise; that gave them a few hours in Qbit time to formulate a credible reason and plan.

A simple plan was agreed—show them the evidence. At the hotel, Tom cleared his throat and went out onto the roof, where they were all waiting for the first sighting. 'Can I have everyone inside right away, there is a major problem.'

Everyone was staring at the horizon, where some small fragments, faint shooting stars, were making an appearance, like a support band. They shunned his request, as they were focused on the first few strains of the opening act.

These young Aussie men were intelligent but annoying. Tiresome practical jokers. This was it—the chance of a lifetime. Front row seats to observe, and hopefully tomorrow to retrieve and analyse some nice sized extraterrestrial meteorites.

Tom insisted. 'We have an emergency—our research and information from Australia indicates we have underestimated the size of the large meteorites by metres and they are due here in less than 30 minutes. Some will not break up on re-entry.'

The NASA scientists dragged their eyes from their telescopes and looked at Tom and Mad Dog as if they were mad. Was this some silly joke? Surely this was not the time for games? Jake was about to say, 'Yes, and there are little green men flying them,' when Tyler registered the look of genuine terror in the boys' eyes.

'The data is onscreen downstairs on Hubble feed.'

There was silence. The CIA agents and locals didn't know what it all meant, but Tyler, Emma and Jake now look stunned. 'Three plus metres? At that size they won't break up on re-entry. That just can't be correct. What data? Why haven't we seen this? Show me—*now*.' Tyler took charge.

Emma couldn't believe it. This just couldn't be so. And how would these guys have found all this out? The CIA agents on the roof didn't know what was happening, but the tense nature of the conversation alerted all their senses.

They flew down the stairs and Tom showed them the

downloaded Hubble images, and it was as simple as that; the meteors measured and time of photo confirmed it. They had been using lower-orbit satellites to capture entry, not Hubble looking away into space. Their chances of survival were not good. Captain Michaels followed Tom but indicated his men should keep watch on the rooftop base.

Tyler spoke, he knew the numbers. 'A projectile diameter of 5 metres will cause a crater of hundreds of metres. We are out of time. Captain Michaels, we need everyone here NOW.'

The Captain spoke clearly into his intercom. 'Emergency situation, everyone to temporary lab now.'

'Get the manager, maybe there is a basement we can take refuge in,' added Jake.

Emma was about to say the obvious to Tyler when he shushed her. Clearly Jake didn't realise the enormity of such a meteor impact. Emma had done her PhD on meteor impacts. They had little chance of survival in a basement, but for now it at least offered hope.

The Earth's diameter is 12,756 kilometres and its axial tilt is 23.45%.

*Good. Data downloaded and they have accepted the danger*, thought Tom. Phase 1 complete.

Confusion reigned; none of the scientific team could fathom how Tom had done his calculations, but he had come up with answers. In fact, he had come up with all the answers. Tom was finding Emma grew friendlier the longer he spent with her. It seemed that, when faced with knowing both the danger and reality of the situation, she seemed the most calm and was prepared to work through solutions.

Stage 2 of the plan. Everyone was present.

Tyler spoke as the commander. 'We have data that suggests the size and intensity of the meteor storm are significantly more dangerous than predicted. Tom and Scott have presented data I have verified. We need to take emergency shelter underground. The meteor storm will not consist of small fragments but rather large ultra high velocity impact boulders that will impact at 25,000 kilometres per hour, like major bombs. This place will be like a war zone in less than 30 minutes.'

'If I might, Tyler, interrupt.' Everyone turned to Tom. 'Scott has come up with a solution. We need to move immediately to the Global Seed Vault. It is 15 minutes by snowmobile—we went there yesterday.'

Emma asked, 'What? Hide in the Seed Vault?'

Tom continued. 'The Doomsday Vault is built 120 metres inside a mountain, and is designed to withstand a catastrophe.'

Most didn't know anything about it but the Chief of Police added, 'It's designed to withstand a nuclear war. The Doomsday Vault is a seed bank as strong as a fortress built into the side of a mountain for the purpose of preserving food sources in the event of a disaster. It has blast-proof doors with motion sensors, airlocks, and metre thick walls of steel-reinforced concrete.'

'Good enough for me—we leave in 2 minutes. Bring jackets and any handy water and food. We must go immediately,' barked Tyler.

Captain Michaels and his men were already running about competently, as this was their speciality—war zones.

Then came a moment of sincerity from Tyler. 'Tom and Scott, if we get out of this, we owe it all to you.'

But Tom couldn't help beating himself up about the fact he had effectively got everyone into this, and there was a high probability they themselves would not survive.

The police officer, midway through putting on his jacket, stopped and addressed the group. 'You know, I'm not so sure about this plan. The vault has the best security available in the world—the lock is electronic, we will never get in. Hope is a great energy, but when it is taken away, the despair can be worse.'

'We will be trapped outside?' asked Jake.

'Can we call anyone en route to remotely open it or get the code?' asked Captain Michaels, stopping to absorb the key information. Outside the vault they would be sitting ducks.

Time for that moment again. 'I can get us in,' said Tom, gulping.

'How?'

'Don't ask.'

'But if you can't, we will be exposed in the open,' pleaded Emma, suddenly preferring the basement odds.

'We got in yesterday. Trust me, we can get in.' Tom looked at her levelly; she stared right back at him.

'We need to go *now*.' Mad Dog seized the moment. There was no time for any more questions or explanations.

'Two on each scooter, you guys just follow us.' The CIA took charge of transport. 'Move, people!'

When his phone rang in Tom's ear, he instinctively still looked around, amazed that only he could hear the loud ringing sound, but it was an electronic impulse inaudible to everyone else.

Mac said simply, 'It's your mum. It's 8.00 am in Sydney.'

'Oh hell, I told her a little white lie—that Mad Dog and I were going out for a road trip to the Outback and wouldn't be contactable.' Tom gulped, ready for the onslaught of questions.

'Hi Mum, yes, yep ... no, not for a few days. Plans changed and we went a bit further ... yes, Mum, Scott is behaving. Look—there is something I need to tell you ...'

'Yes—but will you be coming for lunch this Sunday? Bring Scott along and then you can tell me all about your trip. Bring the photos ... better go, the doorbell just rang. Tell Scott to behave,' she chuckled. 'Big kiss, love you.'

'Mum—' He wanted to tell her everything, but it would put her in danger. 'Love you too, Mum.'

Mac said abruptly, 'Why the hell didn't you tell her?'

'Watto, compose a contingency e-mail if it all goes wrong. I will review it.' Then to Mac, 'I didn't tell her because she will worry. I will tell her when I'm back. We will survive. I will get us out of this.'

Radio waves travel so much faster than sound waves that radio broadcasts can be heard over 10,000 kilometres away before they are heard in the back of a room! Radio waves are long—they vary from 1 metre to 100 metres in wavelength.

# Chapter 33

## Snowmobile dash to Seed Vault

16 March 2015
8.57 pm + 10 seconds

Perseids Meteor Storm in 10 minutes + 35 seconds

Whilst so far nothing visible was happening, there was a tangible sense of panic among the group. It was an eerie, calm panic. All remaining inhabitants of Svalbard, including the policeman and the NASA scientists, were herded by Captain

Michaels and the CIA, with Tom and Mad Dog bringing up the rear, to the safety of the Seed Vault.

Tyler, Emma and Jake had no idea how to even start a snowmobile, and the others were little better, handling them clumsily and warily. A CIA agent who hadn't spoken since they had been in Svalbard, Misha, had stepped forward and in broken Russian English said, 'It's just like driving a car without wheels. Come, I show you. Ok, steer like motorbike, very easy. Up hills you must lean forward to make go up hill. That's it. We go now. I know easier we drive, two on each.' He hopped on a bright blue one.

They all hopped on the snowmobiles lined up in front of the hotel. The engines roared to life. Tom and Mad Dog each grabbed a single, as they knew where they were going.

The biggest known number is Yotta, 'Y' that's $10^{24} =$ 1 000 000 000 000 000 000 000 000

The snowmobile convoy was barely at the end of the main street when the town was hit. Tom and Mad Dog were teleported instantly inside the Great Hall, which was shaking with the impact. The Qbits were visibly shocked.

'Storm's started early,' Alby confirmed.

'What the hell?' yelled Tom. 'Show me trajectories!'

'Mainly smaller random meteors initially, followed by a very high-intensity storm of large meteors in 11 minutes. Initially about 10 meteors per second but when the storm hits the estimated peak, there will be hundreds of larger meteors per second.' It was like a weather report from hell.

'Random impacts, bloody hell! So which direction is best to get out of town?' asked Mad Dog.

'Fast,' replied Newts.

'Fast, isn't a direction!' yelled Tom.

'Just go and we will watch for large incoming meteors and try to guide you,' was all Alby could offer. GG couldn't speak at all.

Back in the real world, several houses were already on fire, where small meteors had impacted wooden homes. There was a deadly fireball hailstorm taking place at one end of the street, so they all instinctively headed the other way.

Alby was now shouting to Tom to take the lead. Tom motioned the direction to the others but the CIA were faster and raced ahead. It was like a battle zone, and they were trained for this.

Tyler held on tight as Misha raced ahead, carving a trail in the snow, showing off. Emma, Jake and the others held on tight, terrified as much by the daredevil speed of the riders carving through the light snowstorm as by the meteors now lighting up the skies.

They all made it out of the small town as the show quickly intensified, with a hailstone-like meteor storm now peppering the snow as they raced toward the mountain vault. The riders weaved across the snow, following Misha.

The Chief of Police was very worried about living. Although he didn't exactly understand what was going on, he just couldn't see how they were supposed to gain entry to the secure vault. He had once visited it and whilst mostly the tour talked of the seeds and science, the vault was noted as being totally secure, like a bank vault. So, unless they had a bank robber with them, he didn't know how they would get in. In fact, when he thought about it, little of the past week made much sense to him. He hadn't even been aware that there was a large CIA base located near his town.

He now understood the earlier enormity of the panic—meteor storms, huge impacts. Initially he hadn't realised what the whole kerfuffle was about. The NASA scientists seemed to be very scared—and even the CIA guys seemed a bit twitchy. But perhaps they were always like that?

They were 5 minutes from downtown Svalbard when GG alerted Tom and Mad Dog that the real storm was about to start. As they headed calmly across the field, a stone of about a metre in diameter was due to impact in 3, 2, 1 ...

The first large meteorite hit the centre of town with the impact of a small earthquake. The sight of this first major impact completely destroyed the main tourist information building, leaving behind what appeared to be a huge crater. As Captain Michaels looked back, the destruction in their wake was the clearest communicator of what the scientists already knew; their chances of survival weren't very good. While snow-mobiles are safest when operated at about 40 kilometres per hour, suddenly the skilled CIA agents accelerated to speeds of almost double that, for, as they say, there was now a clear and present danger. The rest of the hapless riders set off after them, trying their darndest to keep up.

The sky was lit up with shooting stars, and would have been an impressive sight if they could stop to watch, but as they fled through the snow the scene was terrifying.

Suddenly, a meteor struck the snow some 30 metres away from the CIA agent's snowmobile, which was also carrying the Chief of Police. The impact hurled snow and debris metres into the air, leaving an impact crater the size of a bus.

A shard of rock exploded into the snow scooter, sending the Chief into the air. The scooter shot through the snow, instantly crushing the CIA agent. The Chief was thrown clear and plummeted onto the cushioning snow.

Without hesitation, Tom and Mad Dog turned back and Tom quickly hoisted the Chief onto his scooter. The CIA team also circled back, but when they arrived there was nothing they could do for their comrade. He had been crushed to death under the weight of the snowmobile, with snow already covering his body.

They all sped away, darting across the snow as fast as they could go.

Tom had advanced warning of major impacts from Watto, so Mad Dog followed him closely. Small pebble-like meteorites were stoning them with the stinging impact of large hailstones.

Soon, from some 500 metres away, they could see the blue lights of the vault. The remaining snowmobiles all arrived safely as a second large meteorite hit near the town's waterfront. Exciting and terrifying, it wasn't unlike an uncoordinated military attack, as each impact was some kilometres from the next. It was terrifying in its randomness.

The Qbits advised Tom and Mad Dog that more and bigger stones were on their way. They had only a few minutes to get to relative safety. The ground shook as more frequent meteorites pounded the planet. Alby confirmed the storm would peak in the next 15 minutes and last over an hour.

The satellite feed Tom was getting from Alby confirmed the storm was much worse than they had thought. It would be best to stay in the tunnel, as that was the strongest part of the structure, and the command centre about halfway down would be somewhat comfortable and had access to the exit.

After whizzing over the last few hundred metres of snow, they reached the vault entrance, and found themselves staring at the shiny and imposing door, which appeared very uninviting. The Perseids mission had quickly gone from one of scientific research to pure survival, and the trained CIA agents couldn't help but take control. Misha, in a stilted Russian accent, said, 'But we don't have the code to entry, the blast doors are sealed with a digital security code. No code, no entry. I have some C4—let's blow it.'

Tom stepped forward. 'Let me try—I have my iPhone 8 and headphones. I can get us in,' he stated with confidence.

'How are we going to get in? It's secure and the code changes daily. The encryption is the highest level available.' That was as much as the Chief of Police knew about the security of the vault.

'Ahh, it's just a big steel door. Don't panic ... now, where did I put the key?' No one was laughing, the tension was palpable.

Tom pulled out his iPhone and put in his headphones. He turned it on so it would be a convincing prop as he fake-hacked the door code. He pointed the phone toward the keypad as if it were reading the keypad, and moved it up and down.

'It's just a goddamn iPhone.' Tyler was getting very anxious, and Emma wanted to go back to town.

'A telephone and headphones?' The head CIA agent wasn't going to waste time with an iPhone. The door was secure; they needed an impact-entry device.

'Give me 10 seconds. Back home we call it hack and crack. I can get us in, it'll take me 30 seconds tops.'

Soon Misha insisted, 'It's secure—we blow it now. Unless you are truly the wizard from Oz. Stand back, we use C4 now.' The storm was clearly intensifying.

'Tom—you have 10 seconds and then we blow it.' Tyler was clearly getting caught up in the action movie situation.

Tyler now wondered if they should've stayed in the basement, as Jake had suggested. The worst part for Emma was that she knew all about the impact energy and the likely devastation, the fact they were standing outside like sitting ducks terrified her.

Also getting very nervous, Tom had no desire to pretend the hack and crack was going to take 10 more seconds, so he just commanded Alby to open it 'now'. Just as he waved his iPhone, the mechanism clicked. They were in. The CIA raised their eyebrows, impressed. They could use this guy. How did he do that?

The Perseids storm was now in full swing, hammering the ground like hot hailstones, burning into the white snow.

Inside the airlock it was freezing, even colder than outside.

Mac spoke. 'You can only survive in here for 12 hours at this temperature.'

'Great, so we have to die again. I was getting used to the prospect of being alive,' retorted Newts, serious as ever.

'You idiot, you're not "alive", you're a bunch of photons in a quantum state. Tom is the one made of carbon and water—he's the one who will freeze to death. In fact, if it were to get to about 100 °C, he would boil just like a kettle.' GG sipped from his glass of wine and laughed. 'The storm will end in just over an hour, so don't panic, Newts. You will be able to finish your novel.'

The Earth is not perfectly round—the North Pole's radius is 4 centimetres longer than the South Pole's.

# Chapter 34

## Seed Vault Entrance

16 March 2015
9.10 pm + 27 seconds

They raced inside the vault, they could feel the ground shaking like the tremors that occur before a major earthquake. Nevertheless, the vault felt secure, reinforced by the anecdotal knowledge of the Chief of Police and the logic of building a Seed Vault in this remote location, designed to withstand any man-made or natural disaster. This predicament, however, was extraterrestrial, and therefore did not quite fit the specs. And how

> There are millions of observable meteors every day, but most burn up on entering the atmosphere.

did anyone really know, anyway? How could you test such an assumption? No one had ever actually nuked the thing to make sure it worked properly. Logic and emotions were all mixed up for everyone; they may have just entered their burial tomb.

The command centre located halfway up the 120-metre tunnel was comfortable and had basic supplies like coffee and even some biscuits. The next emotion for the NASA team was disappointment—trapped inside with no view of the storm, drinking instant coffee and munching on cookies. The huge samples would be easy enough to locate, but they were now missing out on the visual spectacle they had been so eager to observe.

The Chief of Police was chirpy—all he cared about was that he now believed he would see his wife and kids again. 'Coffee anyone?'

Jake and Mad Dog nodded.

Seeing her disappointment, Tom went over to chat with Emma. 'It was the only safe option.'

Before she could respond, Tyler spoke. 'We all owe our lives to you and Scott. Tom, I will be recommending NASA recognise this at the highest level.'

Captain Michaels, who sat within earshot, agreed.

'It's our fault that you are risking your lives. I wish we had never discovered the storm.' Tom was resolute; this was his and the Qbits' fault. They had put lives at risk—including his best friend's.

Emma thought about this. 'Yes, Tom, it has turned out to be more dangerous than any of us expected. But we had been tracking the storm since you found it. Even we didn't foresee its severity—no one could have. And if we had not evacuated the town, over 2,000 people's lives would be at risk. They couldn't all have crammed in here. We are safe now and you have saved 2,000 lives.'

The CIA agents were nodding in violent agreement. They would have been amongst those unaware and exposed. The sequence of events had meant they now had a chance of survival.

GG was pacing up and down the Great Hall, shaking his head, trying to understand the miscalculation. How did they miss it? They had heard the conversation and knew they had possibly saved thousands of lives, but they had still risked the safety of the group. Alby hooked up to the satellite monitoring the storm and suggested Tom use the terminal in the office so all could see what was happening.

Tom turned on the screen and perceivably hacked into the Seed Vault system. Tyler couldn't believe these guys' skills; they knew how to find scientific events that NASA failed to find, they had opened the vault as if it were child's play, and now they were hacking into the Seed Vault system to get Internet access to watch the storm as if they were logging into a work computer in the public service. *If we get out of this I must hire both of them*, was all he could think.

Now that they had Internet access, they could log into NASA. Tom handed control over to Emma, who punched in her ID and password. Once inside NASA's server, they located the satellite feed they had been using. Emma turned and looked at Tyler in horror as the message came up: 'Due to a catastrophic hardware failure, NASA Satellite B is temporarily offline.'

Things just weren't going well. Suddenly the screen came up with another prompt: 'Our technical staff are working to correct the problem, we apologise for any inconvenience.' The storm had taken out the satellite. She hit the keyboard with both hands in frustration.

Jake was partly relieved they could no longer see the incoming storm; he just wanted the whole ordeal to be over and done with.

Tom and Mad Dog teleported to Qbits.

GG had seen the message too. 'Bloody inconvenient—we have lightning, thunder and meteorites bombarding the planet. It's more than an inconvenience—it's unacceptable!'

Alby spoke to Newts. 'Let's try that nearby Russian satellite we used the other day.'

Alby and Newts linked to the satellite and established a visual feed of the storm, but Tom decided that for security reasons they couldn't share the visual with the others, as they might start to think they were spies.

Alby spoke. 'That Delta Force I mentioned has landed.'

'What?' asked Mad Dog.

'Delta Force. I mentioned an e-mail I intercepted to Tom.'

'Yes, Alby, and we checked—they are the good guys.'

All of a sudden, Alby stood up, his face a picture of urgency he had never heretofore shown. His mind was racing faster than his mouth could utter, '*Herr freund wir sind.*'

Mad Dog tilted his head but Tom waited, listening as though he understood. 'English, Alby.'

'It just got a whole lot worse,' Alby stated slowly.

'But we are ok in here. The vault can withstand a nuclear blast and the largest impact is projected to be 2.5 metres, about the same as a small nuclear explosion. To penetrate this depth would require at least 5 metres,' confirmed Newts. GG nodded and stood next to him in agreement, but due to his very high error rate for the day, he didn't dare speak.

'*Nein, nein—es ist der ...*'

Mad Dog didn't know what was going on. Tom could understand but Mad Dog couldn't. Then an English word he certainly understood came out. 'Terrorist.'

He continued in English. 'Delta Force isn't Delta Force. It's their code name. They have just landed on the island in a boat dodging meteors, and are about to head to the vault. They heard the island was evacuated and intend to rob the vault.'

'What the hell?' asked Tom, looking at the team in the Great Hall all sitting at the table. A tense silence ensued.

'How do you know?' asked Tom again.

'What would they want with a bunch of old frozen seeds?' asked GG, brow furrowed.

They all sat down and looked at the Great Tapestry. 'Let's hear what you know, Alby.' Tom wasn't in the mood for any more anything.

'The short-wave radio message was intercepted by Watto 20 minutes ago from a boat in the channel. Play it back.'

The words 'Delta Force', 'landed' and 'vault' were clear. And it was evident with the short message, 'Mission is a go—get in, get packages and get out', that the objective seemed to be to rob the vault.

'Ok, let's review the port security camera system—there is one on the docks—and see what we have,' Tom instructed Watto.

They watched as four heavily armed men in military gear exited the boat, silhouettes dark in the dim wharf lights.

'Oh hell,' said Mad Dog. 'Not good.'

'We need help. We need to tell the CIA. But I can't just say, "hey, by the way, terrorists are on their way",' said Tom fearfully.

'They won't know how severe the storm is—they might not even make it here. The chance of them making it here alive is at best 50/50. I can e-mail the President, or the CIA Chief?' Alby was unusually unsure of what to do. Everyone was confused.

'Ok, everyone remain calm. What do we have?' Tom asked.

Mac took the floor and stated the facts. 'I now estimate the storm will last just over an hour. The heavily armed Delta Force are 30 minutes away. Eight civilians are in this sealed vault, five highly trained CIA agents, and a policeman. Numbers are on our side. They don't know we are here. The element of surprise is ours.'

'Secure the vault,' was Alby's first instinct.

'Call for help—ignore the possibility for now that the storm might kill them all,' advised Mac.

Tom spoke. 'First, lock the vault door. Second, send the recording to the CIA. Slow them down getting here. And hope the storm blasts them into orbit on their way here.'

Alby said, 'And that's the plan—the whole plan?'

Mad Dog asked, 'What are you going to tell everyone? Hi, guys, we just need to lock ourselves in this icy tomb for a while ...'

Mac wondered, 'How can we slow them down?'

Newts went over to the Great Tapestry and called up the schematic of the vault. Instantly, he moved through the plan and into the system. He punched in the code and the door started closing.

'Tell them it's time locked and can't be left open for more than a few minutes. If they suggest opening it, then tell them it's safer to do so when the storm passes.' Newts was clear; it made some sense in a nonsensical situation.

Inside the vault, when they heard the creaking of the steel doors closing from inside the office, the CIA and NASA teams dashed out of the room. Once they realised what was going on, they quickly ran back in to Tom and Scott, who had remained behind.

'Can you open the door?' asked the commanding CIA officer, his eyes wild.

'Yes easily, from the control system. But it may be best to wait until the storm ends,' responded Tom, gulping nonchalantly.

All in the Great Hall heaved a sigh of relief.

'Ok, now we are safe—they can't get in, and we can get out later,' said Mac.

As Mac spoke, Newts looked concerned, his lush mane hanging limp and worried alongside his furrowed face.

Alby was focused but frantic, searching through all the events occurring worldwide in the last 24 hours, for any clue as to what was going on. He drew a sharp intake of breath when he found that in Oslo the day before there had been a terrible accident. The head science officer of the Svalbard Seed Vault had been involved in a hit-and-run; no witnesses. He had written the algorithm for the security code.

As Tom and Scott listened to this latest information, they were no longer concerned with the door or even the deadly meteorite storm raging outside, they were clearly now terrified of being murdered by terrorists.

Overriding his panic, Tom was exacting. 'Find out who these guys are and what they want with the seeds.'

The Qbits immediately scattered to various parts of the room, trying to solve the new mystery.

'And we need someone to e-mail the head of the CIA to tell him about the terrorists. I suggest GG, as he has the biggest reputation.'

'Done.' GG was a man of action.

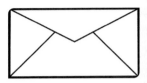

From: GG@Qbits.me
To: O'Brien@CIA.com
Sent: 16 March 2015 3.15 pm
Subject: Terrorism at Svalbard Global Seed Vault

Dear George,

The Perseids meteorite storm intensity is beyond everyone's calculations. I'm sure NASA now knows this. Your team and the scientists have taken refuge in the Svalbard Seed Vault.
As you know, the town has been evacuated except for your CIA staff and the remaining civilians, including top NASA scientists, and the Chief of Police.

We have detected a terrorist act at the evacuated Norway Svalbard Seed Vault, or as you call it, the Doomsday Vault. Here is the sound tape from 'Delta Force' we just found. I don't think they are your QRF.

They do not realise there are people hiding in the vault, nor are they aware of the severity of the meteor storm, which will finish in an hour.

They will arrive at the vault and attempt to break-in in 15 minutes.

You need to warn your agents in the vault NOW.
Please do not waste any time.

Regards
GG

Within a few minutes of O'Brien obtaining the President's permission to do *whatever* was required on foreign soil, Captain Michaels' secure handheld began to crackle with orders directly from Langley of the new mission. The meteor survival mission was now a counterterrorist mission.

Perfect, thought Tom. Now the CIA professionals will take charge in the real world and cut us a break!

Captain Michaels slid his comms unit back into its little holster and gathered himself up, chest puffed out with authority. 'Ladies and gentlemen, we need to get more secure. This area has been compromised by terrorists,' he announced bluntly.

The occupants of the office all looked at one another as if to ascertain which ones were the terrorists, but at this stage none of them really cared about the answer. Let Michaels shoot them; that was what he was paid for. They all just wanted to survive this hellish evening.

Tyler was incredulous. 'What? There is no one in Svalbard but us. And in here we are secure and safe—cold but safe.' They all looked at each other again.

Captain Michaels motioned for the other agents to stand up, indicating that his team was now in charge. This was now a matter of national security. 'An unidentified terrorist group has just landed on the island. We move into the main vault. Take some supplies. We have to move ... now! We have four bioterrorists heading here.'

Oddly, there was general relief to know the terrorist wasn't someone in the room.

Emma spoke. 'They can't get in here, can they?'

The big Russian spoke in stilted English, nodding toward Tom. 'He did.'

'Move, move, move!' Michaels commanded. This wasn't going

to become a scientific debate if he had anything to do with it. Let them come in, and he would blast them back out.

The now terrified civilians grabbed armfuls of supplies and headed in through the airlock vault. Once safely locked behind that, they settled in, arranging some of the boxes of seeds into seats and a table.

Jake had brought the kettle and some cups. 'Coffee or tea?' he nervously asked. He sounded like an optimistic flight attendant on a plane that has gone into free-fall. There was a chuckle in Qbits, as quite possibly the largest meteorite strikes ever witnessed on Earth failed to interrupt their tea break. Public servants.

Mad Dog opted for tea, not being able to stomach any more inferior instant coffee. His mind drifted at that moment, would he ever be sitting back on the wall at Harry's observing the world.

Michaels stationed three men at the entrance and he and one other stayed in the vault with the civilians, who were quiet but nervous.

Inside the Great Hall the debate raged. How do we slow them down? They had the element of surprise, but was there anything they could do from Qbits? Arguments and ideas were flung around the room like electrons whizzing around atoms.

Firstly, as the terrorists left the wharf, the Qbits turned on all the town's street lights, hoping to slow them down and make them a bit less certain that the town was deserted. It also had the effect of blinding them with their night-vision goggles on. Meteors were now mercilessly pounding the whole area.

Then Alby suggested setting off alarms as the terrorists passed the bank and shops as they made their way toward the vault. Alby felt sure this would throw them off.

As an alarm whooped into the still night, the Qbits all

watched proudly. But they barely even paused; they just kept on creeping through the town, their weapons drawn, eyes scanning the landscape. This was what they were trained for.

As they crossed the main street, they ducked behind the general store on the other side and in a team worked their way forward in a fluid motion, watched by the Qbits on the town's security camera. They operated a grenade launcher and in a few seconds the entire bank building exploded in flames. The other end of town had been hit by a large meteor and the fire completed the scene; it was a battlefield.

'Oh geez,' Mad Dog said in awe. Clearly they were heavily armed and willing to make a mess.

Then the terrorists uncovered a stash of snowmobiles stowed behind the hotel, and rode at full speed over the hills and out of sight, dodging minor meteors as they went. The storm was intensifying and how the terrorists managed to avoid being obliterated, or at least knocked from their transport, defied all good logic. Their battlefield experience made it seem like they had actually trained for this once in a lifetime event.

All GG could think was, *where is a big meteor when you need it?*

Then Alby said what everyone was thinking, 'What do they want? Seeds are just not that valuable—unless this is just a terrorist destruction attack funded by foreign military.'

Just as the words fell from his lips, Watto intercepted a message from the CIA to Captain Michaels: 'Polar bear. Secure the Seed Vault packages. All civilian casualties acceptable.'

The Qbits froze in shock. Civilian casualties? Acceptable? What in the hell was going on here?

A deathly silence fell over the Great Hall.

# Chapter 35

## Delta Force on Snowmobiles

16 March 2015

9.30 pm + 3 seconds

The race was on. As Delta Force dashed to the vault, the CIA agents within attempted to fortify and secure the entrance to stop them. They had little choice; it was too risky to go outside in the meteor storm, and weapons were useless against huge balls of rock hurtling toward the ground at 25,000 kilometres per hour.

Empedocles c 460 BC: proposed everything is made from 4 elements—earth, water, fire and air.

They were relatively safe locked in the vault, but they were still vulnerable. Other than racks of crates, there was no shelter within the Seed Vault itself. Thank

God they still had the key element of surprise, which was their major tactical advantage. If the terrorists got through the door, they would be waiting and ready.

Tom didn't want to be a leader, and certainly not a hero; he just wanted to discover things and have fun. He didn't want to be the Indiana Jones of science, he was happy tinkering with his revolutionary storage device. Now, he was trapped by the once-in-a-century Perseids meteor shower and locked in a freezer in the Arctic aptly nicknamed the Doomsday Vault, with everyone looking at each other with fear in their eyes.

Emma spoke. 'It's ok, Tom, we will be safe in here. The door is locked and the storm was only forecast to last about an hour.'

'I guess,' he began. But what could any of them do to help? They had no weapons, not that that would have mattered, because none of them would know what to do with them even if they did have weapons. And Qbits could not help in the physical world. They could only guide and inform.

Newts was monitoring the terrorists' radio; they were on their way. Unless there was a direct or large meteor impact, the last line of defence was the CIA agents in the tunnel.

Alby had established that the leader of the attacking group was Jim Doolan, actually a decorated CIA Delta Force commander who was noted on file as missing in action, presumed dead. What the hell were they breaking into the vault for? Were they in fact good guys coming to rescue them?

As agreed, Alby sent the text message to the attackers' communications devices. 'Gentlemen, your mission has been compromised; a crack CIA contingent based on Spitsbergen is on its way and will be at the vault in 5 minutes.'

As soon as he received the message, Doolan raised his hand to stop the zooming snowmobiles, as meteors blazed through the sky. Trained soldiers, they stopped immediately for their leader. He ripped off his hood and signalled to everyone to take off their communications headsets. The storm was pounding all around them. War zones were their playground, and explosions went with the territory, no matter what caused them.

As soon as they had discarded their devices, the commander issued new orders. 'We are now on full combat alert. Nikolai take the rear, Johnno take point, everyone on guard. Hand signals only—comms have been compromised.'

The Qbits had no idea their electronic scare tactic had done nothing other than alert the senses of a highly trained group determined to complete their mission.

Then a further message came in. 'Jim, they know where your family lives and a squad of CIA are on their way to Glasgow, Scotland, to pick them up. Your military record was a credit— why are you with these guys?'

It was too late to stop now. Jim looked at his team of hired guns and mercenaries and thought for a moment. It came with the territory. The assignment had come from intelligence in the UK; it was clear it was the highest level of covert ops and normal support could not be assured. He figured MI6 would sort it out. CIA, though—what was his old employer doing here?

Back in the vault, the civilians huddled quietly, feeling vague tremors as meteors hit the ground around the shelter. In the Great Hall, the Qbits were doing a similar thing. The suspense was palpable.

Alby spoke. 'Wait, maybe, just maybe, there is something we are missing, like why does the CIA have a minibase and so many serious operatives in an Arctic research town of 2,000 people? Sure, the vault is strategic in case of nuclear attack or a natural disaster, but a permanent 15-man team? That's a serious deployment. Listening to the Russians? I don't think so—satellites do that these days.' He scratched his unkempt head of hair.

'Good question, Alby. Let's search the CIA database and flag anything to do with the Seed Vault,' suggested Mac.

Mac and Newts began quickly rifling through files, which looked like reams of folders flying around the Great Hall. Soon Mac screamed, 'Got it! Doomsday Vault! CIA investment contribution. Seems America contributed $500 million to its construction.'

'Say that again? The whole project only cost $10 million.'

Tom held up his hand to stop all other discussion and searching.

They all looked at each other for a second and then continued to blast their way through the files, throwing them in the air over their shoulders like kids looking for their favourite t-shirt in a clothes drawer.

'What's this DV request for a $500 million cash transfer, signed personally by the previous President? Doesn't say anything, but it's filed in the same area. A deleted e-mail ...'

'So, these guys are after something—but what?'

'We are just guessing—there are no records, no files, and we have searched everywhere!'

'Almost everywhere—check the President's personal files.'

GG and Mac were hunting through all records and communications relating to the vault, looking for a clue, the smallest inconsistency. Was it just a destruction mission? In that case, Tom and Scott were doomed. Or was there a piece of the jigsaw missing? They had been looking for hours, but nothing was coming up.

The diameter of a typical atom is $1 \times 10^{-10}$ metres or 0.0000000001 metres.

Meanwhile, when Delta Force arrived at the entrance to the vault, the abandoned snowmobiles confirmed their suspicions that they had company. And when they tried the code, the door wouldn't open. They tried again. The lock controls had been overridden.

The commander put on his headset and called base, breaking radio silence. 'The mission has been compromised, the code is a no go, and we have ears on us. Armed CIA contingent en route to cave.'

Qbits froze and listened.

The message from base was clear. 'Priority 1 mission, must be completed. Use all force necessary. Get the package and rendezvous at drop point.'

The attackers all peered skyward as the meteors continued to rain down, now peaking at thousands per minute of all sizes. The noise was deafening, but to the trained combatants, already half deaf from military service, this was just business as usual.

'Bloody hell, let's blow this thing and get in and out.' The mission leader looked at his mercenaries; they knew death was an accepted risk.

The Frenchman got out the C4 explosive brick from his backpack and primed it for detonation in 10 seconds. 'Take cover!'

All the Qbits were watching on the security camera, until, as they ran for cover, one of the Delta Force members instinctively turned and shot out the lens.

Now blind and able only to listen, Qbits continued brainstorming.

'Think, guys! What would terrorists want with a vault full of seeds? Do you think they are going to sell 1,000 different strains of wheat on the black market? Are there bioterrorist materials stored here or some bacteria or virus stored in some of the seeds? That would be valuable on the black market ...'

Still rifling through the electronic files, Newts addressed them. 'This does look odd. Around the time the Doomsday Vault was opened, the Americans set up their research base.

The Norwegian Government opened the vault to allow them to check their inventory was properly secure. It notes they had advised the Norwegian Government the US base was manned by a small contingent of scientists with limited security located on the outskirts of Svalbard.'

'Limited security? Fifteen highly trained CIA field agents and only a few scientific staff?' spluttered Mac, reading the latest CIA internal files.

'Why would the CIA want to check a bunch of seeds in a big fridge?' asked GG.

They all looked up. 'Watto, switch to CIA central database.'

'Guys, we have a more critical issue, like the fact that some highly trained madmen are attempting to open the doors to find three CIA agents holding weapons. And if they get past them, they will find us hiding behind a bunch of boxes,' urged Tom with panic in his voice.

'I'm with him, we need ideas,' Mad Dog added. 'Forget the why, let's work out the how—how to survive.'

'I don't believe they are here to hurt you,' stated Alby calmly. 'Don't panic.'

'Don't panic? *Believe*? I really don't give a toss what you believe! You're not sitting in a dead-end vault with four highly trained murderers about to find you! And you're already dead. Or don't even exist. Arrrrgh!' Tom really was panicking.

The Earth's magnetic poles reverse about every 400,000 years. We are overdue for a reversal now!

# Chapter 36

## Entrance Tunnel

16 March 2015

9.45 pm + 43 seconds

The civilians huddled at the back of the room, whilst Captain Michaels and Misha hid behind seed racks on either side of the sealed airlock. Again, if the first line of defence failed, they had the advantage, as they would be waiting if and when the terrorists got through.

Nothing could be heard from inside the sealed airlock. Outside, the door was blasted open and, as the terrorists entered, their senses were on high alert after receiving Alby's e-mail and seeing the

The human heart beats about 100,000 times a day. The average human blinks 25 times per minute—4 million times a year. Each second 10,000,000 cells die and are replaced in your body.

snowmobiles. Someone knew they were on the island. Communications were being intercepted. Anything could happen on a compromised mission.

The vault had been designed to withstand a nuclear blast and the doors would withstand nearby explosions. The design flaw communicated to the ex-head of Delta Force was that the security mechanism, once destroyed, left the doors unlocked. No blast could destroy or open the doors themselves, but by destroying just the security entry system, the doors would be unlocked and could be manually opened. They had to have this fail safe because, in the event of nuclear disaster, access would be required by survivors, who wouldn't necessarily have the code. It had to be secure but practical.

The four had fanned out as the door opened, preparing to enter. Half an hour earlier, before receiving the e-mail, they had been quite relaxed; the mission was a highly paid walk in the park—no one around, crack the vault, and walk in. None of them even knew what they were there to collect. The ex-Delta Force leader knew the locations and electronic identification of the packages, as he had deposited them. At the end they would all be $500,000 richer, all for a couple of days work. That was enough for the mercenaries. They knew all they needed to know. Now, after receiving a short text message it had turned into a proper mission. But that was the nature of the business—expect the unexpected.

They had a schematic of the vault on their PDAs. With infrared glasses on, they would hit the lights with the first shots. They moved into position.

On the inside of the vault, the three CIA agents had their weapons ready, adrenalin flowing, nervous but confident. No one would expect them to be inside the sealed vault. The cold air assisted their heightened alertness. As the door smoothly opened, they had the 'weapon of surprise', which won most battles. They also had the disadvantage of having no cover in the tunnel, which was a straight 120 metres down to the vault. They were totally exposed.

The door opened, guns were aimed and ready. With a volley of shots, the lights in the tunnel went dead. The tunnel was now pitch black. The CIA agents had state-of-the-art weapons but without their night-vision goggles it was never going to be a fair battle. Delta Force deftly despatched the agents and coldly stepped over their remains as they proceeded toward the main storage vault.

With a swooshing noise, the airlocked doors slid open. Inside the vault, all Captain Michaels could see was darkness. He could hear Delta Force lurking just outside the doorway, but he didn't know how many were there, what kind of weapons they had, or whether they were about to execute him too. A stand-off.

Then a voice spoke loudly. 'We have night vision and we can do this either way. Drop your weapons and we will not use ours. Come out into the open. Failure to comply will result in a bad outcome.'

Michaels was faced with a decision. If they killed him, it was the end of the battle. No matter how lucky they got, all the scientists would be executed. His orders were clear; civilian casualties acceptable. But if he fought now, no one would survive—not even him.

'You have 10 seconds—10, 9, 8, 7, 6, 5, 4 ...'

'Wait.' Michaels had no choice but to surrender.

'In the open—now. Where we can see you! Drop your weapons in the open.'

He had no choice. Obviously his comrades were dead. Night vision. Outnumbered. This whole mission was not meant to be a mission. Meteor storm, Doomsday Vault, terrorists. Michaels and Misha stepped out from behind the racks.

'How many others?'

'Nine unarmed civilians, hiding from the meteor storm, in the back.'

The lights were flicked on immediately.

The mercenaries were trigger happy. 'Let's finish off the job,' said one.

'We take what we came for and leave!' Doolan yelled.

'Tyler, bring out the civilians,' ordered Michaels coldly.

'Delta Force, stand down,' grunted Doolan, wiping his forehead with the icy sleeve of his jacket. He looked at the group of scientists and hotel staff. 'Why are you all here?'

Guns were pointed directly at them.

'Yikes,' went GG.

'Oh my God,' panicked Mac. Newts and Alby sat down.

Tom and Mad Dog were with them. 'Answer them, Tom. Someone has to, or they will panic.'

They were all too terrified to speak, so Tom nervously began. 'We are scientists studying the Perseids meteor storm.'

Doolan interrupted. 'Inside a Seed Vault with armed guards? Why are you really here? Answer me or I let Delta 2 here find out the truth.'

The man behind him gave a sly smile, with his gun clearly pointed at Tom and Mad Dog, as the other two fell in behind them.

'No one move or reach for anything,' said the guy Doolan had called Delta 2.

'State your mission,' Doolan asked again. 'Who do you work for?'

Tom answered carefully. 'NASA, and we were sent here to collect meteor samples to work on the age and composition of the Earth. We have ID. The security was part of NASA's requirements. We are all hiding from the meteor storm, as it is much worse than forecast.'

Delta 2 spoke. 'What the hell is the CIA doing here? I don't like this, let's deal with these guys and get the packages and get out of here.'

'We seize the packages. Delta 2, come with me. Deltas 3, 4, you guard the hostages.'

The total number of bacteria is estimated to be 5 million trillion trillion, or $5 \times 10^{30}$.

Doolan collected everyone's ID cards, before herding them toward the waiting Delta 2.

'We might need a hostage in case more agents turn up. Take him and secure the rest,' Doolan said, pointing at Tom.

Delta 2 grabbed Tom roughly around the back of his neck, digging the muzzle of a gun into his back, while the others were herded to the office and tied to the chairs with plastic tape.

Now the Qbits really panicked. Tom as a hostage? But what if those Neanderthals harmed him?

Tom was petrified.

Inside the Great Hall, the search continued. If they could establish why the terrorists were there, then it just might help them survive. Newts and Alby were rifling through all the President's deleted e-mails at light speed—reading some 10,000 e-mails a second on his computer, looking for anything even vaguely relating to the Doomsday Vault.

There was one e-mail sent around the same date as the cash withdrawal, from the President to the CIA Chief arranging to meet in Belgium, but it had nothing to do with the vault.

'It's a dead end,' said Alby, as he slumped in his chair with hopelessness.

'Belgium?' repeated Mac purposefully. Everyone just stared at her. 'Well, Antwerp is in Belgium and is the world's largest diamond centre, with thousands of diamond companies based there.'

Pennies began dropping like meteors.

Tom assembled the facts: 'The President, $500 million in cash, CIA, Antwerp, Seed Vault, packages ...'

Newts had now found an obscure file called Polar Bear Study Project. 'The project was personally sanctioned by the President. The expenditure approved was $500 million at his discretion.'

They all sat around the Great Table, pondering all this new information and its implications.

'They may have stored diamonds in seed packs!' cried Tom.

'It's a robbery,' said Mad Dog. 'These aren't terrorists, they are thieves.'

'$500 million worth! That's about 5 kilograms or 10,000 carats of high quality diamonds,' stated Mac.

'But why diamonds? Search the CIA again for any e-mails preceding that date. All deleted e-mails and files included.' Alby wanted to know why.

'Who cares why they are here?' asked Mac.

'Understand the motivation, understand the goal.' They were hired guns.

'Terrorists, thieves or maybe a secondary government organisation. Might be an inside job, no one seems to know about the hidden diamonds. Even took us minutes to work it out, with access to everything.'

Mac added, 'Tom, you must not let the others know. We will get out of this, but all of us need to work together. It's best the others think a rescue is imminent.'

'Watto, tell us about diamonds now—all background.'

# Great Tapestry

**Diamonds**

Value: $1 million     $100,000     $10,000

Diamonds are just carbon but are the hardest substance on Earth.

1 kilogram has an estimated street value of $100 million.

Diamonds are 100 times more valuable than gold.

Diamonds are commonly judged by the 'four Cs': carat, clarity, colour, and cut.

If a diamond is 'cooked' in an oven at 763 °C, it will simply vanish.

A diamond is 58 times harder than the next hardest mineral on Earth.

About half of all the worlds' diamonds come from Africa.

Belgium is the international diamond trading capital of the world.

The only way to cut diamonds is with other diamonds.

Back in the vault, all Jim Doolan could think about was revenge. He had accepted the MI6 mission willingly. He was one of the best and his former employer, the CIA, had attempted to terminate him twice in the last 6 months. They had forced him into hiding, to change teams.

The first suicide mission the CIA had sent him on, he had suspected from the start it was going to be a bad gig, but the second assignment alerted him that something just wasn't right. They were trying to retire him. And now the CIA would pay for trying to terminate the services of one of their best European undercover agents. They knew he knew about the diamonds. He was one of the agents that had coordinated the package transport from Antwerp to Svalbard and the same O'Brien was now in charge of the entire agency. Another country would now get the secret diamonds. Revenge.

He had known from the pickup and drop off what they were doing. He was one of only three people who knew about the seeds' real purpose and value. The other agents had mysteriously died on missions the next year. He had pieced together O'Brien's plan—no loose ends.

Doolan's search didn't take long. They fanned out in the US section of the vault, focusing on the wheat seed section. They scanned the barcoded seed packets for confirmation—they were listed in the inventory as apricot kernels, and they were exactly where he had left them. He opened one and checked the contents, grabbing several fistfuls and putting them into small dark pouches and into his khaki pockets for his and his team's own insurance and 'bonuses'. He nodded to the other two, who spontaneously high-fived. Even Doolan was pleased at the outcome. It was confirmed; these were the packages.

'Delta Force, grab all the packages and move out.' Then Doolan spoke to Tom. 'Listen this isn't like the movies. Do what we say, you live. Otherwise, you die.' He was direct. 'Now, come with us.'

The Delta Force members shoved what looked like ordinary A4 envelopes into their military backpacks. The US Government Doomsday insurance policy had just been cashed out.

It is estimated there is 0.01% chance of finding intelligent life in the Universe.

# Chapter 37

## Entrance Tunnel

### 16 March 2015
### 10.15 pm + 18 seconds

Emerging from the Seed Vault, they ushered Tom ahead of them at gunpoint. As they passed the command centre, the Delta Force commando guarding the tied-up members of the group emerged, locking the door behind him.

Thales of Miletus 624 BC-547 BC: mysteries of the Universe are mysteries because they are unknown, but not because they are unknowable!

The Delta Force commander knew it wouldn't take the CIA agents more than a few minutes to unbind themselves and free the others. It didn't matter, as they wouldn't pursue them without weapons, and any help was hours away at the earliest. They would soon be clear; mission successful.

Rich and avenged. Doolan felt some disappointment at having killed innocent agents, but it had been necessary to complete the mission.

As they moved down the tunnel toward the entrance, they felt a severe tremor. A large meteor had hit close by, causing the vault to shake violently.

'What the bloody hell was that?' asked Doolan, looking at Tom.

Tom spoke up. 'The meteor storm—it is forecast to end in about 15 minutes. Might be worse impacts to come, but it's safe in here. The vault is designed to withstand all impacts.' He now needed to help the terrorists stay alive and needed them to recognise the risk, as he wanted to survive.

They couldn't wait. There were risks in everything. 'We keep going,' said Doolan.

Inside the Great Hall, they were busy identifying the Delta diamond thieves.

'The guy at the back was thrown out of the military for excessive force with prisoners,' informed Newts.

'Forget all that—how do we get out of here?' cried Tom. He was terrified and not interested in details.

Mac tried to calm him. 'We need to know what we are up against.'

'Due to our ability to speed up your biomechanics and our jujitsu training, we now have your reflexes operating at about twice the normal speed. We can't dodge bullets, but pretty close to it. We can basically flinch to avoid major damage and do it fast enough to be pretty sure that any damage is survivable,' said Alby.

'*Perhaps*, but ...' piped up the ever-accurate Newts. Mac frowned at Newts to shut him up.

Alby continued. 'Focus on the guy to your left. His service

record and profile suggest he is the most likely to want to hurt you. Calls himself just Black Angel, Angel for short. Real name John Black. He is psychotic, thrown out for stabbing his commander on a mission. He keeps score and claims to have executed 250 bad guys on missions. How do these guys turn out like this?'

'Tom—focus. Know your enemy, the *Art of War* by Sun Tzu,' added GG.

Alby spoke then. 'All are highly trained ex-military special operations. Three commandos and a Frenchman we haven't yet identified. The Delta Doolan—the commander—has an exemplary military record and went covert CIA many years ago. He is believed dead after he was sent on what you might call a suicide mission and hasn't been seen since. Unusual for a guy like this to go renegade. I think he also led the team that placed the diamonds here. The thing is, all the members of the team on project Save Polar Bear seem to have been killed in action in the last year.'

Tom felt a gun jab him in the guts. Sure enough, it came from his left. He doubled over. The commander gave a stare that even Black Angel hesitated at. He looked away; it was just a bit of fun.

Using small torches, they marched toward the entrance in the pitch darkness, past the dead CIA agents lying in pools of now frozen blood. Black Angel kicked the two on the right as he passed them, as if to check they were dead.

The commander moved to the point, leading them to the entrance with their guns raised. The entrance was the most vulnerable part of the vault; a tunnel with nowhere to hide. They knew from experience that the sooner they were out in the open, the safer they were. Then to the boat. They increased speed along the tunnel, jogging to cover the last 50 metres to the entrance.

GG was screaming now. 'Tom, there is a meteor about to hit! It's 2.5 metres and by my calculation will land only 100 metres away. Do not leave the vault. It's big. Tell them. *Now*.'

Tom didn't feel great about warning these buffoons of the danger, but he had no choice. He needed them to survive so he would have a chance.

As he spoke, they all turned their guns on him, as though he was threatening them—even the commander. It was their training. He was terrified.

'There is a major meteor about to hit. Bigger than the last. Huge blast. We need to stay in here. Don't open the door.'

The Delta Force commander looked at him suspiciously. Was it a trick? How would he know? Decisions. Leadership. NASA scientist, non-military, and the last blast had shaken the whole structure. All the facts lined up. 'We wait. If it's a trap, Black Angel, he is yours.'

The Frenchman didn't like it. 'Non, we are in ze tunnel.' He pointed at the bodies a few metres behind them. 'Too exposed.'

'How long do we wait?' the commander asked Tom.

'Impact in less than a minute,' stated Tom. He couldn't be too precise or they would wonder how he knew. 'The storm is to end in 10 minutes, and the largest meteorites are predicted to be over in the next 5 minutes.'

Now everyone was not so much scared as on guard. Was it a trap? The mission had been compromised and the CIA was waiting. What if the agents broke out of the office whilst they were sitting ducks in the tunnel? No one spoke.

Earth turns faster at the equator and slower near the poles.

After 45 seconds, Black Angel and the Frenchman wanted to move and looked restlessly at the commander. The commander looked at Tom, who shook his head softly, as if to say, 'Please wait.'

# Chapter 38

## Seed Vault Command Centre

### 16 March 2015
### 10.17 pm + 50 seconds

Inside the vault office, everything shook violently, like they were being hit by a major earthquake. Items flew off shelves, their chairs rattled and jerked around, and their hearts nearly leapt out of their chests. The lights also went out. The vault's power supply had been disrupted. They waited for the emergency generator. Nothing happened. No lights. There was pitch blackness inside the Doomsday Vault.

Quantum physics assumes the world is inherently probabilistic and that some events happen without a cause.

'Must've been a direct meteor hit,' said Emma once the ground had stopped shaking.

Captain Michaels was busy breaking the leg on his chair, and trying to wriggle his hand free.

'Perfect!' he whispered, as he pulled his arm free from the plastic tape.

The others could hear noise and assurances from Michaels but could see nothing. They were terrified. What if Delta Force came back?

Now completely free of his bonds, Michaels rummaged around for the emergency pack mounted on the wall, and found the torch. He dashed to release his colleague first, and then they quickly untied Emma, Tyler and Scott, and the Chief of Police, who released the others.

Soon they had found enough torches for everyone and some emergency blankets, but still no emergency power. It was getting cold very quickly inside the office.

Jake spoke first. 'We can't stay here.' It seemed like a statement of the obvious but at least it had now been said aloud.

It was easy to escape from the office into the tunnel, as the door was secure but not blast proof. A disabled electronic lock and a strong shoulder was all it took.

With the door open, they all headed inexplicably in the direction of the explosion. The site was horrendous. A heavy white wall of snow now lay between them and freedom. The snow had been blasted back into the tunnel several metres; they would never dig themselves out. There was no sign of Michaels' men killed in action. They must have been buried somewhere under the snow.

Looking at the mound of snow, it dawned on Mad Dog and the others that the doors had not withstood the impact of the direct meteor strike, which had hit almost immediately after they had been left in the office. Everyone knew the sequence of events. Tom, his best mate, closer than his own brother, was dead, buried in an icy tomb. And they were trapped with no way out. There was air, but for how long no one knew. He hung his head, so as to be out of sight of the others, and wiped a tear from his eye. His mate had given his life for him, but it had been for nothing.

Mad Dog felt very alone. It was cold and dark and the Qbits weren't answering Mad Dog's thoughts. No Tom, no Qbits; they had quickly become part of his life. But this was all their fault. *Damn the Qbits! Where were the Qbits?* Right now he was experiencing a cocktail of mixed feelings. He wished he had never heard of the Qbits. They had killed his mate, and now he was going to die as well.

Emma put her arm around him for comfort; no one spoke.

'Tom is the bravest man I've ever met. I'm so sorry. He ...'

Mad Dog just nodded in agreement. 'He was like my brother, we did everything together, maybe he got out ...'

The other two bowed their heads with respect. They were alive purely due to Tom's bravery.

Michaels gulped as he gathered his thoughts. 'We have air. Find the emergency generator—there must be one. Get it working. Our exact location is known by HQ. There must be an emergency beacon system. Find it. There is basic food and plenty of water.'

The checklist and instructions seemed to give everyone hope. Buried alive but maybe it was survivable. It now seemed their security escorts were the right guys to have around. They scattered to search the vault, storage area and the command centre.

Emma just couldn't believe how cold it was becoming suddenly. The vault was designed to be a fridge but the office area had been 20 °C before the power went off. They were back in there now and it felt just as cold as the tunnel.

They sat there, four helpless scientists, helpless but intelligent, entombed with two highly trained agents, a small town Chief of Police and the hotel staff. All communications were down, they had some food and water but they couldn't live too long in a sealed fridge. One by one, over the next 24 hours, hypothermia would set in. They had to keep moving; if they fell asleep they may not wake up. Without power to the tunnel and office, there was no heating and the vault was designed to maintain minus 18 °C.

Captain Michaels spoke with authority, but what he said made them laugh, even in this moment of crisis. 'We have options. First, if we try and light a fire and find fuel in the office, we should be ok for a while. Then we could build an igloo.'

'Igloo!' scoffed Jake, who was quickly silenced by a glare from Michaels.

'There is plenty of soft snow at the cave entrance. The igloo will allow us to radiate our body heat, raising the temperature to 15 °C.'

Mad Dog thought that this last part was something that Newts would have added—dwelling on the detail when really it was the idea that mattered. He desperately missed his best mate and his new friends.

They all looked at each other, as if to determine whether it was some kind of sick joke. But all at once they realised the good sense in it; by camping inside the igloo the air temperature would rise due to their combined body heat. It was how the Inuit people survived. There was a glimmer of hope. Food and water weren't the issue, just the freezing cold. The command centre room was like an office with several desks in it and one of the agents had matches. Once the fire was started, it warmed the entire room.

Next they had to establish how long the fuel would last. An igloo would take several hours to build, so if they had no sign of help it was agreed that in 3 hours, before the fuel ran out, they would expend the energy to build an igloo.

The CIA's last communiqué before the collapse meant that help was en route. What they didn't know was how deep the cave-in was.

Get warm, get organised, and survive. They must survive and honour Tom. He had saved them, so they must survive. The story must be told. His mum deserved that, the world needed to know. CIA, diamonds, terrorists. Mad Dog would make sure it was headline news. Scumbags.

Mad Dog kept saying under his breath, as if hoping it would help the Qbits hear, 'Tom, you there?' There was no response. Just silence.

# Chapter 39

## Entrance Tunnel

16 March 2015
10.17 pm + 53 seconds

The vault didn't just shake, it roared like a bear being declawed. The tunnel walls moved visibly, but held fast. They could hear the noise through the vault entrance like the rumble of speakers at full volume. The door and the entrance to the vault started creaking like they weren't going to hold back the blast. The ground was shaking violently.

99.86% of the mass in the solar system comes from the sun. The planets make up less than 0.14%!

'What in hell?' said Black Angel.

Tom gave him a look that said, 'I told you so.'

The commander spoke. 'Any more?'

'No more major ones near here,' replied Tom. No point in lying; he wanted to stay alive.

The commander nodded. 'Then we move.'

The doors opened, but revealed no great devastation. Oddly, the snow and ice now hid what had impacted just moments earlier. Tom couldn't help but mentally note where the impact had occurred, in case they were able to retrieve a sample later. There was now an eerie calm, with the sky still being lit up by minor meteorites.

The Delta Force proceeded cautiously, looking around for evidence of the blast. It doesn't matter how tough you are, when the Earth is angry, everyone gets scared, and survival is no longer an exercise in skill but completely random.

Suddenly, they heard a hissing, cracking, crumbling sound, and realised in horror that the entire mountain of snow was slipping down towards the mouth of the Seed Vault. They immediately rushed over to the snowmobiles. Everyone jumped on one, including Tom, and raced off away from the mountainside as fast as they could go.

'What the crap in hell was that?' shouted Angel above the roar of the snowmobiles.

'Avalanche,' stated the Frenchman flatly.

'Well, duh,' laughed Black Angel, despite the fact it had been he who had asked the initial stupid question.

Tom couldn't help thinking no matter how highly trained these cowboys were, they were still as thick as planks.

Tom held on tight to the snowmobile, as it was clear what they would do if he tried to run. They raced toward the wharf just outside of the town, with the storm finally easing off.

Just as the wharf came into view, one of the Delta Force was suddenly hit by a meteor large enough to throw him from his vehicle but not to kill him. Black Angel dashed back and snatched up his colleague with military precision, pulling him onto his own snowmobile.

In less than 10 minutes, they had reached the high-speed boat, with meteorites still whizzing past them and smashing into the dense snow around them. It was like artillery fire.

'So,' Tom began nonchalantly, as they clambered into the boat. 'Exactly how far am I coming with you guys?'

Doolan grabbed Tom roughly by the jacket and slyly slid a small sealed pouch of uncut diamonds into Tom's jacket pocket. 'You saved our life. We will drop you further up the channel.'

Tom was relieved. He was still a prisoner, and he was about to be abandoned in the middle of nowhere during a meteor storm, but things were looking up. Perhaps he was going to live.

The dinghy sped up the channel towards the waiting helicopter, which Delta Force would use to exit Svalbard. Rich and avenged, they would all vanish.

Tom zipped into Qbits in a panic. 'Where is Mad Dog? Why isn't he teleporting in?'

'We don't know,' said GG sadly. 'We can't communicate with him. Either all the power is down in the Seed Vault, meaning there is no electromagnetic field to transport on, or ...' He didn't need to finish. Or the Seed Vault had become a tomb. Scott Maddocks was dead, buried in the vault.

# Chapter 40

## Delta Force Escape Boat

16 March 2015
10.28 pm + 33 seconds

The boat sped along the channel, dodging small meteor missiles like in a war zone. Black Angel was having a great time going at full speed, with everyone else being thrown around. Tom hung on for dear life. No need to tie him up.

The storm was still in full force, but only minutes remained. Meteors now bombarded the ocean like hot rocks dropped in a bath tub. In the distance a large meteorite hit the ocean with the force of a bomb that could destroy a US warship. Even in the dark the water displacement and massive

> Water is the only substance occurring naturally on Earth in 3 states: solid, liquid and gas. It freezes at 0 °C and vaporises at 100 °C. Ice floats because frozen water is 9% lighter than water.

steam cloud were visible about 500 metres further ahead. Black Angel steered into the wave.

'The storm ends in 115 seconds.' GG was unusually precise.

'But,' he continued, 'there are three remaining large meteors, and the last one is going to be big, and nearby. It is a metre in diameter and its trajectory is about 500 metres in front of you. It may not hit the boat but in 56 seconds if it doesn't hit the boat at this speed the wash and impact may tip the boat.'

'What?' Tom didn't like what he was hearing.

'You need to take your chance now, Tom,' insisted Alby.

'Chance?'

'We should start anticipatory thermogenesis,' exclaimed Mac. '*Now!*'

'What?'

'Meteor storm ends in 55 seconds,' added Watto, as if to confirm GG's statement.

'No more incoming large impacts on the radar.'

'Perseids ends in 52 seconds,' said Alby. 'But Mac's right.'

'1.1 kilometres northwest, 25 degrees from shore,' added Newts.

'15 minutes and 30 seconds at your swim speed,' added Alby.

'What?'

'You must escape from the boat. You need to jump over the side as either the meteorite impact, or more likely they will kill you. You know too much.'

'But you said ...'

'We can't risk it, their mission orders were clear—no survivors.'

Suddenly Tom was in the Great Hall. 'You have 1 second to explain. Starting now.'

The Qbits all looked around nervously, as they made to elaborate.

'It's clear from all the communications and e-mails. You need to get as far away from these Delta animals as you can. And as quickly as you can. They mean to kill you—those are their orders.'

'But ...' argued Tom.

'No! No buts. And the funny thing is,' began GG, hesitating at his poor choice in words, 'that the CIA *also* has orders to kill all the civilians at the end of all this!'

Tom didn't know what to say. Damned if he did, damned if he didn't. One thing was clear—he had to get the heck out of there and alert some type of authority—anyone—to come and sort this out before the CIA got hold of them.

Tom was steely. 'Well, tell me all about this anticipatory thermogenesis then.'

# Great Tapestry

**Delta Force Vision**

**Arctic Water Survival and Anticipatory Thermogenesis**

The Arctic water temperature is below zero.

Body heat is lost 25 times faster in cold water than in cold air.

Cold shock is the physiological response to sudden cold and may cause a heart attack.

Survival time in water is 5 to 10 minutes, if you don't die of cold shock in 47 seconds.

Humans' standard operating body temperature is 37.5 °C.

If body temperature drops by even a small amount, hypothermia sets in.

At 35 °C you will be unable to write your own name.

At 33 °C you become irrational, throwing away survival gear.

By 32 °C you will collapse.

At 30 °C loss of consciousness with probable cardiac arrest.

By 28 °C irregular heartbeat, by 20 °C your heart stops.

People use anticipatory thermogenesis to raise their body temperature by up to 1.5 °C.

Probability of surviving 1.1 kilometres swim at minus 1 °C is less than 50%.

As far as Tom was concerned, the decision was made. He instructed Mac to do it, and do it now. There was no time to waste faffing around. Soon Tom was starting to feel hot and bothered in his arctic gear, as if he had a fever.

'Tom, anticipatory thermogenesis is complete. I have raised your body temperature by 1.5 degrees.' Mac was businesslike.

'Tom, the bow wave will make it harder for them to shoot you in the swell,' added GG, trying to sound comforting.

'What?' asked Tom, horrified.

There was no time for GG to dig himself in any deeper, because suddenly the boat was airborne, flying over the 2-metre wave caused by the meteorite. As the boat came down, the hull smashed into the sea. Another wave came as everyone held onto the side for safety, hands off guns and on the boat for the sake of self-preservation.

Self-preservation was an amazing thing. The water at zero meant Tom would survive for a maximum of 15 minutes, but probably less, as he might well have an immediate heart attack. Even with a high-tech wetsuit, Tom would survive less than 30 minutes in the icy waters.

'Jump ... now!' screamed the Qbits in unison as the boat again lifted at the front.

Tom looked around; the men were all looking forward and hanging on.

Meteor storm, freezing water, murderers, diamonds, scientists coming back from the dead ... this must be a nightmare, this whole thing is a dream. Tom looked out at the horrible, dark water lapping violently around the boat.

'Jump!' they screamed again. He felt that if they could have pushed him, they would have. Suddenly he fell off the back of the boat. *What the hell?* he thought, as the icy water stung his throbbing body. A small meteorite hit the water nearby. And another.

'All clothes off, Tom, you will swim faster and all they will do is freeze you quicker,' stated Alby.

Tom knew they were right, as he felt the weight of the heavy, soaked, freezing NASA jacket and pants. He quickly unclipped his vest and pants and was now in just his thermal underwear, thrashing about in the water. He had only been in the dark water for a few seconds when the reality of the icy water hit home. His hands and feet stung with the cold.

Mac spoke slowly and clearly. 'Sorry, Tom, I know it is still freezing water, but you can survive 15 minutes. We can control your heart rate to make sure you don't get cold shock.'

'But you said it will take longer than 15 minutes to get to shore,' Tom whined.

'Swim! Move, Tom, it will warm your blood flow. Swim now, as hard as you can.'

The cold water was like having sharp needles stuck in his nerve endings. The air exploded out of his lungs with the cold. His heart began beating hard and fast as he started swimming.

Mac spoke again, to calm him. 'We are letting your heart rate go up to warm you up, keep swimming. Newts has you on GPS lock for shortest distance to shore. Don't fight stroke direction, Newts is guiding you in. Shore in 14 minutes.'

The boat swung around for an instant, with a searchlight now panning the water. They hadn't planned on that. The beam of light was scanning directly towards him.

'Dive, dive down now, Tom,' screamed GG, with an urgency and seriousness like none of the Qbits had ever seen. Tom took a breath and dove 2 metres under the icy waters. It was the most eerie sensation, being in that freezing pitch blackness, with a faint stream of light moving through it. He could hear and sense the boat's proximity.

Suddenly, the light snapped off and the boat turned and

continued speeding down the channel. They had obviously left him for dead.

Newts was calm and mechanical as ever. 'We need to overcome friction and wave—it is much more pronounced when part of the body is above the water, so keep moving and stay under for as long as possible.'

'The last large meteorite will impact in 15 seconds. Swim, Tom, the impact wave from the meteor in 30 seconds will help you make the shore,' directed GG. 'The boat is heading straight toward the impact area.'

Tom burst out of the water like a killer whale breaching, lungs on fire and freezing all at once.

'*Cripes!*' he said.

'*Swim!*' the Qbits screamed.

The impact of the large meteor in the distance was eerie. After an initial splash, as if someone had thrown a large rock into a calm river, the ocean seemed to take a while to transmit the result. The wave looked like a surf breakup as it surged toward Tom.

The boat was unceremoniously tipped upside down and, with engine still running, it whizzed around in the water, going nowhere.

The wave quickly carried Tom a good distance but not far enough to reach the shore.

After 12 minutes of swimming, the strength of Tom's strokes began to fade. He was so cold and tired, he just needed a little break. Then he could swim harder.

The Qbits could sense his system was slowing down with the cold; even they were getting cold inside the Great Hall. No one spoke. They just willed him on. Only 300 metres from the shore, they could see the dark outline of the town wharf.

He was fading quickly now. He had been swimming for 13

minutes, but hypothermia was setting in. It was so quiet, just a nanonap was all he needed to rest, warm up, then he could do the last 200 metres and save the others. Yes, that was the plan—rest, warm up and save them. He started to slow down.

'*Swim!*' they all implored, but he wasn't listening. His eyelids slid shut, he stopped swimming. He drifted under the water. So cold, so tired. His metabolism was shutting down, his heart rate slowed, he was being frozen. The shore was only 100 metres away now, the stairs to the wharf now visible.

Suddenly, Tom opened his eyes to a huge guitar riff and a supersonic drum roll. The noise was deafening. It was like trying to go back to sleep next to a construction site. Then the words of AC/DC *It's a Long Way to the Top (If You Wanna Rock 'n' Roll)* started bellowing into his ear. It was Scott's favourite late-night party song. The distinctive bagpipes came next. His best friend, Mad Dog, dead. He needed to get back to tell the story. It was so loud that everyone sat there stunned, except for GG, who was sitting at a drum kit, cranking out the chorus. Loud enough to wake the dead.

Now wide awake, Tom resumed his swimming, faster than ever. He quickly reached the wharf and dragged himself ashore.

He knew he had to keep going so he moved as quickly as he could down the wharf to the main street. He was relieved when he saw some shop lights and it appeared emergency generators had automatically switched on. He stumbled towards a ski clothing store and in a single fluid motion he picked up a heavy rock and hurled it through the window. The alarm sounded immediately. He jumped over the shards of glass into the store and began to search for the warmest clothes he could find. He found ski pants, a jacket, gloves, a beanie and ugg boots, and

The tentacles of the giant Arctic jellyfish can reach 36 metres in length.

threw them into a pile, ready to put them on. The outfit wasn't really a fashion breakthrough, but it would quickly restore his body temperature to the normal range.

Tearing off his sodden thermals he quickly stripped naked. Tom was just about to put on his new outfit when he caught sight of something creeping in the window he had just smashed. Tom crept behind the counter of the store, scanning the shelves for anything he could use as a weapon.

The massive polar bear blended almost perfectly with the white snow in the street. It had caught the scent of something tasty and was standing on its hind legs, sniffing. It stood over 2 metres tall. Its nose was twitching in the air.

Tom then heard inside his ear, 'Polar bears are found mainly in the Arctic Circle. They weigh over 500 kilograms and can run at about 50 kilometres per hour. They are the world's largest carnivore.'

'Enough, Watto,' Tom said to Watto internally. 'How do I get rid of this thing?'

Inside the Great Hall Watto had assembled a flurry of information mostly dealing with how polar bears faced starvation and extinction, but this wasn't really the time for sympathy or information.

'We could flash the lights in the store and make the alarm louder?' suggested GG. Tom had a feeling that with all the flashing lights and noise outside, that wasn't really going to have a lot of impact on the massive beast.

He felt about among the various bit and bobs in the cupboard under the counter—scissors, a letter opener, all worse than useless. Meanwhile the bear stalked its way further inside the store, hoping to find the source of the lunch aroma.

Tom peered up over the counter to find the bear's head almost level with his, looking directly at him. There was no mistake. This wild animal was shopping for only one thing in the store.

'Tom, the emergency kit! It will have a flare gun in it! It's standard issue in the Arctic,' cried GG, who was looking on in earnest.

Almost instantly as Tom's hand landed on the emergency first-aid kit, he wrenched the unlocked box open and rifled through it looking for the flare gun. Soon enough, he held it in his hand, but then hesitated, unsure how to approach this next bit.

'Jump up on the counter and shoot the bloody flare!' yelled Newts, getting caught up in the drama. 'Into the air not at it.'

Tom immediately leapt onto the counter, still naked as the day he was born, attempted to shout a lame hoarse battle cry, and fired the flare into the ceiling and watched it ricochet around the room. Tom fell to the floor like a panicked kid who had misfired a firework. The bang and bright smoking flash terrified the unsuspecting animal and it immediately turned tail and hotfooted it out of the store, bounding off into the distance.

Still exhausted from his swim, Tom sank to his haunches on the counter, gathering his thoughts. How many near-death experiences could one guy have in one day?

'Ah, Tom?' began Mac hesitantly. 'We have a pretty good view of all this on the Great Tapestry right now,' she continued awkwardly.

'May be time to get your kit on,' finished GG.

Having momentarily forgotten he was completely nude, Tom hastily leapt from the counter and pulled on the ski pants and top, annoyed and shy at the same time.

He could hear the Qbits giggling childishly in his head.

'Grow up, guys. I could have been killed,' he scolded them.

'Ah, but you weren't. Who knows if that bear will recover, though, after what it just saw,' said GG.

Tom appeared in Qbits. 'I don't want to hear a word of this ever again, ok? *Ever again!*'

Trying to suppress their smiles, they nodded obediently.

All water originates from when the Earth first formed, so you are drinking 4-billion-year-old water. We drink on average 75,000 litres of water throughout our lives.

# Chapter 41

## Entrance Tunnel

### 16 March 2015
### 10.42 pm + 21 seconds

Tyler and Jake found the emergency generator and power was restored. Immediately the ring on Mad Dog's finger tingled lightly. Then he zapped into the Great Hall, looking right at Tom and the Qbits. Mad Dog immediately broke down into manic, relieved laughter—Tom was alive! His best mate had survived! He grabbed Tom, hugging and squeezing him tight. Tom weakly hugged him back, just so relieved to see his friend safe.

There are approximately $10^{80}$ atoms in the Universe and 75% of the Universe is hydrogen.

As Mad Dog pulled away, he couldn't help but think that

something horrible had befallen his friend after all. *What was he wearing?* The ski jacket was bright red, with bright yellow ski pants, the gloves were electric blue, the ski cap was fluoro orange, and the ugg boots were pink.

Mad Dog double over in laughter, tears streaming down his face as he pointed and slapped his thigh in pure relieved mirth. One by one, the scientists joined in.

Tom looked himself up and down and back at Mad Dog, not quite sure what all the fuss was about.

'We lost all communication because you had no electricity— no electromagnetic transmissions to and from the vault. The generator must be operating now, is it?' Tom was trying to plan to get Mad Dog out, but Mad Dog was still laughing too hard, in pure elation.

'What the hell are you laughing at, Dog?' Tom asked.

'Nice camouflage gear, Commando Jackson,' teased Mad Dog. 'How did you ... what happened?'

Tom, scanning his gear with a more critical eye, realised he looked like a clown in a circus.

The Qbits giggled.

'Long story ... later. You ok in there?' asked Mac. 'Careful of hypothermia.'

Tom grinned and shrugged. 'Feeling a little toasty now, but otherwise quite comfortable.'

'No wonder that polar bear went screaming off into the hills as soon as he saw you, Tom. That outfit probably half-blinded him!' suggested GG mischievously.

'Um, yeah,' responded Tom sheepishly. 'Yeah, he certainly didn't seem too fond of it.'

As agreed, the Qbits kept straight faces and didn't breathe another word.

Once Mad Dog had managed to get his laughter under

control, he got back to business. 'Well, it's not too bad in the office, either—no hypothermia. It's quite small and we have lit a fire using files and desks as wood,' said Mad Dog. 'But we can't get out. The CIA want to build an igloo to keep warm using the tunnel cave-in snow, if we start to run low on fuel. I tell you, these guys know their stuff.'

Visible light wavelength is longer so we can see it 0.000001 metres to 0.00000001 metres.

'Igloo?' GG asked. They didn't have much call for igloos in Italy.

Tom was still focused on his friend's predicament. 'I can't get you out. The snow is 10 metres deep into the tunnel.'

'No need to worry!' cried GG. 'I have located a Norwegian Navy ship just off the coast. I will give you their coordinates and you can mayday them,' GG explained.

'You really think they'll believe me?' Tom faltered. It had been a big day, and he just didn't know who to trust anymore.

'Tom, you must alert them to the NASA people and local Norwegians trapped inside the Seed Vault! They cannot refuse you—they are military!' Alby chipped in.

'Do it, Tom, they can come dig us out and then we can have a nice sit-down and a cuppa,' insisted Mad Dog.

Still only half convinced, Tom slipped out to find a two-way radio in the hotel office and made the call.

He returned proclaiming proudly, 'Cavalry is on its way! They said they'd send the chopper and some kind of machinery I've never heard of.'

'We know, we were listening,' GG said. 'Good work, Tom!'

'All over,' breathed Tom with relief. It had got pretty hairy there for a while, to say the least. He was exhausted.

Alby observed with obvious pleasure, 'Everything is back to normal.'

GG agreed. 'Yes, Tom is dressed like he is going to a bad

taste party, Mad Dog is contemplating making an igloo in the Doomsday Vault entrance with his friends from NASA and the CIA, terrorists are floating around dead in the harbour with hundreds of millions of dollars of diamonds in envelopes, and the Earth has been smashed by a once-in-a-century meteor storm. So all is normal. I need a drink.'

The Qbits all laughed.

'What's your poison, Mad Dog?'

'Scotch, GG. Make it a double.'

'I'm going for a long hot shower,' added Tom.

'All right for some,' joked Mad Dog.

'I guess I need to contact the CIA so they know I'm alive. We must not mention the seed packets. The CIA knows, but I get the feeling it could result in a bad outcome for us if we admit that we know.'

After a bit of e-mailing and creative storytelling, the CIA soon received news that Tom was miraculously alive and having a shower at the hotel. The navy rescue team was en route and the fire had successfully warmed the office; combined with the heat of many people in a confined space, it was for the moment cosy.

By the time morning broke, the navy had snowploughs operating and within several hours they had punched a hole through 10 metres of soft snow in the entrance of the vault. As they filed out one by one from a small ice tunnel they had carved, there stood Tom with a beaming smile from ear to ear.

Emma was the first out. She was so overwhelmed to see Tom there, all she could do was run over to him and hug him tight.

She said, 'Wow, that was the bravest thing anyone I've met has ever done. I can't believe you sacrificed yourself for us.'

Mad Dog strolled out after her. Tyler followed, who shook Tom's hand, pulled him towards him for a hug and said, 'Tom, we owe you everything.'

Mad Dog whispered so only Tom could hear, 'Really really *good* LUCK.' Tom shook his head with a wry smile, Mad Dog was irrespressible.

Out loud for all to hear he added, 'You're a good man, Tommy, an outstanding scientist and my best mate.'

Jake was next and grabbed him with both arms like a boy hugging his mother. He didn't speak.

Then Captain Michaels came over, shaking his head in disbelief, and shook Tom's hand. 'I would have you on my team any day. What you did was brave—you saved us, Tom. Thanks.' Michaels then moved off to the head of the QRF to get an update. He wanted Doolan caught and brought in. He would deal with him personally; he had killed three good men.

Misha marched out last. 'You—you did real good. You want a job?' He smiled and slapped Tom on the back.

Squids are superconducting quantum interference devices that confuse us.

Tom beamed at the high praise.

'Thanks, Misha. I'm just so relieved everyone's ok,' began Tom, glancing around sheepishly. They all nodded in absolute agreement.

'To the hotel!' shouted Mad Dog.

# Chapter 42

## Hotel—Spitsbergen, Svalbard

17 March 2015

5.45 pm + 21 seconds

Safely back at the hotel they couldn't believe the random devastation. It looked like what they imagined a war zone would look like after an air raid, with buildings smouldering and large impact craters dotted around. At one end of town, the once brightly coloured buildings were completely destroyed.

After everyone had a few hours rest, they spent the evening in the hotel bar, eating, drinking, and reliving the previous day's events. In a quiet moment Tom looked at Emma and he reached into his pocket and withdrew a large meteorite fragment. 'I got you a present—missed by this much.' He motioned with his hands firstly close then progressing to arms wide apart.

Emma's face cracked into an immediate grin. 'Tom Jackson—who are you?' she asked, before planting a kiss on his cheek. He was quite enjoying all the attention.

Once the boys had had time to unwind, CIA operatives squeezed in beside them at the table and shook their hands fervently, the glimmer of patriotic zealotry in their eyes.

The Delta Force leader—the real one—regarded all of them thoughtfully before asking, 'So, what in H-E-double-hockey-sticks do you think those terrorists were up to, anyhow?'

For want of intelligible phrasing, both Tom and Mad Dog merely gazed blankly at him, unanswering, until Captain Michaels picked up the slack. He had received confirmation that the electronic tracking had located all the 'packages' and the envelopes had been sealed and floated and were being recovered at that exact moment in time. No bodies were found just the boat. Michaels' orders directly from George O'Brien were to question the NASA team and all civilians to determine what they knew and report directly to him but there was no need to document the event.

While Tom and Mad Dog were under no illusions as to the likelihood that any trace of the Delta Force members would ever be found, they nodded in feigned gullibility and submitted to the authoritative pronouncements of the CIA.

'They just left me when they got on the boat,' Tom recounted. 'They said their mission was completed and took off. Who were they and what did they want? Are there rare seeds of value hidden in that vault?' Tom ramped up his doddering scientist persona to throw them off the trail—now he had to do everything he could to ensure they were safe from the good guys.

They stared mutually into one another's eyes; Tom's open

and innocent, Michaels' scrutinising. Tom couldn't help thinking on some level Michaels knew they knew, but he nodded in acknowledgement as Tom spoke, as if in tacit agreement that this would be the official line henceforth. After all, Tom had saved their all-American asses.

With full military pomp, the Delta Force commander added, 'Son, there sure were some highly valuable rare hard-to-find seeds stored in that vault—irreplaceable, we've been advised.' He stroked his moustache as he contemplated the unutterably harsh ending he imagined had been in store for the seeds. 'You are one lucky man,' he emphasised. 'Do you know what kinds of plants could have been created from those seeds?' The silence greeting his rhetorical question said it all.

Michaels drained his Coke Zero and turned to leave, before remembering one last question. 'Oh—do any of you know what the hell a Qbit is or a GG?'

Again, Tom and Mad Dog resorted to blank expressions, until Tyler answered, 'It's something they are experimenting with in quantum computing, I think. Why?'

But the agents' eyes had already glazed over. 'Ah, it's nothing,' said Michaels, flummoxed. He didn't give a raccoon's hoo-ha about quantum computing, and he had never seen one implicated in a terrorist threat. Without another word, the agents departed.

Tom and Mad Dog spent the next day locating meteorite fragments and watching the satellite footage of the storm. The mission had been a success; the storm had been captured by satellite and they had collected over 100 kilograms of meteorites. Tom and Mad Dog were even given souvenirs, which was a direct breach of NASA protocol, but Tyler, Emma and Jake didn't care. They owed the pair a far greater debt than a couple of little space rocks.

When scouring the beach area 2 kilometres from the town, Jake had found Tom's NASA jacket, dried it in his room and returned it to him as a parting gift.

The NASA crew had decided to throw Tom and Mad Dog a little going-away party. Most of the townsfolk had returned, so the hotel was full of revellers. Everyone simultaneously toasted that the town had largely been spared outright disaster and mourned the destruction of the post office and the bank. NASA announced it would donate the funds to rebuild them as a kind of thank you for letting them take all the meteorite samples. And it would include a new science lab and museum dedicated to the day's events. They would be famous here forever.

By the end of the evening, Tom and Mad Dog had been invited to come and work the summer at NASA. Maybe they would.

After he had dawdled back to his room, searching for his key in his jacket pocket, Tom found a small package. Instantly familiar, there was no need to open it. Tom's mind raced. The Qbits were silent, except for GG's whistle as he stated quietly, 'Estimated street value is $1.5 million.'

Tom's reply was definitive. 'No one is to know—not even Mad Dog. We work out what to do with them later. Like you guys—they don't exist.' Alby raised his hand as if to differ when Tom put up his hand to halt the conversation. There was to be no debate on any of it.

Early flights meant fleeting farewells after the late night. The Qbits were excitable all the way home. No mention was made of the envelope hidden in Tom's jacket pocket. What a trip, they thought. Science, adventure—what was next? Immediately after take-off, the boys found themselves in the Great Hall.

'What's wrong with GG?' asked Mad Dog.

Mac explained. 'Well, apparently Italian researchers want

to exhume the body of Galileo Galilei and extract his DNA to determine what caused his blindness just before he died. GG thinks it might hurt and wanted to be there ...'

Tom rolled his eyes. 'And where's Alby?' he asked next.

'Alby has been working on this idea of video teleportation. It allows him to do video conferences and look real—alive. It's pretty cool.'

Alby was hunched over a desk in a room he had created in the corner. When they wandered in, he was doing an interview with Suzy. They made sure they stood just off camera, in awe as Alby prosecuted his case to the daytime TV queen. Suzy was more powerful than the President.

'Watto, show Suzy interview with Alby now.' They all sat in the Great Hall watching.

Suzy was probing, trying to discover whether Alby was just a character actor. Was he prepared to be tested to see if he had the knowledge of Albert Einstein?

Alby insisted that he and his colleagues were there to help good people. His friends, who went by the names Newts, Mac and GG, were Qbit descendants of great scientists like him.

Suzy was determined to get him into the studio but Alby explained they lived in another universe entangled with hers.

'So, I have a scientist with me who is going to test your ability to think like your relation Albert Einstein, ok?' Suzy prepared him for the challenge. 'We have some questions sent in from viewers.'

'Great, ask me anything—I like helping. And I intend to live forever—so far, so good,' stated Alby confidently.

'Our first question comes from an Italian university. Mr Gal writes, how do you feel that they might have now confirmed that neutrinos can travel faster than the speed of light? What you have called the speed limit of the universe? Does this mean Einstein's theories might be past their "use by" date?'

GG and Mac chuckled as this was the last thing Alby would want to discuss even though they all believed these most famous theories would probably be modified rather than just discarded.

'Mr Gal indeed.' quipped Mac smiling. Even Newts gave a late smirk realising the joke.

Once the interview was concluded, Alby closed up the portal and turned to find everyone watching him.

'What were you thinking? Are you insane?' asked Mac, with uncharacteristic lack of level-headedness.

Alby shrugged and spoke calmly. 'We agreed—no one can ever find us. We don't need to hide. I'm just putting the world on notice that Qbits are here to help, online all the time. They can ask us anything. I'm promoting science and thinking.'

He looked at them all in turn, as if it all made complete and utter concrete sense.

It was hard to argue, as there was no loca-tion, no link to Tom and Mad Dog, and the world could do with a little help occasionally— as had been proved repeatedly over the past few weeks.

Insanity: doing the same thing over and over again and expecting different results.

So Tom didn't object—there was nothing he could do.

# Chapter 43

## Flight Home

### 19 March 2015
### 6.45 am + 59 seconds

After a 24-hour flight they landed back in Sydney at 6.30 am. Once they cleared customs (with a slightly tricky explanation of the huge shards of extraterrestrial rocklike material in their hand luggage), they exited the terminal to find their parents waiting for them, excited to see their sons who had been working with NASA. After the meteor storm was reported on the news, they had explained that they hadn't been able to tell anyone about the assignment, as NASA had insisted on the

> Relativity means the faster you go, the shorter and younger you are.

utmost secrecy. But now they were local celebrities. They were proud they had got the job done, but were relieved to arrive home safely. The Qbits lapped up the attention.

# Chapter 44

## Great Hall

26 March 2015
2.01 am + 32 seconds

Tom hadn't slept at all well since getting back and was almost automatically waking at 2.00 am. It was an inner concern that random events could get out of control if left unmonitored for even a night.

Tom smiled at Mac. 'I guess it's not every week you survive a once-in-a-century meteor storm, save the planet's seed bank—the future food source of the

Quantum physics assumes there is an irreducible randomness built into nature.

world-from-terrorists and stop a $500 million robbery by accident.'

'Ok, report Watto, what have they been up to whilst I've been asleep? One by one.' Tom rolled over in his trademark crumpled bed sheets.

Watto commenced reporting on the Great Tapestry—one by one like a school teacher reporting the various students' progress.

'Mac has been siphoning off drug money from accounts in the Caribbean and redirecting it to the Cancer Treatment Research Program at Paris University. Institut Curie is a leading research centre specialising in the treatment of cancer. It is located in Paris, France. So far $5 million has been donated.' Mac smiled at Tom.

'Newts gave Cambridge University $5 million anonymously to research mathematics. The source of the cash was an online fraud operation in Russia.' Newts nodded as if to approve his evening's work.

'Alby last night released to the Swiss Government details of the contents of ex-Nazi safety deposit boxes and the location of artworks stolen by the Nazis in World War II and the bank concerned is determining how to release the funds when it sells the artworks. Top-secret documents previously thought to have been destroyed were mysteriously e-mailed to Israel to assist in the investigation. Raphael's *Portrait of a Young Man* was looted from the Czartoryski Museum in 1939. Its current whereabouts were unknown until yesterday.'

'And what about GG?' asked Tom lazily, stretching his arms.

'Nothing to report.'

He had learnt that in Qbits if everything seemed to be going well, he had obviously overlooked something.

'Nothing, really? Well where is GG?'

Newts interrupted. 'Tom, the South Pole has had a major event and an ice island the size of a small country has broken off and is melting and floating towards New Zealand. New Zealand is only part of the issue—if it keeps melting and moving, the sea level will rise several metres and millions may drown. We need to get it to float back towards the South Pole.'

Alby added, 'Did you know Antarctica contains 90% of the planet's ice? It's the major reserve of fresh water on Earth. Also, about 99% of Antarctica is covered with ice at an average thickness of 2,500 metres, and in some places as deep as 4,776 metres. If the ice layer melts, all the Earth's oceans will rise 70 metres above the current level.'

*Great, more snow to deal with,* thought Tom. And then he thought to himself, *is this how it's going to be from now on, always using science to solve the world's problems?* He smiled. How great would that be?

'Has GG e-mailed the President?'

'Yep,' the reply came in unison.

'What the hell?' said Tom, pointing to GG dressed in his snow gear. 'You guys don't get cold!'

They all laughed.

'We just need to give the big iceblock a nudge in the right direction,' replied GG.

'It can wait until morning. I'm going back to sleep. Work out a plan.'

When Mad Dog wandered into the kitchen the next morning and saw the look on Tom's face, he knew something was up, especially as he was wearing his NASA ski jacket and cap. Nodding, he confirmed, 'Harry's—coffee.'

**Man needs science—science doesn't need man.**

**Tell someone something is impossible
and that will get them thinking!**

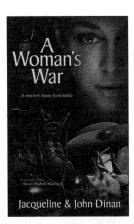
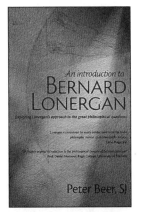

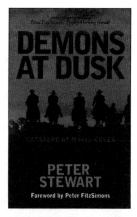

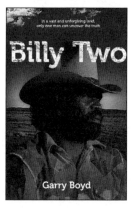

# Best-selling titles by Kerry B. Collison

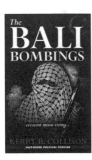   

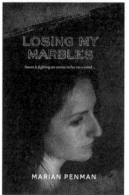

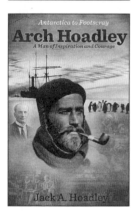
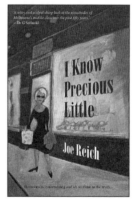